The Palestine Conspiracy

To Jester, this is a book about peace.

Best regards,

BY

Robert Spirko

Olive Grove Books, Medina

The Palestine Conspiracy

All rights reserved under International and Pan-American Copyright Conventions. Published in the United States by Olive Grove Publishers, Medina, Ohio.

www.atlasbooks.com

The Palestine Conspiracy
ISBN 0-9752508-0-9
Copyright, 1987, 2004, by Robert Spirko

Olive Grove Books is an imprint of Olive Grove Publishers, Medina, Ohio.

Printed & distributed by Bookmasters, Inc. Mansfield, Ohio www.bookmasters.com
1-800-BOOKLOG for book orders

Cover Artist: Ryan Feasel, BookMasters, Inc.

The Palestine Conspiracy

The Palestine Conspiracy

Other books by Robert Spirko

The Hour-Glass Effect

The Palestine Conspiracy

SYNOPSIS

This chilling spy-thriller will take you into the armed camp of a Bedouin chieftain, who becomes the leader of the Palestine Liberation Organization, aided by a wealthy Saudi family who wants nothing less than nuclear parity with Israel and equality in terms of human rights.

Rick Waite, a UPI reporter discovers a secret plan to destroy Israel then gets himself kidnapped by the PLO. Armed with this secret intelligence message from the Israeli Mossad, Waite and his new Bedouin friend, Ahmed, embark on a search for the truth as to what this "secret message" means for the Middle East. As the two hook-up with a mysterious Red Cross worker, Adrienne, they rescue a Palestinian youth caught in a deadly crossfire between Israeli snipers and the PLO. With the Middle East peace effort in a shambles and the region on the brink of nuclear annihilation, Israel and the Palestinians must come to grips with the question is it better to live together than die together in the lands of Abraham and Solomon? Will the Mossad let them live to see the creation of a Palestinian State? Will the duplicity of a secret agent make all their efforts in vain?

THIS IS THE PALESTINE CONSPIRACY.

ACKNOWLEDGEMENTS:

This book is dedicated to Jean McIntyre, the singular person whose teaching methods had a direct impact on my ability to think, create and put on paper words that made sense. She was a brilliant English instructor and a graduate of Bryn Mawr College who taught English at Kent State University from 1961 to 1965. I understand she obtained a Ph.D. in English literature somewhere in Canada. Upon a chance meeting with her on campus before the beginning of spring semester 1962, she asked why I had signed up for her again. I answered, "Because, I can't write, and I know you can teach me." I have long since lost track of her, but for whatever it's worth and wherever she is, I am sincerely grateful.

To my wife, Rita, and family, whose loving support and understanding enabled me to finally produce this book, and to mom, who always believed in me.

And, to those who love and honor peace whether they be Muslim or Jew, Asian, or Christian, Hindu, or any religion of this earth.

Robert Spirko, author

The Palestine Conspiracy

FORWARD

This book was first copyrighted and completed on October 20, 1987, before the events of the Persian Gulf War and the Iraq War. It is an analysis set to a novel format of the Middle East at the time prior to the beginning of major military action in the Persian Gulf by coalition forces, and the Palestinian Intifada. The book predicted all of the above several years before they happened. Mr. Spirko's predictions have proved beyond a shadow of a doubt the real need for both sides in the Middle East to come to the conclusion that this continuing course toward war is a futile cry for help as both sides attempt to destroy each other where wars have been the norm since the beginning of civilization.

Mr. Spirko developed a peace plan offered to the Camp David participants where both sides could have achieved compromise in a workable solution to a Palestinian State plus a compromise on Jerusalem which would have satisfied both sides with the City serving as a simultaneous capital for both States.

With his idea, coming close to agreement, both sides finally capitulated to pressures from their various political factions and walked away from the Peace table in failure – Chairman Arafat embarking upon a worldwide tour to garner support for his position, and Ehud Barak, failing to resurrect the issue of the Palestinian "right of return and compensation for lost land and homes" in the West Bank.

Thus, three years of new bloodshed and bloodletting

have ensued, dragging America into the
fray in the role of conqueror and peacemaker following
the Sept. 11 cataclysm.

Mr. Spirko's book discusses all the issues of the
Middle East in a way that can be understood and
appreciated by the reader worldwide, weaving these
issues into a formidable spy-thriller that takes the world
to the brink of nuclear Armageddon.

The Palestine Conspiracy

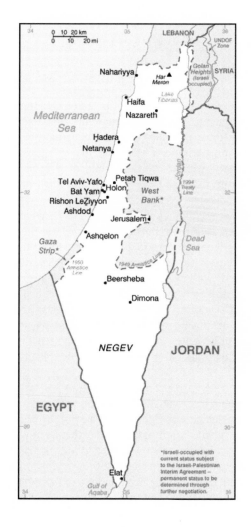

The Palestine Conspiracy

CHAPTER 1

Dhahran, Saudi Arabia: May 3. 07:27 a.m.

General Abdulla Necomis carefully studied the military map just handed to him in the situation room.

The muscular, dark-skinned general was a career fighter pilot who had taken charge of the Saudi Air Force three years earlier, and had developed it into a formidable fighting force in less time than any of his compatriots had imagined was possible. His sharp intelligence and quick military mind had enabled him to shape the Saudi Air Force exactly the way he wanted, molding it into a formidable fighting force that could attack and kill an enemy in the skies above his homeland with amazing precision and organization. But, it wasn't always that way. Before he had enrolled in flight school in the United States back in the 1970s, quickly advancing to the top of his class learning the technical, delicate and tough skills required for tactical air combat, the Arab pilots were no match for the Israelis.

His stern psychological nature as a Muslim cosseted an inner satisfaction in believing what he stood for and what he was fighting for, a cause he projected to his subordinate Saudi fighter pilots, that he now trained.

As a brash, young fighter pilot, he had flown several combat missions against the Israelis during the war with Egypt, having been on loan to the Egyptian Air Force at the time, and had distinguished himself by

10

downing two Israeli jets in less than twelve combat minutes. In actuality, combat time was far different from real time, because, in the mind of a fighter pilot, with adrenalin pumping at full throttle, and death measured in milliseconds, it was startlingly instant, compressed, and could freeze the inexperienced or poorly trained pilot. There were no miscalculations to be made, unless, of course, you were simply inept at your trade. And, if that was the case, Necomis knew he and his pilots wouldn't be alive very long going head-to-head against the Israelis, or Allah forbid, the Americans.

Yes, it had been quite an achievement for an Arab pilot, and it had never, ever been done before. The Israeli command had considered them inept in the skies whenever they encountered them. But, after the 1973 combat experience with the Egyptian Air Force, the Israelis saw a much more advanced fighter pilot in terms of skill than ever before. With Necomis leading the patrols over the Sinai, with his two quick kills, the whole world knew the Arabs were getting better, and that they could fight, at the very best evenly; and at the worst, winning occasionally.

On the very next combat mission, Necomis shot down three more Israeli jets without taking any hits, and so the young pilot became a national hero to his fellow Saudi Arabians and Egyptians as the whole world watched with fascination.

But, now, as he interpreted the intelligence data coming into the situation room, he knew a far greater challenge lay ahead. On the computer screen, in sharp

11

green contrast to the black consoles, was direct and growing evidence that Iraq was planning to attack the Saudi oil depots along the Persian Gulf. With new intelligence data mounting, Necomis' military sixth-sense told him that something important was transpiring behind the scenes.

Was it one of Iraq's major bluffs? Something they were patently good at? If they did attack, it would mean war between the two Arab countries. But why would they do such a thing after the Saudi's had negotiated a peace for them with Iran, and had secretly financed the war for them? If they attacked the oil fields, the move would be tantamount to one of the biggest surprise attacks since Pearl Harbor. The Iraqis had amassed hundreds of warplanes near Jalabah, a 15-minute flight across Kuwait and the Persian Gulf. Necomis knew he had to protect these precious radar stations along the gulf, and more importantly, the three new AWAC planes recently purchased from the United States now flying round-the-clock on patrol high above the oil-rich deserts of Saudi Arabia. The AWACS were Necomis' early warning against a surprise attack
and his most valuable military hardware if an air war erupted between the two countries. A suicide attack by Iraqi forces on his planes, while they sat on the ground at Sarti Air Base, would be fatal. Necomis knew he would have to mobilize Special Forces on the ground to protect them at all costs, readying his fighter planes to take off at a moment's notice. He picked up the special link telephone.

"Connect me with King Fasaid," he barked in Arabic, "and use the scrambler."

"Yes, sir," the aide obeyed with a Saudi accent.

12

The Palestine Conspiracy

"Good morning, your majesty," Necomis said. "You are well, I pray? Praise be to Allah."

The king acknowledged Necomis and thanked him for taking his call so early and without delay. Necomis waited for the king to finish, then politely interrupted him explaining why he had telephoned.

"I am asking your permission to put our forces on Green Alert and move 5,000 special anti-terrorist forces to Sarti?"

He knew before asking that the king would give him the permission he needed. His majesty was insightful, and Necomis knew the king trusted him as a loyalist who knew about war.

The king replied calmly, "Surely. But, I will want to meet with you immediately at my palace in two hours. I will have my personal helicopter at your disposal."

"Your majesty, I have ordered the secret police to keep a constant surveillance of all Iraqis in the country to prevent the sabotage of our AWACS. And, I have already activated a Special Forces unit to surround the palace in order to prevent any attempt on your life."

"Do you really think that is necessary, general?" the king asked.

"I must take extreme measures, your majesty. Our intelligence sources say the Iraqis will stop at nothing to assure the success of an attack."

"I understand. I shall see you in a few hours. Goodbye, and may Allah be with you."

General Necomis hung up the red telephone and motioned for an aide to enter the room.

The Palestine Conspiracy

"Place all Saudi forces on Green Basic. Do not make any attempt to disguise it. If the attack comes, I want the entire world to know we were not taken by surprise," snapped the general.

"Yes, sir," the aide replied coming to attention. He saluted and moved swiftly from the situation room.

Necomis analyzed the reason the Iraqis might decide to launch an attack against them. The Saudi's had financed Iraq's war with the Iranians for seven years before they finally sued for peace on Iraq's terms. The Iraqis, with the help of American arms, had overrun two provinces near Basra, a key oil loading facility, and had captured entire territories along the Iraqi coast. Up to that point, it had been a debilitating "war of attrition" on both sides. When Iraq had finally gained the upper hand, Iran's defeat had devastating effects among their people in numbers killed and wounded, and it had shattered their confidence. At the same time, Iraq's military pressure on Kuwait had put mounting pressure on Saudi Arabia to use its government to negotiate a cease-fire. Why were the Iraqis now willing to risk everything by attacking the Saudis?

It didn't make military or political sense, unless, of course, the Iraqis had a hidden agenda.

King Fasaid pushed aside the knife-and-fork he kept at the table for his American guests, and in deference preferred to eat Bedouin style. He dismissed his servant with a sincere, polite dignity; always treating them with common respect even though it wasn't necessary. He often prayed with them at the holy mosques not wishing to forget the fact that he was himself of simple, humble origins. But, now, even as the royal monarch, he could not deny that he was the sole head of the immensely wealthy Saudi Royal Family, which headed the most economically advanced, powerful Arab country in the Middle East. And, most importantly, he didn't have to share that power with anyone.

* * *   * * *

The helicopter moved with dart-like quickness as the jet engines roared under the strain to cover the 200 kilometers from the air base to the palatial grounds. General Necomis changed into his military fatigues for the flight. He was feeling more relaxed now that he had spoken with the king. It would be a pleasant flight to Riyadh. He snapped shut the briefcase handcuffed to his wrist with the top-secret documents inside, and prepared to meet the helicopter now streaking in over Dhahran Airbase at nearly 280 miles per hour. He stepped outside the barracks into the Arabian heat where it was already 91 degrees Fahrenheit in the shade. Once airborne, the air would quickly cool down at higher altitude, but he was used to the heat. He had grown up in it.

As he waited for the helicopter to touch down, his aide brought him his .45 caliber service weapon, which he strapped onto his side. Standing crisply at attention, the aide saluted him and took two quick steps backward and kicked in his heel. Two royal guards leapt from the helicopter as it touched down near Necomis' barracks.

The Palestine Conspiracy

"How fast can you get me there?" he shouted above the din of the whirling copter blades and climbed in behind the pilot.

"35 minutes at maximum speed," the pilot shouted over the roar of the engine.

Dust engulfed the helicopter as the gyrating rotors picked up speed. Once Necomis was securely aboard, the pilot throttled-up for take-off.

General Necomis watched the barracks and the air traffic control tower recede in the distance as the helicopter gained speed and altitude sharply pulling away from the airbase. He was amazed how fast the new American Halcyon attack helicopters were. He had personally flown them and remarked to his co-pilot that it was like flying a World War II fighter plane, only with a much tighter turning radius and more control and maneuverability.

The pilot flipped on the radar deflector, a special device used to avoid radar detection by neighboring countries, switching on a spray device that spewed-out super-cold liquid nitrogen over the exhaust so that Russian and U.S. reconnaissance satellites would not be able to track their departure from the base with infrared sensors.

While en-route, General Necomis determined that the Saudi's must not be caught by surprise, but he would be unwilling to bring the Americans into the fray for fear of looking weak in the eyes of brother Arab countries. He would request their help only as a last resort. Other Arab countries would oppose American involvement both ideologically and politically. Therefore, a plan had to be developed with the king to make it look as though the Americans had been drawn into the fight if the Saudi's needed help. He would think of a way to do this, if necessary.

The minutes ticked by. He checked his watch again. It was 0830 hours. He would be there in less than ten minutes now. Riyadh, the capital, could already be seen from an altitude of 5,000 feet. As the palace came into view on the pilot's three-dimensional target scope, Necomis nodded at the superiority of the American technology used in tracking the enemy and launching missiles at their intended targets. Necomis braced himself for the swift descent to less than 300 feet above the ground in less than thirty seconds. Although he had experienced far more G's in a jet fighter, the effect was still exhilarating as the Halcyon approached to within five miles of the palace. He would be there in less than a minute now.

Meanwhile, King Fasaid had finished dressing and glanced out his palace window catching a glimpse of the battle helicopter roaring in over the palace. He went out onto a balcony and watched it circle to the north, then land with a slight bounce near the security entrance.

Security forces swarmed around the helicopter as it touched down. They quickly escorted the general inside with a flurry of military hustle. The Special Forces unit grimly did what it had been trained to do with precise movements. Necomis observed how well disciplined they were. Safely inside, he dusted the orange desert sand from his uniform, slapping at his pant legs in a gesture of frustration.

"Sir!" the lieutenant spoke in Arabic. "King Fasaid awaits you in the situation room."

"Thank you," Necomis saluted back. "Take me to him immediately."

The Palestine Conspiracy

The two were escorted into a vault-like room, reinforced with concrete walls and blast-proof doors, about the size of a small airplane hangar, but with a low ceiling so it could withstand the initial blast of an attack from the air, and built underneath the palace. Earthen ramparts, fortified with land mines, surrounded the entire bunker, a virtual impenetrable fortress, which could function on its own if it were, cut off from outside support. That earthen wall was again surrounded by crack Special Forces trained in anti-terrorist tactics and hand-to-hand combat. Each soldier carried Israeli-made Uzi machine guns, stun, smoke and incendiary grenades to counter any

attempted assassination of the king and his family. They also carried automatic pistols with cyanide-tipped bullets. Each also had, as a last resort, a hardened

steel knife to be used in close-quarter fighting if a fight-to-the-death was necessary.

It might well be.

General Necomis stepped into the situation room. Several top aides to the king were already present, but no other military advisors had arrived yet. That was good. It would give him a chance to communicate his strategy to the king without the interference of others less well informed. He, and only a handful of intelligence officers at Dhahran, knew the hard, cold facts.

As he turned the corner, he glimpsed the king standing near a computer terminal. Necomis raised his hand immediately in obedience, and bowed in Bedouin fashion. Walking briskly across the room, he politely embraced the king in the traditional greeting of the Bedouin from side-to-side.

The Palestine Conspiracy

" My king, it is good to see you, even though I bring serious news."

"How serious?" the king asked.

"Your majesty, the Iraqi's have amassed two hundred attack fighter-bombers on the border near Kuwait within striking distance of our oil fields at Dhahran. They have positioned two divisions of army regulars for imminent invasion at the seaport city of Bushire where they are poised to move across the gulf following an air and naval attack by their forces. And, if needed, they can move through Kuwait with ten divisions of artillery and tanks units, swinging south to capture Dhahran unless we move troops to the north to defend the border."

The king grimaced as he listened intently to the details from Necomis.

"What do you recommend?" the king gestured in a smooth, sweeping arm motion inviting Gen. Necomis to sit next to him on two comfortable, cushioned chairs flanked by a pair of tea tables.

Necomis didn't miss a beat.

"My plan is three-fold. First, we must let the world know that Iraq is positioning for an attack on the major oil supplies; secondly, we must move five fighter squadrons to the Dhahran Air Base to counter the threat across the gulf. We must do this under the auspices of air force and naval exercises so as not to arouse suspicion by the major powers monitoring our movements. And, thirdly, we must protect the three AWAC aircraft at Sarti Air Base at all costs. One aircraft must be flying around-the-clock relieved by the other two at eight-hour intervals. I have already directed my officers at Sarti to take this step to preclude a surprise attack against us. I have also mobilized 20,000 men forming a perimeter around the airbase complete with tank units and flame-throwing capabilities to protect against an Iraqi sapper squad intent on destroying the AWACS.

"Excellent, General," the king said looking appreciative at his well thought-out initiatives. "Now, do you really think they will attack?"

"What in the name of Allah are they trying to accomplish? Why would they do this to us after all we have done for them?"

General Necomis had already anticipated the king's questions in the helicopter. They were answers he didn't want to give. But after sifting through all the possible reasons, he could come up with only one plausible explanation.

"They know they can win, your highness. For years they have been in a secondary power position in the Persian Gulf, just prior to the Shah's fall from power. Now, Iraq has the military power to enforce

control over the entire oil supply in our region," he explained.

"After the bitter war with Iran," he continued, "I didn't think they were eager for yet more fighting because of heavy casualties. Somehow, their fanatical leadership must think they have an unmistakable advantage over the American forces and us in the Gulf of Oman. I have not yet determined what that edge might be, your majesty, but intelligence continues to work on it every hour," he said.

Necomis turned his attention to the computerized command desk near the king. Everything was ready in case of a national emergency.

The Palestine Conspiracy

"Thank you for briefing me on such short notice, general," the king said as he slipped on his white dress gloves.

Turning toward him and coming to attention, Necomis answered obediently, "Your majesty, it is my duty to you and our people."

"My staff has prepared a room for you, general. You may continue to operate from the palace as you see fit. I have given instructions to all palace guards and government staff to grant you any requests."

"Thank you your majesty," Necomis saluted crisply. "You are indeed gracious. Praise be Allah."

General Necomis would remain at the palace for the next several days coordinating the military moves and to be in constant touch with Saudi forces if it became necessary to act. He would brief other military staff as they arrived adding further defensive countermeasures as necessary. He truly was a military genius. The king had been gracious to him, and he would remember it with his life, if necessary.

CHAPTER 2

In the region of Palestine: Beirut, Lebanon: May 1. 8:07 a.m.

Ahmed wept.

He remembered the day when his father had brought his family to the great Jordanian Plain to watch over the sheep grazing in the desert grass.

Many generations of Palestinians before them had performed the same ritual of breeding and herding the sheep and livestock establishing the nomadic traditions of the Bedouin life in the desert hundreds of years before the birth of Christ and afterward, during the reign of the great prophet, Mohammed.

But, he could not understand why this had to happen.

Why brother had to fight against brother, and father against son. Entire Bedouin families pitted against each other in a tangled web of frustration and treachery, as a foreign evil crept insidiously into their vast nomadic homelands.

They fought among each other despite ancient Arab teachings, forbidding warring among their own tribes. Yet, in their larger hatred of the Jew, each tribe knew by events foretold by the prophets, that they would someday unite against a greater enemy. Each knew it was their destiny. Each had been taught this for centuries.

22

The Palestine Conspiracy

And now the enemy loomed. An enemy rose from the ashes of the Old Testament. An enemy who challenged the very rights to the homelands of Mohammed, Solomon, and Pharaoh.

As the soldiers lowered Akram into the simple, unmarked grave, his body wrapped loosely in white linen burial cloth, his mother cried-out uncontrollably.

"Allah! Allah!" she sobbed. "Forgive my son! Forgive the many sons who kill their brothers."

Ahmed came to her side and embraced her in her moment of crisis. Then he turned away. The thought was painful, for he knew what that moment meant. He knew he would never see her again. It was something every Bedouin son had been taught from childhood. Suddenly, she looked old and weary to him. She must now go into the desert to live the rest of her years with a family Ahmed would never know. It was the Bedouin way. It was Bedouin tradition. And it was now that Ahmed would take Akram's place as the eldest son. Now, he must hold his head straight and choke back the tears that welled-up in his eyes. For his time had come. His time had come for his people.

Months passed by, and Ahmed traveled to the village of his birthplace, Pariahe, to visit his many cousins to divide the lands and flocks left behind by Akram. The journey would take four days and four nights. And, as the sun burned into his face, he rode the awkward gait of the single-humped camel, his body balancing rhythmically in a clumsy, almost drunken tilt as he reflected on what had happened.

He remembered that terrible day.

The Palestine Conspiracy

The tragic incident was imprinted on his heart and in his mind. An inner voice forced him to extract every detail about that day in a therapeutic attempt to purge the guilt from his conscience. Wincing into the glare of the sun, he remembered how the PLO bullets meant for an Israeli courier had cut down Akram, as he continued his journey toward the village.

On that evening, the Israelis had stormed through the western streets of Beirut with lightning-like speed, penetrating the PLO reinforcements as if they hadn't existed. The attack, a deliberate violation of a delicate cease-fire arranged earlier had been sudden and carried-out with the usual precision of the Israeli military.

Not one country in the United Nations had called for a pullback to the original cease-fire lines as the invasion intensified in its ferocity. Moving with stunning quickness, the Israelis had captured the entire west sector of Beirut in less than 10 hours. They attacked with tanks, joined by a deadly barrage of artillery fire and bombs delivered by jet fighters, meting-out their brand of retribution for the slaughter of Israeli prisoners-of-war three days earlier.

His brother, Akram had been caught in a deadly burst of machine-gun fire by his own militiamen who had moved near the enemy lines in an attempt to cover the assault. Akram had been hit on an Israeli motorbike while trying to deliver a message to his PLO sector commander.

Working secretly behind Israeli lines observing troop movements and listening to coded radio transmissions, Akram had sped-by a burnt-out checkpoint in his attempt to rejoin his brigade when his own PLO troops, reacting with deadly accuracy, mistakenly opened fire on him with their Russian Kalashnikov's. Even Ahmed had mistaken him for an Israeli as he came up on them by surprise. Ahmed's own bullets tore Akram from the motorbike.

If only he hadn't been wearing an Israeli uniform . . . he might have recognized him in time . . . and warned the others. But, it had been too late as the bullets ripped through his body, shattering his bike, spinning him out of control in the streets. He remembered how he had lifted Akram's crumpled body from beneath the twisted motorbike, begging Allah to spare his life. But, in an instant, he knew he would never speak with him again.

As he embraced him for the last time, a message he had been carrying slipped from his courier's pouch. Ahmed picked it up and secretively tucked it underneath his PLO shirt away from the eyes of other nearby soldiers. He didn't know why he did this, but it was an action he himself would later question? At the time, he felt the need to conceal it, and he did.

Knowing he could do nothing more for his brother, Ahmed placed the body near a deserted fountain and propped himself up against the cool shade of a fig tree, away from the heat of the day and the searing fire of hatred in his heart. He needed to be alone, to wash away the burning anger that was building inside him. His breath caught in his throat, trembling as he unfolded the secret message. He glanced around to be sure no one saw him reading the scrawled note.

It was handwritten in Hebrew.

Akram had been clever to disguise the dispatch so that if the Israelis caught him, he could say he was from

Israeli intelligence delivering secret military communications.

Ahmed pondered its meaning. It made no sense. Perhaps, he should take it to the PLO commander himself? But, whom should he trust? Why was Akram so determined to risk his own life to get the message through? Who was the message intended for?

It read: "Intercept David and Goliath. July 24. God be praised."

What did it mean?

* * *   * * *

London: May 2. 1:23 p.m.

A half-continent away, British intelligence was preparing for Mrs. Thayer's secret visit to the region of Palestine. It would be the first state visit to a nation, which geographically didn't exist. And, it would mark the first time a British prime minister would visit with a major PLO leader under any conditions. It would be an historic first for the British government, one that would shock the world. An attempt to negotiate a peace settlement in the Middle East.

Not since 1955, in the aftermath of Suez, had so much excitement marked the preparation for a secret departure from England such as this one. The British prime minister had made a unilateral decision to hold preliminary talks with the PLO, a bold and calculated move she knew would be criticized by Parliament, Europe and the United States. But, at least it was some kind of an initiative. Any peace initiative had been sadly lacking in the years subsequent to the Syrian and Israeli invasions of Lebanon.

The Palestine Conspiracy

There had been no real movement on anyone's part in the Middle East for years, and the affair had deteriorated so badly, that something, anything, had to be attempted. Mrs. Thayer had already received assurances from close friends of PLO leader Fasi Etebbe that he was willing to make concessions on the issue of recognizing Israel's sovereignty in exchange for the creation of a State of Palestine to co-exist with Israel.

Even she knew that Fasi would be tempted by such a proposal. Both parties could announce the meeting at the same time. Thayer knew it would give pre-eminence to the idea for the creation of a separate Palestinian state, and that if conditions were right, it might get broad support from the United Nations, and third world countries and the Soviet Union.

In 1920, England had proposed against the partitioning of Palestine, in a failed effort to placate the Arab world; and established the Palestinian Mandate. Decades later, when the Haganah broke out during the great in-gathering, Israel decided right then and there to declare itself a state confirming the great Exodus of 1947-48.

So Thayer's actions would be a historic move on Great Britain's part.

Palestine. Finally, its own country again.

It's own borders.

Perhaps the time was now, in exchange for the ending of world terrorism.

Mrs. Thayer knew there was nothing to lose and everything to gain. For Great Britain had long ago forsaken its role in the region. But, if the plan worked to perfection, she could once again establish Britain as a dominant world leader in the Middle East. Britain's prestige would be bolstered. And, if the strategy worked, she analyzed, England's Middle East presence could again be asserted with access to military bases and Arab oil interests.

London: 10:00 a.m.

"Brian, intelligence picked up some unusual activity by the Saudi's this morning. What do you make of it?" Geoffrey asked while studying the computer printout from ICE.

"Well, it's a problem," Brian replied. "We don't know what to make of it yet. ICE is still trying to figure out what the hell is going on."

Brian, still angry from a late-morning spat with his girlfriend, continued, "The activity is at Sarti Province. The Saudi's have beefed up their units to 20,000 men, but we don't see any troop carriers to fly them anywhere. It's as though they've gone to green alert and didn't try to disguise it."

"Yes, old boy, it certainly looks that way. Our casual observers picked it up yesterday," Geoff said in a subdued voice. "Even the dozy yanks noticed, too."

Geoffrey, brushing back his blonde hair, reached into his desk, lit a cigarette, blew out a puff of smoke, and took a deep breath.

"It's as though they wanted us to see something. But there doesn't seem to be much to it . . . eh, Brian?"

"Anything from the Iraqis?" Brian asked.

"Nothing. No troop movements by either the Iraqis or the Iranians since their cease-fire two years ago. It's probably nothing to worry about. Kind of like being paranoid, this intelligence business, huh?" Geoff said sarcastically.

"You mean pretty soon you get used to it," Brian laughed.

"Exactly!"

"You're probably bloody right," Brian responded. "But look, just to be on the safe side, I'll make some inquiries through Saudi channels just to reassure myself."

"Jolly right! Now go home and get some sleep. You'll need plenty of rest for the trip to Beirut. Is Adrienne staying at your flat these days?" Geoff asked, already knowing the answer before he finished asking the question, then added, "it'll be a long while before you get some of that again, unless you find a pretty little PLO terrorist ready to give herself to the crown."

"You cheeky bastard," Brian countered as he swung open the door remembering the argument. "At least I do get some every now and then."

Geoffrey laughed at the good-natured insult.

Brian checked his watch. He was supposed to meet Adrienne at his flat at 3 o'clock. He had just twenty minutes to get there. Geoff interrupted again.

"When are you scheduled to arrive in Beirut?"

Brian answered halfway out the door.

"2100 hours. It should be quite an exciting ride. You know the RAF. When it absolutely, positively has to get there overnight, drop the bloody bloke from 20,000 feet."

His laughter echoed through the corridor, down the steps and out to the waiting cab, which would take him to his flat where he hoped Adrienne, would be waiting for him. She usually let herself in with the extra key Brian had given her.

Even though they had no serious plans and both were free, Brian felt something more than just a wistful romance. He knew he could count on Adrienne when he needed her, and more importantly, he felt he could trust her with his innermost thoughts.

Maybe Geoff's suggestion about knocking one off was a good one at that.

Adrienne was beautiful, brunette, alluring, her face delicately featured in elegant English refinement, an obvious inherited trait from a family of nobility. Her body was made to be touched. And when she was with him, he loved to put his hands on her olive-skinned breasts and feel her nipples harden. She enjoyed that. They had slept together on the second date before either of them knew it would evolve into a serious relationship. It really didn't matter to him if it was love at first sight, or if they both just liked to fuck, but it really didn't matter to her either. It was what they liked to do.

Now, three years later, he felt himself getting more deeply involved. They both felt it. Only Brian loved her more. And, they both knew that, too. He hoped she would be on time.

The lurch of the taxi jolted him back to reality as it screeched to a stop outside the apartment building. Brian tipped the driver and brushed past the doorman, jumped the front steps, and entered the lobby elevator. The door swung shut and the elevator lurched toward the third floor. Adrienne was probably already undressed and waiting for him in bed.

The Palestine Conspiracy

Suddenly, the elevator stopped, the light flickered and then went out.

"Damn it." Brian muttered. "Of all the stupid times," bemoaning his predicament.

A fuse must have blown in the basement. Nothing to get alarmed about. Adrienne would have to wait a bit longer, remembering a scene he'd seen in an Alfred Hitchcock film. The caged elevator was vintage. It was the kind they used in Paris at the turn of the century when hotels were built with a central atrium. There was nothing to do but wait for the power to come back on. Eventually, the elevator light flickered back on, but the elevator still didn't budge.

"Hmmm," . . . I might have to give this thing a bit of a coax."

After several attempts to shake it loose by jumping, and about to give up, the elevator suddenly
and unexpectedly started moving again on its own. He let out a sigh of relief when he finally reached the third floor.

He walked down the hallway to apartment Number 10.

Number 10.

A strange coincidence.

Brian lived at the same house number as the British prime minister. But that was as close as the comparison got. He smiled a "so what" to himself. What his address lacked in the way of British top-secret state-of-the-art communications equipment, it surely made up with the lovely Adrienne waiting for him inside. It was a fair trade-off, he surmised. Even Denis would choose his flat tonight over Number 10 Downing Street.

The Palestine Conspiracy

Brian keyed the door and stepped inside, noticing that the lights were already turned down and the living room curtains completely drawn. He heard slight noises in the bathroom, and taking off his trench coat, he spotted Adrienne stepping from the shower wearing white panties. She was absolutely stunning standing their nearly naked, not knowing that he was peering in on her. Beads of water, reflecting the lamplight, glistened from her heavy breasts. Brian pulled her from behind and into his arms, feeling her buttocks with his other hand. The move startled her, so he

covered her mouth then kissed her. She kissed him back.

"Brian, you silly beast," she pretended to resist, "you scared me half to death. You simply are the most unpredictable one."

"Yes, and a large one at that. But we both enjoy these little carnal surprises don't we?" he said responding to her warm embrace.

"Uhmmm . . . " she breathed life into his mouth and caressed the hair on the back of his neck. "That feels good."

He gently brushed his hand over her nipples and kissed the nape of her neck. His breathing quickened as he slipped his hand around her back, fingers sliding beneath her panties feeling the warmth between her legs. Now, her breathing became more intense. Their lips met again in deep passionate kisses.

She knew from his strength that he would take her then and there in the hallway if she didn't coax him into the bedroom. But, before she could utter a word, he lifted her up, and began undressing her, slipping off her underwear, tossing them to the foot of the bed, and gently placed her on top. Then he stretched out his body full length while she undid his necktie, took off his shirt and pants, all in one careful movement so as not to break the romantic rhythm.

Adrienne now felt the movement of his penis. She knelt down by it as he lay back on the bed and took him into her mouth. His penis was so large, that each time she did it; she was surprised at her own accomplishment.

At his urging, she increased the stroking, up-and-down, faster, and when she felt he was ready to explode, she moved on top of him and they made love rocking back and forth until they were both exhausted.

"God, that was fantastic," she sighed. "What am I going to do while you're away for three weeks?"

"I don't know, lovey. We'll both have to make do, though. I suppose we'll have to watch a lot of telly."

"Do they even have telly in Beirut?" she chided.

"I dunno. From what I've seen on the BBC lately, they could do with some serious coverage from the Middle East these days. Maybe an interview with a famous Arab head of state," he joked, moving closer and kissing her on the buttocks.

"Can you believe it?" he raised his head. "The prime minister of England meeting with the leader of the Palestine Liberation Organization to discuss ending world terrorism. It could be the breakthrough the world's been waiting for."

Adrienne paid no attention to him and without as much as a reaction, ordered, "Go to sleep, or you won't want to get up in the morning . . ."

She covered her mouth realizing what she had just said.

The Palestine Conspiracy

Brian smirked.

"I can always get up for you."

She leaned her head on Brian's shoulder, her words drifting off in mid-sentence as she closed her eyes.

Her words were far more serious than she had realized.

The man listening through the headset in a nearby basement flat jerked upright and motioned to his friend. He could not believe what he had just heard.

"Moshe! Moshe! Wake up! We've got to transmit to Tel Aviv. Where are the code books?"

"What's this? You're always waking me up for something! Never do I get any sleep!"

"My friend," Moshe said, "If this means what I think it does, General Sharn will decorate us himself. Hurry, we must transmit!"

Nooka unfolded the portable transmitter and began sending the coded message Moshe had just written. His eyes widened at the significance of what he was transmitting.

He paused for a moment, and then repeated the transmission a second time to make sure that the message was accurately received at Israeli intelligence.

CHAPTER 3

Beirut: May 2. 3 p.m.

Ahmed moved through the streets with a cunning and purpose he never imagined he possessed.

He had to get to his American friend. He knew Waite might be able to help if he could locate him. He had met Rick Waite, an American field reporter, while running errands for the UPI bureau in the west sector several years before joining the PLO, but he couldn't be sure that Waite would remember him. Except, he knew Waite would probably remember the special favor he performed in getting Waite through the PLO lines for an interview with Fasi Etebbe, the legendary, fanatical leader of the Palestine Liberation Organization.

Surely, he would remember Ahmed for that. It was because of his special effort that the interview could be arranged in the first place, one that subsequently made a name for Waite as a legitimate foreign correspondent. Waite hadn't seen Ahmed much afterward with the tide of war changing back and forth during the ensuing years, but Ahmed hoped Waite would still remember the favor, and then, by association, him.

Ahmed knew that Waite was one of the few men who might be able to help him find out what the message meant, a message, he sensed, meant for more than himself. He climbed onto his bicycle, flashed his identification pass to a Syrian guard standing near a barricade dividing the combat zone from the neutral sector, and started off in the direction of the once familiar American embassy where Waite used to hang out when he was in Beirut.

As he pedaled his way toward the PLO lines, he could hear the occasional bursts of sniper fire hitting the ruins to the left or right of him. Quickly pedaling through Beirut's side streets was an extremely risky and dangerous ordeal in itself. Rubble from the battle was everywhere, and he couldn't help but notice the hundreds of old men, women and children picking their way through it in a desperate struggle for survival in a constant attempt to escape the punishing bombardment that increased in intensity everyday.

The people would hole up for days and weeks at a time, cowering in their ramshackle hideaways, with a deep-seated resignation, firmly rooted behind the little protection of the smashed houses and buildings in order to play out the masochistic game of survival for yet another day. They peeked from their hideouts like cornered rats, waiting for a lull in the bombardment so they could leave their dwellings for a few precious minutes. Death and danger were the only constants. Sleep was impossible. And to make their situation even worse, their hunger was killing them at a faster rate than the enemy's shelling.

When they did manage to come out, they scavenged desperately for food, clothing and any other necessities they could take back to their families. It took raw courage to do this everyday praying to stay alive as the Druse shelled them, then the Israelis, and then the Syrians on top of that. Sometimes, even its own PLO factions would mistakenly return fire. But, even that risk, the daring gamble of venturing out into the open in broad daylight couldn't be stopped. They did it because they needed to survive, and they couldn't stop themselves. Neither could the Israeli's stop from shelling them, either.

When the shelling did pause, the inhabitants of Beirut seemed to ooze from the rubble like ants pouring from an anthill and scurrying about their business with a job to do, and nothing could or would stop them until that job was finished. Some even bargained with Israeli soldiers for scant military rations. With diminishing confidence, they would climb from the depths of their underground hiding places and crawlspaces for a just a few hours of freedom and sunlight. Indeed, these were trapped and tormented humans living like feral animals under brutal conditions.

In the midst of it all, the young played children's games while the older ones practiced a deadlier form of play, taunting each other with hand carved wooden machine guns they knew someday would be the real thing to a real enemy. A new generation of warriors was being born.

Ahmed pushed down hard on the pedals of his bike trying to escape more quickly from the west sector knowing that with each passing second a sniper's bullet could kill him instantly. Frantic with fear, perspiration pored from his face, neck and back as he swerved his bike through the craters left by the artillery shells, pock mocking the northern sector now only three miles away. It was well within reach now, and he remembered where the United Press International office stood. He hoped it was still there.

As he neared the building, he saw it was still standing, leaning a bit in a fragile sort of way.

But, was it still functioning inside?

Ahmed parked his bike alongside a half blown away brick wall and quickly glanced over his shoulder to see if anyone had followed him. After casually smoking a cigarette and loitering for a minute or two, he flicked the cigarette to the pavement and crushed it beneath his foot. Then he briskly walked down the alleyway looking for the hidden doorway he knew existed somewhere in the shadows.

Getting darker and more difficult to see, he carefully made his way through the alley sidestepping the broken glass and boards. There . . . in the shadows . . . was the doorway. Ahmed pushed aside the two boards blocking it, and slowly squeezed through the opening, catching his breath as he came out the other side, then slowly crept up the stairs not wanting to make even the slightest sound. Halfway up, he heard noise coming from the second floor room where the bureau was located. He inched his way forward along the railing until he could just see over the landing and peered toward the office doorway. A man was sitting near the doorway reading an Arabic newspaper and drinking a bottle of Pepsi. His Kalashnikov rifle propped against the wall, the soldier appeared completely unaware of any intruder near him. Ahmed studied him carefully knowing he was an Arab who might kill another Arab simply because he was being paid to do it. Suddenly and without warning, Ahmed didn't have any choice but to come out into the open as he heard footsteps pounding up the stairs below him. Others were returning, and he was caught in the middle. He had to move fast. Standing upright, Ahmed tried to assume an air of confidence by asking loudly.

"Excuse me, I'm looking for Richard Waite, an American field reporter with United Press International. Is he here?"

Clearly startled, the guard bolted upright from his sitting position taken by surprise at the sudden appearance of Ahmed.

"Stop! Not another step further!" the guard commanded in Arabic grabbing for his rifle. Regaining his composure, he pointed the Kalashnikov at Ahmed's chest and pushed him back a few steps with the tip of the bayonet.

"Who are you?" the sentry demanded loudly. "Where is your identification?"

"I arrive in peace. I am looking for a man named Richard Waite, an American field reporter. He is here, yes?"

"But who are you?"

Before Ahmed could answer, two large men rounded the top of the stairs on a dead run. One grabbed Ahmed, pinning him against the wall, while the other kicked his feet out from underneath him. Ahmed's head hit the floor with a splat. He instinctively reached forward with his hands to protect his face expecting the full force of a combat boot. But, none came. Instead, he heard a familiar voice. Praise be to Allah. It was none other than Richard Waite's reverberating in his ears. The sound was almost too good to be true.

"Ahmed. Dear God, is it really you?" Waite said

as he pulled the other man off Ahmed and began apologizing profusely. He helped Ahmed to his feet and straightened him up.

"God, it really is you," he said after getting a good look at him in the light. You are a sight to behold! I heard you were dead . . . killed in a PLO ambush a few days ago. What in God's name happened to you?"

"It wasn't me," Ahmed said quavering, still frightened by the assault, eyeing the sentry uneasily. It was my brother. It was he who was killed. A terrible accident. It should have been an Israeli. Dear Allah, what am I going to do to atone for it? It may have been my own fault."

"Calm down, Ahmed. Tell me what happened to bring you here. Start slowly. Why are you here? Why have you come looking for me?" Waite asked.

"I need your help. But, we must talk privately."

"Of course. Quickly . . . into my office. I'm sorry about the attack on the stairs. Abdul, our sentry, is our only protection from factions we're not certain of these days, including the PLO. We can't even trust the Israelis anymore. They know we're still operating somewhere in Beirut and they would rather have us out. They haven't found us yet. But, when they do, we're sure they'll put an end to our operation here," Waite said.

"But I am the PLO. And, I have come for you."

Waite laughed. Ahmed hadn't changed any.

"Now tell me, why did you risk your life by coming here today?"

They sipped coffee while Ahmed explained what had happened to his brother.

"He was carrying a message from Israeli

intelligence. It read, 'Intercept David and Goliath. July 24. God be praised.'"

He showed Waite the message.

"I must know what it means? Have you any idea?"

"Offhand, I don't. The only thing I know about David and Goliath is from scripture, that David killed Goliath with a crude type of slingshot. That's hardly what a coded message would mean, would it? As for the date, it could mean anything. Can I borrow it for a few days? I have a friend at the American embassy that might be able to analyze it further or put it through crypto graphics to see if it contains something else," Waite asked, sensing he had found a story.

He realized he might be holding in his hand a piece of Israeli intelligence, which could be viewed as evidence if it contained anything of military importance. He had a hunch it did.

Ahmed didn't know whether or not to trust Waite with it. It was his only copy. He offered to copy it for Waite instead. But, the wily, experienced reporter bluffed his way past the offer, flatly refusing, saying only that the embassy would think it was a phony.

"I cannot," Ahmed said quickly testing Waite's intentions. "My brother's blood is on this paper and my conscience, along with it. He must have thought it necessary to die for. I cannot give it to you."

"But . . . Ahmed," Waite parried, "Who else can you trust beside me? Look, once before we trusted each other. We must trust each other again. I owe you a lot for the Fasi interview . . . and, I promise, I'll do my best to find out what the message means."

Ahmed was silent for a moment. He had no other choice. They both knew the reality of the situation.

41

The Palestine Conspiracy

Ahmed had to trust someone sooner or later, a person with no particular political interests. Perhaps, an American field reporter with hopes for a big story could be trusted. He knew Waite's reputation as a meticulous and honest reporter. He had worked with him before. That was reason enough why he sought him out in the first place. He also knew Waite was not a member of the American CIA who might double-cross him. Perhaps, he could be trusted. Ahmed finished drinking his coffee and extended his hand with the piece of paper.

"All right. I shall put my faith in two persons."

"Two persons?" Waite replied.

"Yes. You . . . and Allah. This time only . . . you come first," Ahmed said expressionless.

He instructed Waite, "Give me your word you will show no one but your contact at the American embassy."

Ahmed knew if he was to trust Waite with such a secret, he had to appeal to his journalistic ethic. To a reporter, to disclose a source of information was unthinkable. It was a gamble, but a well calculated one with the odds on Ahmed's side.

"Agreed. On my word as a journalist," Waite spoke in an oath that would convince the Supreme Court, and shook Ahmed's hand, and took the piece of intelligence.

"I must leave now," Ahmed said. "The PLO will miss me. I've already been gone far too long. They may be suspicious of my whereabouts."

Ahmed left Waite's office and walked past the guard who had struck him. He felt like hitting him with his fist, but he stoked his pent-up rage because he had more important things to do. Besides, how could the guard have known who he was? Ahmed descended the stairs and went out into the alleyway being careful that no one had seen him leave. Back on his bicycle, he made his way through the streets back toward the PLO lines, making a mental note of the gunfire in the distance.

It was nearly 10 p.m. Curfew. Things were beginning to quiet down as they did every night, except on the rare occasions when the Israelis or PLO unleashed heavy barrages of artillery at each other to punctuate the passing of a ceasefire deadline or the start of a sudden attack.

When he finally arrived at his unit, no one had missed him. He had been lucky this time. Everyone was busy digging in for the night. There would probably be more fighting in the morning if the Israelis decided to strengthen their position inside the sector. If they did, it would mean a full-scale assault on the PLO positions, including artillery, air strikes and tank fire.

The PLO was not prepared to handle that kind of attack. They all knew they would be easily overrun.

Ahmed was tired, hungry and disheveled, but needed sleep too much to do anything about it. He dug in behind a makeshift cement bunker for protection and fell asleep thinking about the day's events. His perspiration drenched khaki uniform stuck to him as the night cooled down.

CHAPTER 4

Tel Aviv, Israel: 9:47 a.m.

Col. Yitzhak Arial hung up the red telephone and pressed the switch on the computer panel. The computer instantly came alive displaying a map of the entire Israeli air defenses showing more than 800 jet fighters poised for combat. In the event of a military attack, the squadrons would be summoned to mount air raids at an enemy off shore or deep into Lebanon, Jordan, Syria and even Saudi Arabia, if necessary.

He studied the map, especially the secret installation in the Negev Desert where they tested their nuclear arsenal. At Haifa, a secret navy installation with major implications for the defense of Israel was strategically important. Ten squadrons of Israeli built supersonic Jericho F22 fighters stood by on the flight line ready to defend the port city against attack.

Two full squadrons of attack bombers capable of carrying nuclear bombs lay in wait below ground, ready at a single command from Tel Aviv to be raised by elevator to the surface in less than two minutes and be airborne toward their pre-selected targets. Pilots and flight crews slept on the premises around-the-clock, keeping an eerie vigil over the security of the tiny nation.

Occasionally, to break the monotony, maintenance crews would challenge the flight crews who prepared the warplanes to a soccer match in the depths of concrete and steel below the airbase in what looked like the giant innards of a Star Wars movie set. Peculiar as it was, the underground hangar resembled the insides of a nuclear-powered aircraft carrier transplanted below the sandy, but barrier reinforced soil.

It was considered attack proof from a nuclear blast, although it had never been tested. They hoped it never would.

Col. Arial pressed more buttons on the control panel and studied the configurations on Israeli troop and air concentrations positioned to meet an unknown enemy. At a glance, he knew that Israel was overextended in Lebanon, and if the bloody fighting continued with the PLO in Beirut, more ground and tank units would have to be deployed if the Israelis were going to maintain their push into that area. Rear forces had to be protected from counterattack. Israel felt Egypt would stay out of any escalation with Syria and Jordan, if they got into the fray, but prudence still dictated that several squadrons of interceptors and attack bombers be kept at the ready along the Suez-Sinai Peninsula as a precaution. Libya, absolutely, could not be trusted to stay out of any new war.

Col. Arial picked up the telephone. After consulting with other military staff commanders, he decided to put Israeli forces on a first stage alert. Every Israeli male and female knew what that meant. It was the prelude step, which notified the nation that an emergency situation existed and ordered the increased readiness of all military reservists and other needed civilians, which could be mobilized immediately.

The control panel in front of him lit up with the

ominous code words displayed at different points in Israel connected to other military command posts by computer.

"General Sharn," he spoke into the telephone, "we have no reason to believe that something unusual is going on inside Saudi Arabia. We are simply taking precautionary measures to protect our units from rear attack if we penetrate Lebanon any further. We are taking further steps to continue to analyze the Saudi buildup, however."

"Has the defense minister approved these measures?" Sharn asked.

"We already received an approval from Prahoe as long as Israeli army units are considered to be in danger. The prime minister has also been notified."

But, Gen. Sharn already knew this, because he had been briefed on the emergency procedures the military used in such cases and he outranked him. Arial wondered why he had even asked the question?

Shali Prahoe, the defense minister, was a generally cautious man who had never been involved in a general mobilization such as the one, which occurred during the Six Day War with Egypt in June of 1967. Perhaps, he had put Sharn up to the question just to be sure he followed military chain-of-command even though Arial was justified in taking the action alone. Prahoe had been in the army during the more serious Yom Kippur War in which Israel lost more than 2,000 soldiers dead in three weeks of fighting. The consequences of that war in which Israel had nearly been defeated by an Egyptian surprise attack and one in which the Egyptian army advanced across the Suez Canal, left its mark on the total Israeli population as nearly every family felt the sting of death.

After a harrowing two days, Israel devised a brilliant counterattack, which finally forced an advancing Egyptian army to surrender after being surrounded, and cut off from supplies in the sun-scorched Sinai. It was either surrender or die without food or water.

Still, the Israelis knew the Arabs were getting better in tactics, and if they couldn't bring about a peace settlement with the combined Arab nations, they just might lose the next war. Egypt had inflicted the heaviest casualty toll against the Israeli army since the fighting began in 1948. That fact alone seemed to be the singular reason why Israel had signed a peace treaty with Egypt's Anwar Sadat and tried to get other Arab countries to join the peace treaty. However, the Arabs remained divided and would not put their seal of approval on the treaty. Such a treaty, to be valid, would have to recognize one important factor missing in the Egyptian-American-Israeli accord, the recognition and formation of a future Palestinian State.

Gen. Sharn thanked Arial for informing him of the action he had just taken and placed the telephone receiver back on its hook.

Sharn paced the floor of his apartment. My God, a step closer to another war. Will this madness never end? How many Jewish mothers will bury their sons this year? How many Jewish fathers will say goodbye forever to their sons in a general mobilization? What kind of people were these who lived in the Middle East, these Arabs and Jews who didn't care what happened to the lives of their children?

He had to find out what was really going on. He

would meet with Israeli intelligence leaders tomorrow morning to find out why it was necessary to order a first stage alert. It could wait until the next morning, but then he would want precise answers from his military planners.

* * *   * * *

Haifa: 2 p.m.

The Jericho F-22 fighter thundered down the runway gathering speed until its sleek nose pierced the overcast sky, its wheels lifting off the ground and tucking underneath its wings. The afterburners glowed in the overcast as the pilot continued a steep climb out over the Mediterranean. His reconnaissance mission would take him over the Sinai regions, south along Suez, and over Saudi Arabia near Tebuk.

The Americans had communicated with the Israeli government on a troop buildup at Sarti, but as yet, had seen nothing extraordinary at Tebuk, another large airbase. Just in case American spy satellites were wrong, Israel wanted to make sure. The Israelis were looking for something else.

Two more reconnaissance planes blasted into the skies at 30-second intervals following the same flight plan of the first F-22. They would fly at 80,000 feet undetected using radar absorbing materials and jamming devices, which would let them penetrate Saudi airspace with ease. Nothing would show up on the Saudi radar screens. Not even the AWACs, which the Saudis had purchased from the U.S., would see them. The U.S. had given the Israeli's their best technology in a mutual understanding between the two countries. This

The Palestine Conspiracy

is where the secret agreement would payoff.

The three planes linked up at 40,000 feet and continued their climb toward the Sinai undetected. A tanker plane would refuel them over the Red Sea, and again on their return trip to Haifa.

"Gabriel 1, 2 and 3, climbing out to 41,000 feet. Over," the lead pilot acknowledged to military command in Tel Aviv. "Affirmative. Proceed to sector 2 on your chart, refuel, and report upon completion at vectors D2643. Over," the command center replied.

"Roger. Beginning radio silence."

The three jets cruised at subsonic speed to conserve fuel, and reached their rendezvous point at the assigned vector with the tanker plane already waiting at 35,000 feet, slightly below them and in the sun. Breaking radio silence, the pilot spoke into his helmet microphone.

"Gabriel 1, 2 and 3 arriving for a snack."

The tanker pilot waggled his wings and responded, "Pull alongside and drink up. We'll see you on the way back for an early breakfast. Over."

"Roger, snack 1."

The three reconnaissance fighters moved up behind the wings of the tanker plane, one off each side and the third behind the tail. They hooked up with flexible refueling booms where they would take in the extra fuel for the round trip. After five minutes, the lead pilot, watching his fuel indicator point to full, broke away from the tanker and waited for the others to finish. Seconds, later, when they had finished taking in the precious liquid, they broke away from the tanker and rejoined their flight leader.

They continued their climb to 70,000 feet, quietly pulling away from the tanker and leaving it behind over the Red Sea. The fighters, glimmering in the sunlight, gracefully turned eastward toward Saudi Arabia. The tension mounted as the pilots switched on their radar absorbing technology and began transmitting a false jamming signal, which would disguise their presence over Saudi airspace. At precisely 3:31 p.m., the Israeli jets entered Saudi airspace flying at approximately 650 knots. There would be no radio communication with Tel Aviv until the mission was over. Each copilot checked his infrared camera equipment and laser guided computer systems. Everything was working perfectly, but they would have only enough fuel for one pass over the target. They climbed to 80,000 feet for the run. The target was coming into view, some 12 minutes ahead and 130 miles away.

* * *   * * *

At Sarti, General Necomis' plan to activate the AWACs had already begun. One AWAC radar picket had already been in the Saudi skies for more than an hour. Two others were fueled up and ready to go. The AWAC cruised at 500 mph at 35,000 feet. Technicians intently watched the luminous radar screens in the darkness, searching the skies toward Iraq.

Minutes ticked off as the technicians flipped switches and monitored computer readouts.

One of the radar technicians rubbed his eyes as the debilitating effects of constantly staring into the video screen began to take its toll. He needed a break. But he knew another technician would relieve him in only minutes, so he relaxed again to finish out his watch.

The AWAC swung in a wide arc over the Shaqra Desert, northwest of Riyadh, the Arabian capital, and far enough inland so as to be protected from the range of any incoming missiles in an attempt to knock them down. It would circle constantly for seven more hours and then land at Sarti while another AWAC would take its place at 35,000 feet and continue the unending vigil.

The planes were Boeing 707's converted to AWACs, fitted with four engines, burning fuel at the rate of six gallons a minute. The AWAC was a flying radar station, which could monitor anything in the air above and below it for a radius of 250 miles. It had become an integral part of the Saudi air defense system, which the President of the United States had authorized in exchange for world stabilization of oil production and to counter any threat of an oil cutoff by Iraq.

The radar sentry rubbed his eyes again, looked at his watch and realized his crewman was late to relieve him. He blinked his eyes to clear them. He blinked again, and peered more closely at the screen. Suddenly, his head snapped back in astonishment. There, in the right front quadrant of the screen, were three blips at 70,783 feet above the AWAC and to the northwest, closing at a speed of 644 knots toward the interior of Saudi Arabia. He adjusted the control knobs and switched on the anti-jamming device that permitted the computer to fine-tune the display and ignore the false signals the rogue fighters were transmitting in an attempt to foil the system.

Could it be an atmospheric aberration, he wondered? The weather was perfect over Saudi Arabia, no unusual atmospheric conditions to interfere with radar and no sunspot activity reported by weather observers at central command.

He leaned over and touched the toning device to identify the three blips vectored in on Tebuk, 120 miles from the three reconnaissance planes. My God! The toner shrieked with a shrill that astonished even him because he knew it was no drill. The computer had identified the aircraft on the console screen. Three Jericho fighters were on a heading toward one of Saudi Arabia's most secret and sensitive areas.

He jumped to his feet, exclaiming in Arabic, "Israelah! Israelah! Targets at 11 o'clock!"

Holding his headset with one hand, he simultaneously pushed an alarm button, which automatically sent an emergency signal to scramble fighter planes at Tebuk. Allah be praised, he still couldn't believe his eyes!

At Tebuk, jet fighter pilots raced to their planes, helmets flying and chairs strewn aside as sirens wailed the alert. The engines of their F-16 interceptors had already been started for them by their crew chiefs. They clambered up the sides of the planes and strapped themselves in.

The base commander radioed the AWAC.

"This is commander Atohl at Tebuk. What have you identified?"

"Sir," he spoke excitedly, "three confirmed Israeli intruders, Jericho fighters at 70,400 feet showing a heading of 278 degrees, 110 kilometers from your point."

"Are they out of range of our interceptors?" the commander asked. "What do you think they are up to?"

The Palestine Conspiracy

He had only minutes to contact General Necomis and decide what action to take against the Israelis. A staff aide announced to him that Necomis and the king were standing by on the military hotline for consultation.

"This is commander Atohl," the voice spoke urgently into the phone mouthpiece. "Israeli warplanes vectoring in on our position, sir."

"How many are there? What altitude?" Necomis wanted to know.

"Three Jericho fighters climbing to 80,000 feet, well out of range of our interceptors. They've already been scrambled, sir."

"What is their intent?" Necomis asked.

"We don't know. They have maintained radio silence thus far."

"Do you think you can lure them down?" Necomis asked.

"I don't think so. We've been tracking them for five minutes, and they have held a steady course. What do you think they are doing here, general? Do you think they're off course?" the Tebuk commander wanted to know.

"Nonsense! No military plane in this part of the world is off course 300 miles, especially if they're Israeli!" Necomis thundered back into the intercom. "They're too precise, too good for that! Ready the antiaircraft missiles, and standby to fire them!" he ordered.

The king, listening over the intercom, said nothing, but agreed with the general's decision. Yet, he wondered if Necomis would ask his permission to attack before actually ordering the countermeasure.

The Palestine Conspiracy

Necomis spoke slowly and carefully into the mouthpiece, which connected him to the missile batteries at the airbase. He wanted no mistakes in the communication. An aide was tape recording the entire conversation by Necomis' order. It would provide an accurate account of the event after it was all over.

"Your majesty, do I have your permission to launch the attack?" Necomis finally asked the king.

The question reassured the king of Necomis' loyalty to him and the royal family.

"General, proceed with the attack. It is an intrusion of Saudi airspace in violation of international law. These are military planes capable of significant damage to our nation. You may launch the attack when ready."

"Thank you, your majesty," the general said respectfully. He nodded to the aide standing by at the firing control. The missiles were at the ready in their firing positions, their radar units and heat seeking systems precisely matched to their high-altitude targets fleeting across the sky at near super-sonic speed.

The base commander, the AWAC technician and the aide all held their collective breaths. If they missed the attacking planes with the radar seeking system, the missiles were designed to transmit a signal to an orbiting satellite 22,500 miles in deep space, which would instantaneously send commands to the missiles' homing device to lock in the target by laser corrected guidance and infrared sensors. The satellites would guide the missiles to their intended targets. The system, operational and fully tested a few years prior by the American military, was nearly infallible and had a kill ratio of 99 percent. Three planes; six attacking missiles.

They would not miss.

"Standby to fire," he ordered.

The base commander at Tebuk stood with his eyes transfixed on the radar screen linked by satellite to the AWAC plane.

Meanwhile, the three Jericho's nosed their way to 80,000 feet and the copilots completed their checklist of the camera equipment on board. Everything was working normally.

"Antiradar device on, signaling response set, interference terminal on, we're virtually invisible," one of the copilots mused.

Confident that no one could see or track them from the ground, he squinted out the cockpit window and could see the target 20 miles away. The Israeli crews would soon begin what amounted to a bomb run over Tebuk using laser-guided cameras through a bombsight.

The lead pilot looked at the digital stop clock in his cockpit and switched the plane over to autopilot. The fighter would be held on a steady course for the recon run which would take approximately two minutes. The plane had to hold a steady course to ensure clear, high-resolution pictures for intelligence experts in Tel Aviv. No deviation, not the slightest.

The copilot leaned forward and peered into his target scope, much like a World War II bombardier, and sighted the target just ahead. The computerized targeting system was already calculating the estimated arrival over the target . . . three seconds, two seconds, one . . . cameras on.

The equipment in the three planes switched on and a slight whirring sound could be heard inside the cockpit reassuring the pilots that everything was working correctly.

After a minute, halfway over the target, one of the copilots broke his radio silence . . . "Missile lock, attack mode, sir!" he spoke calmly into the headset.

Necomis had given the order. The Hawk missiles had been fired from their launch sites at Tebuk.

"How close are they?" the command pilot responded matter-of-factly.

"20,000 feet. A lock on us, sir!"

He knew what that meant. They must break off the target and evade if they were to have any chance of escaping the deadly blasts that were sure to follow in only seconds.

"Six missiles," the copilot interrupted. "Five seconds apart, twenty seconds to impact," he said becoming more agitated.

Instantly, the command pilot gave the order to break off the attack. But, he alone would take a calculated gamble and continue his run over the target. To continue with the entire squadron would be like murdering his own pilots. If the others broke away now, the missiles would lock onto the two other planes, which would be lower and closer. With effective countermeasures, they could evade the oncoming missiles, recover, and head for the safety of the Red Sea. He needed only 45 more seconds to photograph the entire target. It was a chance to complete the mission. But his life and the lives of his fellow pilots depended on the technology built into their planes.

The two trailing planes suddenly rolled to the right, broke off the target, and began a sharp descent to get below the attacking missiles. The Israeli pilots fired white-hot flares from the rear of their planes to divert the heat-seeking missiles. The radar-deflecting configuration of the Jericho's should have made the planes invisible. But, something had happened? How had the Saudi's detected them?

The command pilot continued his run over the target while his co-pilot observed the missiles closing in on their position.

"Captain, five missiles veering off toward the other planes, it's working!" he shouted. "One is still with us. We must take immediate evasive action!"

The captain pressed his right forefinger to the front of the stick and fired two flares perpendicular to the tail of his aircraft, then two more in quick succession. But, the last missile ignored the heat from the flares and continued to lock onto the Jericho hot thrust, guided to its target by the satellite overhead, correcting the missile's trajectory to match that of the evading F-22. The satellite high in the sky continually scanned and disregarded the false jamming signals and decoy flares, homing in on the attacking Jericho.

The copilot's eyes widened. He knew before he could speak. The two other evading Jericho's exploded on his radar screen as the Saudi missiles found their mark.

"Jehovah!" he screamed aloud over the headset.

"Abort the run!"

The captain interrupted.

"Quiet, and concentrate! Only 30 more seconds over the target!"

"It's too late! Red 2 and 3 are hit! Missile closing in! Five seconds!"

Before the captain could move his control stick, he glanced to the side of the cockpit and saw the Angel of

The Palestine Conspiracy

Death onrushing in the form of a Hawk missile. It was over in a split-second. The explosion was thunderous. The pain never felt. All three Jericho's had been destroyed over the target. There would be no refueling, no rendezvous over the Red Sea, and no return home to Israel.

Israeli military personnel watched in stunned silence as the three planes disappeared from their radar screens. They knew what had just occurred. Their flight commander had taken a calculated risk and lost. The mission was a failure.

How had the Saudi's tracked their planes by the AWACs? They weren't supposed to have that capability. Six Israeli pilots dead, three Israeli planes destroyed. The whole world would know about it in a few hours.

Military officers in Haifa were stunned by the failure. Defense Minister Shali Prahoe was quietly informed at his residence and notified the prime minister. All hell would break loose in the next few days.

One of the Israeli intelligence officers, hands clasped over his face, tried to control his disbelief when he suddenly heard the tele-scanner start up. His attention turned to the printer, which began producing photographs of the target run over Tebuk.

The flight commander had switched on the transmitter to send the pictures by satellite to Israel ground stations some 900 miles away. In an instant, before his death, he had transmitted the results to the intelligence center. The photographs were coming in.

The intelligence officer looked at the remarkable clarity of the photos, and immediately saw that the mission not only was a failure, but that the crisp still photographs showed nothing unusual at Tebuk. Everything appeared normal, except for one thing. Israel now had six dead pilots and three downed aircraft on its hands to explain to the world . . . and for nothing of any consequence?

At Tebuk, there was tremendous jubilation as the AWACs radar tracker announced over the intercom that the Hawks had destroyed the Israeli intruders.

"Congratulations, general!" King Fasaid praised. "You have served your country well today! You will be rewarded for your actions. I must now make preparations to announce to the world what has just taken place," he said.

"Your majesty," Necomis said boldly. "It is a great day for the Saudi armed forces. But, what will we tell the world? We don't know what the Israelis were doing in our airspace."

"We'll make them explain," the king responded. "We will demand to know. We will take our case to the United Nations. The whole world will be outraged at Israel . . ."

CHAPTER 5

London: May 4. 6:00 a.m.

Adrienne snuggled closer to Brian and draped her arm over his chest. She heard the clock radio click on as the sun began to seep in through the balcony window. The early morning breeze gently lifted the curtains from the wall giving ethereal warmth to the room.

Brian stretched, stirring slightly in his sleep, reaching toward the radio, fumbling at the snooze alarm. Shutting it off, he rolled back and closed his eyes again. Adrienne knew he had a military flight to catch at 8 o'clock. She wished she could lie there with him the rest of the morning, but if she let him sleep any longer, there would be a mad rush to Langehorn Air Base, and she didn't relish the thought of that.

"Brian," she whispered softly in his ear. "Time to get up."

Brian gripped the covers tightly; mumbling at Adrienne, then fell instantly back to sleep. She rubbed his chest with her hand and kissed him on the cheek. Her hands and head moved slowly beneath the covers until they reached his sensitive area. She could hear his breathing quicken as she massaged him, feeling his excitement building as he slowly aroused in his sleep. She knew it was every man's fantasy to be awakened like this, and she was good at it.

After thirty seconds of this, he was fully interested

in what Adrienne was doing and amused by it all. But now, he would take control of the situation as he reached down and stroked her hair and ran his fingers down her back until they reached her buttocks. He slowly reached his hand around her thigh and gently moved it between her legs until she began to sigh with pleasure. Her breathing became more urgent as he felt her move underneath his hand. Adrienne moaned with shortened breaths punctuated with slight shrieks of pleasure as he positioned her to straddle him in the opposite direction. They began their lovemaking in earnest, oblivious to whatever emotional discharges their sounds had in the adjoining flat. During the twenty minutes they excitedly aroused each other's pleasures, Brian had to reach over twice to turn off the snooze alarm. God, that irritated the hell out of him. The buzzing was absolutely unnerving.

"Son-of-a-bitch," he muttered to himself continuing to kiss her breasts. She had thrown every ounce of strength into the morning's lovemaking session and was now spent in an orgasmic frenzy. She wanted to lie quietly with him now, letting the breeze cool both of them down.

But she saw Brian turn and look at the clock. 6:36 a.m. Time to head for the airbase.

Sweeping the covers aside in one motion and planting his feet on the floor, he asked, "Are you seeing me off at the base this morning?"

"Uhmmmm. . . " she replied sleepily. "Of course, love. Do you think I'm an ungrateful lover?"

"Well, how about getting me a bit of breakfast, while I take a shower," he said turning on the television.

Adrienne rolled from underneath the covers and

eventually made her way into the kitchen.

Brian showered, toweled off, and shaved before returning to the bedroom. When he got there, breakfast was waiting for him in the form of two poached eggs, rye toast, coffee and a fresh glass of orange juice.

Marvelous. Adrienne could be fantastic at the whole thing. Marriage. It was a serious step for both of them. But it might be nice. He had never been married, and he was already 30 years old. Perhaps his mother was right? Maybe it was time for him to settle down and raise a family?

But, he would miss the excitement of the espionage work in her majesty's service. Maybe he could do the less dangerous assignments. No more counter-intelligence work. The thought intrigued him for a moment.

"Well, you sure did go all out this morning in more ways than one," he said with silly sarcasm. "What's on the tube this morning?"

"It's the same stuff every day. I don't see how people can watch it to tell you the truth."

"Yeah, it would get to me. Imagine if you were married. You'd be at home watching it every day," he teased.

"Are you serious? That's the absolute last way in the world I'd spend the rest of my life," she responded while getting dressed.

"Imagine, me. A house mum tied to the soaps all day long, with loads of laundry to boot."

Brian laughed. It was her tender spot.

She was particularly bright in her job as a reporter for the London Times. And, she could be tough as hell when she had to be, too.

The Palestine Conspiracy

"Oh, all right. Don't look at me that way," he said. "I was only kidding."

As they ate breakfast, talking over their plans, a BBC announcer came on.

"We interrupt this program to bring you an important news announcement. Reuters News Service in Riyadh, the capital of Saudi Arabia, has just learned at a news conference held by that country's defense minister, that they have shot down three Israeli reconnaissance aircraft over the desert airbase of Tebuk.

"The attacking planes were shot down by six American made Hawk ground-to-air anti-aircraft missiles, all hitting their intended targets. The planes were destroyed, according to Saudi Arabian defense officials, and the pilots are all presumed dead. Saudi forces have been placed on full alert for any contingency measures that may need to be taken. The government of Israel has made no comment on the announcement, but is expected to do so within the hour.

"Saudi Defense Chief Patri Sakhul showed outrage at the attempted penetration of Saudi airspace and indicated that King Fasaid had been kept fully aware of the developments as they were occurring. Sakhul stated that Fasaid gave his direct authorization to shoot down the aircraft over Saudi territory.

"In a statement released by the king, and I quote, 'Saudi Arabian territorial sovereignty was violated by the Israeli government for unknown reasons. The warplanes attacked from the Red Sea and deliberately over flew top-secret military installations for the purpose of taking reconnaissance photographs. There is nothing of significance to hide at Tebuk, and our country asks for a complete explanation as to the incursion. We are, thus, requesting the United States to apply immediate pressure on the Israeli government to disclose their reasons for this unwarranted and unprecedented flight into our airspace. We have also formally requested through the United Nations that a full-scale investigation be conducted and that full details be discussed at an emergency session of the General Assembly so that Israel can respond to the charges.

"'I repeat, Saudi Arabia is a peace loving nation which acted under international law and fully within its rights as a sovereign nation to protect its borders. Saudi Arabia does not seek or intend any retaliation against Israel for its act of aggression. World opinion will agree that our country acted with rightful and prudent force in not taking any further action against Israel.'"

The BBC commentator ended the bulletin with other reports flowing in from the Middle East describing surprise and anger from other neighboring countries condemning Israel for what had just occurred.

Brian could not believe what he was hearing.

Did ICE miss something big in the works? He and Geoff had wondered about that the day before. He quickly got dressed.

"I've got to get to Langehorn fast."

Adrienne was shocked by the terse announcement on the telly. Brian would be in more danger than ever now. Why did he have to go to Beirut anyway? Was Thayer's meeting with Fasi that important? Perhaps she could find out more? But she knew that would make Brian angry. He became incensed with her when she pried into his affairs, which was none of her business, especially when it involved top-secret intelligence work. He hardly ever talked about it with her, but he had let it slip out last night.

Most of his work was of a highly sensitive nature, and he let her know that under no circumstances did he want her involved in it, especially since she was a Pulitzer Prize reporter at the London Times. It was simply none of her business. She would even badger him with the fact that he would never really trust her with highly sensitive information because she was his girlfriend. Being a journalist outweighed even that trust. Their relationship was predicated on her not asking too many questions. But it didn't matter now. She would disregard that and make the attempt anyway while accompanying Brian to Langehorn.

Like clockwork, once inside the taxi, she started in on him.

"Brian," she began, "do you think the Israelis could have strayed off course over Tebuk?"

His answer was direct. "Hardly!"

"You mean you think it was deliberate?"

Brian knew her methods and knew what she was up to. It really pissed him off. But, he ignored his anger for the time being. And, Adrienne knew that he knew, but they both continued the charade, the cat-and-mouse game, as the cab weaved its way through London's traffic.

It began to drizzle.

"Yes," he answered crisply. "But what could it mean? And why would they be so interested in Tebuk to risk losing three advanced fighter planes like the Jericho's unless they were concerned about something of extreme importance."

"You mean something that was a distinct threat to

them?"

"Yes, Adrienne," he answered, irritated at her every parry and thrust, pressing him for every detail that she could.

"I would bet they were looking for something very important to risk a mission like that and then have it blown to hell by the Hawks," he said.

"Have you ever seen what a Hawk missile can do to its target? Of course not."

"I saw a defense film once when I was sixteen years old. I was in high school. It was horrible," she said turning to look out the cab's window. "How can men do that to each other?"

"Very easily . . . and very precisely when precisely many lives are at stake," he said grimly. The cab squealed to a stop near the main gate. A green-brown military command car pulled up to meet them. Brian leaned over and gave Adrienne a warm, passionate kiss and then left the cab, shouting through the rain.

"I'll be back in about a month. I'll wire you from Beirut," he yelled getting into the command car. "Take care of yourself."

* * *　　* * *

Geoff was inside the command car and gave him a huge grin.

"So you took my advice, after all?"

"Well, it's going to be a long four weeks without her. Did you hear the news?"

"Yes, I heard it about six hours ago, long before you and the public got it. I was going to call, but I figured you'd be busy with Adrienne. Anyway, I felt it could wait until you got here. There's not much we can do about it at this point, anyway," Geoff said.

"How does it change our plans?"

"It doesn't. It just complicates things a bit more.

"Has intelligence come up with anything more on Sarti?"

"Nothing. That's because the Saudi government isn't talking.

And they won't until this thing has run its course or until they can wring as much propaganda out of it as possible."

Geoff was right on that score. He was always right about things like that. He had become an invaluable trusted military assistant to Mrs. Thayer. She paid him very well to analyze worldwide events, and in the process, he had become her top political, international and trusted advisor on world affairs. He had pretty much assessed the situation in the Middle East as one of unceasing futility and frustration for the Arabs in their attempt to establish a Palestinian State - a state where Palestinians could live within their own secure borders and subject to their own self-rule.

"How's Maggie reacting to the news?" Brian asked matter-of-factly.

"Well, she certainly didn't expect this. She's nearly beside herself. The timing couldn't have been worse. But she's decided to get on with it anyway. It's a tough call, but you know her. She's tough. But, there's one thing she is worried about, and that's that we won't be able to keep this damned trip secret much longer. I suppose she'll want to move up the timetable. You haven't mentioned this in any way to your girlfriend have you?

"Of course not," he lied with a convincing-enough tone.

But he had. In lying to Geoff, he felt it wasn't something he was compelled to tell the truth about, and he simply shrugged it off mentally. He knew she wasn't a security risk.

Adrienne took one last look at the main gate of the giant airbase and instructed the cab driver to drive her back to Brian's flat. There she could relax and pull her thoughts together for tomorrow's day at The Times.
Things hadn't been going well for her lately. The stories she was working on were cold, and there had been nothing new in the way of exciting assignments for weeks. In fact, the boredom was so great, it was beginning to become routine, and routine to a foreign correspondent or investigative reporter was just unnerving. In fact, it was beginning to drive her a bit bonkers, but as a savvy journalist, she recognized it and adjusted to it. Sometimes, in the news business, news just disappeared for a time before it surfaced
again in some ugly way that only the world could understand when it was witnessed and reported. That's the way it was lately, it had just gone into the doldrums and Adrienne was just living with it.

The drive back was just as boring as on the way in, and to make it worse, the driver was mired in early morning rush hour. As they waited, she watched the rain pelt the pedestrians scurrying about London, when her thoughts drifted back to a much earlier time. She stared blankly at the raindrops beading up in a neat random collection of droplets on the cab's window and remembered a very different time and very different place when she was an orphan child growing up in an English family.

She had been brought to England when she was nearly fourteen, and could only vaguely remember bits and pieces of her background since the plane crash.

As hard as she tried, she could remember only a few fuzzy details of the horrible crash. The rescue people had pulled her from the wreckage, near death, explaining to her that it had left her with a partial amnesia. At her age, Adrienne really didn't fully understand what had happened to her or much of anything about the syndrome. She was told only that her flight had originated in Riyadh where she had purchased a boarding pass for the flight to Nicosia. Her passport and all other personal belongings had been burned in the crash. Indeed, she and a few other passengers were lucky to be alive.

The last thing she remembered was the DC-10 gyrating out of control on its final approach to the island capital. She remembered being seated next to a middle-aged Turk traveling home to Ankara from the Middle East by way of Nicosia. She had been intrigued by his angular features, his thick black hair, his bushy eyebrows, and sun-darkened skin which made his nose seem to curve even more downward, like a bent cavalry sword. His deep-set eyes and bushy mustache made him the epitome of an imagined evil character from an Arabian Knights tale.

She knew instinctively it was wrong to judge a man in this way, but she couldn't help herself. At only fourteen and traveling alone, she was easily influenced and the things she had seen in Riyadh had given her more misfortune than she would have liked for the rest of her life. Indeed, the entire mysterious adventure had been a rather frightening experience for her, to say the least.

And, so she had focused on the Turkish who sat beside her. He was a large, imposing sort, and his appearance made her so uneasy that she could not bring herself to make eye contact with him.

Yet, as the flight progressed, she somehow managed to summon up the courage within her to finally speak to him in a steady, unfaltering voice. After each exchange of information about themselves on the three-hour flight, she began to feel more comfortable with him and actually began enjoying the
conversation. She actually thought he was smart, wise and educated, compared to those she was used to in the desert. In fact, she thought he must be a teacher.

As the flight neared Nicosia, she was beginning to feel a little sad that the flight would soon end, and that she might never see him again. She was happy that she had started the conversation with him, even though he was a stranger, a foreigner and a non-Islamic

But what Adrienne couldn't know was that she had been a victim of another kind of international intrigue as she secretly made her escape on that flight from the thieves who had sold her in the Riyadh slave markets. After being raped repeatedly by prospective buyers, she had struggled against impossible odds to free herself during one of their many drunken orgies and escape.

It had taken her months to earn enough money working on the streets to buy a plane ticket for Cyprus and eventual freedom. Like a true Bedouin, she would be free again to roam other lands, because she vowed never to return to Saudi Arabia.

As the plane began its final approach to Nicosia, Adrienne felt the aircraft shake slightly, swaying from side-to-side. She, and the other passengers weren't alarmed by the vibrations at first, and attributed it to air turbulence. As their breaths caught in their throats, they reassured themselves that it was part of the normal landing approach. But the vibrations became more intense, and in an instant, the flight attendants were running to the rear of the plane to escape the sudden decompression of air.

Something was drastically wrong. There had been an explosion in one of the cargo compartments, blowing upward and outward. The cargo outer doors had exploded in a small fireball, causing a rapid, sudden decompression and loss of air speed. The plastic explosives had gone off exactly as the terrorists had planned when the plane descended below 500 feet. The altimeter bomb had worked to perfection. The PLO had set a deadly trap, and Adrienne and the other innocent passengers and crew had been caught in it like insects in a spider's web.

The pilot struggled with the controls to bring the plane back on course, but he was desperately losing airspeed, which would cause the plane to stall unless he immediately added more engine thrust. He pushed forward on the throttles - all the way forward - knowing it was already too late. He shoved hard on the yoke to get the nose down as the engines revved to power up. He had done the right thing and obviously was a good pilot. Most pilots would have erred immediately and pulled the nose up sharply, guaranteeing a stall of the plane's airspeed. But, even these expert efforts weren't enough to save them. The split-second delay had cost them dearly, and the pilot sensed it.

"Damn! " he exclaimed into the mouthpiece.

The plane's nose pitched downward. But, the co-pilot watched in horror as the airspeed indicator came up a bit, and then faltered. There was too much drag on the aircraft. The plane began to stall and fell awkwardly toward the runway, now only one-and-a-half miles away while the cockpit-warning device droned in the background.

PULL UP, PULL UP, STALL, STALL, STALL . . . ADD POWER, ADD POWER. .

The DC-10 plowed through the gray overcast toward Nicosia Airport and its grim encounter with the ground, its passengers frozen in fear and their fate sealed in the hands of an experienced but helpless pilot as he stared at death through the cockpit window.

For a split-second, Adrienne looked through the plane's window and glimpsed the runway lights in the distance. They seemed to twinkle, a contradiction in what was really happening to them, a bit of time frozen so that there could be no forgiveness at their speed and altitude. That moment transcended her fear. And, she imagined herself still safely on the ground watching her own aircraft tumble out of control toward the airport.

Suddenly, she was shocked back to reality as the jet plunged sharply to the left and downward, beginning an uncontrolled descent. The passengers screamed with terror. Baggage and loose materials flew everywhere inside the cabin. In a panic, Adrienne grasped the hand of the Turk. He, too, clung to her.

The Palestine Conspiracy

At that moment, she knew she was going to die. It was to be her moment of death. She would die beside a stranger, a man she didn't know. But, if that was Allah's will, she could not change it.

The pilot pulled back on the yoke with all his strength now in a final act of desperation. His co-pilot radioed that they could not make the runway.

"Flight 577! Can't pull up! Airspeed 120! Losing altitude! Adding full thrust! Too late! Too late!" he screamed into the headset.

The pilot saw the ground come up with sickening speed and realized he was already dead before the plane hit the ground. The nose of the DC-10 mashed into the soft embankment and piled up a layer of mud several feet deep, pushing it ahead of the nose, and underneath the fuselage. The two-day drizzle may have been a factor in sparing many lives as the plane caught fire now parallel to the missed runway. The rain had soaked everything and large puddles of water near the runway drenched the entire plane from wingtip to wingtip, and entire fuselage threw up a giant wave of spray. The spray quickly extinguished the flames as the plane skidded out of control.

If they were to be lucky, they had to be lucky twice. And they were. They had added only enough fuel at Riyadh for a one-way trip. The plane's fuel tanks were nearly empty. That fact alone saved the lives of many on board.

Adrienne couldn't have realized how lucky she would be as the plane slid across an adjacent runway then back onto a grassy apron where it came to its final resting place. The floor below her collapsed, the fuselage broke apart. But, they had chosen seats in the tail section, and that section - the entire rear of the plane including the vertical stabilizer - had been torn away from the main part of the aircraft and had come to rest in a puddle of muddy, oily water only a few inches deep. An eerie silence enveloped them and the other passengers who were alive and still fastened in their seats. Adrienne and the Turk were still locked together in a white-knuckle death grip when the tail section came to a thunderous and heart-pounding halt.

A few others, strapped in adjacent seats near them, had also survived. She tried to focus on a distant light as rain pelted her face, hair and eyes. She looked up and saw nothing but darkness in the night sky. The roof of the aircraft had ripped away, exposing survivors to the downpour, but it was a refreshing feeling, a reawakening of life splattering over her entire body, wetting her down as though she had just stepped into a shower. Her eyes twirled in a daze of fear and excitement as she lost focus for a moment. She reached up to wipe the rain from her mud-splattered and bleeding forehead. It was then that she realized she was still holding the hand of the Turkish man she had been talking to only a few moments before. She looked down at the severed hand of the Turkish man and let out a terrifying scream, fainting in a split-second of horror.

When she later regained consciousness at the hospital, the episode had left its mark, and she could not remember anything about the crash. Doctors and nurses had worked feverishly to save her, but her memory lapses would continue for the next decade.

The Palestine Conspiracy

She knew nothing of her real name. She had used a false name on her identification when she boarded the plane at Riyadh. There were no papers to identify her. The thought of not knowing her true identity would become a daily trial to her while employed at The Times. But, she hadn't let it interfere with her life. She hadn't talked with Brian about it at all, because she hadn't felt the need to. He had met her parents, and they all got along rather well. That's all that mattered to her for the time being. But some day, there would be a time, that her curiosity would arouse deep within her, and when that day came, she would tell him, or anyone else, what it was about herself that she kept secret in the dark complex of her soul.

The taxi driver pulled to an abrupt stop. The jerking action brought her back to the present. She paid the driver, and stepped into the rain. She hurried inside to her apartment, and once there, slumped onto the sofa curling up into a ball. She slept until noon, emotionally spent from the morning's hectic pace and painful remembrances.

CHAPTER 6

Beirut: May 5. 5 p.m.

In private, Waite handed Ahmed's message to a friend at the U.S. embassy and asked him to interpret it.

The message was written in Hebrew.

His friend, a professor of languages at American University, would provide Waite with a precise translation.

"What does it say?" Waite asked without trying to appear too eager.   "What does it say?" the professor replied categorically, "or what else might it say?"

The professor read the translation aloud.

"Intercept David and Goliath. July 24. God be praised."

He repeated it like an oath to Waite again.

"It could mean anything. Certainly there is not enough there to hide some sort of code. Its meaning is beyond my understanding, but I could have the embassy staff run it through CIA's crypto graphics just to make sure."

Waite had learned nothing new, but he certainly couldn't take the chance of it getting into the hands of the CIA now. Journalists just didn't let those things happen.

"Where did you get it?" the professor pressed him.

The question caught him by surprise and startled Waite.

The Palestine Conspiracy

"Uh. . . a friend of mine is studying Hebrew . . . a fellow reporter . . . he . . . ahhh . . . wanted a literal translation . . . I knew you could provide me with one, so I brought it to you," he said shifting nervously on his feet.

"But any Jew could provide you with the proper translation, why come to me?"

The professor knew he was lying, but being the good friend that he was, he understood there must be a good reason, and didn't challenge him any further. Such were the necessities of maintaining a good friendship, and the professor didn't want to ruin the relationship between them.

"It is rather an odd message though, isn't it?" the professor went on hoping to get Rick to volunteer the information. "I mean, it's written on Israeli military intelligence paper. Where did your friend get a supply of that?"

Waite felt himself go cold. That tidbit of information was entirely new to him; the professor had unwittingly corroborated Ahmed's story. Waite had promised not to breathe a word of this to anyone, but now the professor knew. The only salvation Waite had was that he had confirmed Ahmed's integrity. There was so much treachery going on in Beirut these days, even among friends, that nothing could be taken for granted regarding personal safety. He could clearly sense the professor was suspicious.

"Well, you see, my friend is studying Israeli history at the university; his girlfriend is in the Israeli army. He happened to write down the phrase on a piece of military paper she had and stuffed it into his pocket," he tried to explain convincingly.

"Well, look, I've got to get going. I'm already late for a meeting with my bureau guys, and the shit's going to hit the fan if I don't show up on time."

Waite thanked the professor and left the embassy wondering what to do next? Had he convinced the professor of the simplicity of the message? He wasn't sure.

The embassy had been a regular stop on Waite's daily beat in Beirut; he hoped his impromptu visit didn't arouse the professor's suspicions too much - too much, to mention it to one of his other friends stationed there - members of the CIA.

So, he still had the peculiar message in his possession and it was not going to go away. He still had to deal with it. The professor had more or less verified that fact that it was indeed probably from inside the Israeli intelligence apparatus. Perhaps, it was in some sort of Hebrew code. Waite walked casually past the marines guarding the embassy's perimeter, not too fast, not too slow; he did not wish to arouse any suspicions. Once clear of the main gate, he climbed into his old, beat up, rusted-out Volvo, the standard run-about in Beirut these days. The car actually belonged to the UPI bureau station. Despite its condition, it ran pretty well, and it was one of the few useful tools available to his crew in getting to the outskirts of the city whenever there was an attack or bombing to cover. Covering those kinds of events was always extremely dangerous, running roadblocks, obstacles, mortars, or just plain getting around the interior of the city. Because he was a reporter, a well-known foreign correspondent, they could kill him at any time they chose. By either the Israeli's or the PLO. It didn't much matter once you were dead. He was an obvious target for gunners of all factions, and he could be taken out by any of them whenever they wanted to and for whatever reason they wished. Everyone knew who Rick Waite was these days. He was well known to all of them, on every side, and there were at least four factions that could be identified. Then, there were the fringe elements that had their own agendas. Who knew what groups they represented?

He spun the Volvo one-hundred eighty degrees in the courtyard, zigzagging his way through the anti-terrorist barricades set up in front of the embassy wall designed to stop any terrorist squads from moving easily into the compound, and drove onto the main boulevard speeding past scores of bicyclists. The Americans had learned an expensive lesson years earlier when a terrorist drove a truck loaded with dynamite straight into the lobby of a Beirut hotel where two-hundred and fifty marines were bivouacked, blowing it up, killing most of them.

When Waite got past the final barricade, he felt a wave of relief sweep over him. He had not intentionally violated his promise to Ahmed. At least not yet. He let out a deep breath. The secret message was indeed stolen from Israeli intelligence and had been written on courier paper. It would have to be deciphered, but by whom beside the American CIA?

The possibilities raced through his mind. If it was a valuable piece of Israeli intelligence, then it had to be something very important, and that might mean a big story.

One person was already dead because of it. Ahmed's brother had risked his life to get the message to the PLO. He must have considered it very important to pay for it with his life.

Waite drove the Volvo at breakneck speed avoiding the hundreds of pedestrians along the side streets. He tuned-in one of the many local pirate radiobroadcasts on the car radio. The radio had a short in it somewhere, and he had to intermittently pound his fist against the dashboard to get the antenna to make contact with the radio jack as he listened for any announcements of new fighting in the city.

Suddenly, everyone on the streets started jumping-off their bicycles and running into the small shops and adjacent alleyways. Waite swerved, narrowly missing a bicyclist cutting across his path. He spun the wheel to the right, slammed on the brakes, but still hit the curb as the Volvo spun out of control. The next thing he heard was the explosion of the car's right front tire.

"Damn!" he shouted, straightening the wheel. When he finally screeched to a stop, he got out, looked at the skid marks, and inspected the tire while scores of others ran in his direction and past him to take cover from the sound they had quickly learned to fear.

Waite heard it, too. No spare in the trunk to put on, and no time to spare now, as he instinctively looked up, and joined the rest running for cover.

As his adrenalin pumped through his body, a reflexive mentality took over from his old combat days in Vietnam. He had heard that sound plenty of times before during the Tet Offensive.

The Palestine Conspiracy

Incoming 140mm Katusha rockets. Russian-built. And, deadly.

The familiar whooshing sounded like an old friend to him, but he knew there was no time to waste. His instincts told him that this one was on target and only meters away. He had heard the sound so often in Vietnam, he could gauge how close they were going to hit. He had never been wrong. The sound got louder, and the menacing ringing in his ears told him that he would be dead in seconds if he didn't soon find decent cover among Beirut's burned-out store fronts. In real time, he knew what it meant. He sprinted away from the car in what now had become a foot race against death.

Running as fast as he could toward the protection of a nearby barricade, he heard the "karump," "karump," "karump," sound of the mortar shells closing in on him, exploding only meters behind.

Others jumped headfirst behind the concrete barricade at the end of the street. He did the same. Then, he looked back just in time to see the bureau's Volvo get blown to smithereens, erupting in a giant fireball. More mortar rounds began pouring in, steadily creeping toward them in neat orderly intervals, spaced about two meters apart.

The barrage was coming straight at them. If the shelling didn't end right then-and-there, the next rounds would be on top of them in a matter of seconds.

He readied himself in a tight, low crouch. He would have to make another run for it. To stay there meant certain death. He peeked over the barricade, and drew sniper fire from across the street further pinning him down. They must be Israelis spotters. He barely got his head down in time. Again, he risked peaking over the barricade to spot them. His car was now an unsightly inferno; smoke billowing out through the windshield and windows that were all blown out. Then, he saw the snipers just above the smoke and to the right.

"Shit," he said. "One of the few usable cars in Beirut, and the fucking Israelis have to go and blow it up."

No use worrying about it, his most pressing problem was staying alive. Waite flinched as two more mortar rounds inched their way closer. Christ, he had to get out of there. Gingerly, he peeked around the side of the barricade and identified where the sniper fire was coming. The muzzle flashes were about three hundred yards away originating from a partly destroyed building. Two snipers were firing away at them, spotting other targets in the same area for Israeli artillery. The whine of a rifle bullet ricocheted off the wall, and another closer one made him duck again for cover.

He had been through this before, but this was the closest he'd ever been to death. He didn't want to get any closer. Perspiring profusely from his neck and face; he realized if he had waited at the car a few seconds longer, he would now be dead. And, if he kept fucking around sticking his head out into the open, one of those damned snipers was going to get lucky and blow it off.

Like it or not, he had to move. He watched the mortar shells progress moving closer to his position and he knew he had to abandon the spot or perish.

If the mortars didn't get him the snipers would. Just as he was about to make a run for it, he saw a Lebanese youth dart into the street from an adjacent barricade with the same idea. Waite prayed the kid would make it, hoping the sniper's aim would be off. The youth was on a sprint. Waite saw the irony in it immediately. A boy, who had grown up in Beirut's streets and who had crossed that street countless times, was now on a life-or-death mission, just to get to safety. Waite guessed he was about twelve. As he ran, the sniper-fire picked up. Bullets licked at the boy's heels as he zigzagged his way through the rubble crouching low to make himself a more difficult target. This boy surely knew what he had to do and he was pretty good at it.

Halfway across, the Lebanese boy knelt to catch his breath. In an instant, Waite knew it was a fatal mistake. You don't stop moving. In an instant, two successive shots smashed into the boy, the first, standing him up - the second, throwing him back against the stone pavement. Blood splattered from his back and chest as he struggled to get up.

"Son-of-a-bitch!" Waite screamed at the Israeli gunners.

"Oh, God damn it!" his eyes fixed on the boy gasping for breath.

He didn't know what possessed him to do the foolish thing he would do next. But he figured he'd never forgive himself if he let the boy lay dying in the street without a chance to live. In the next instant, Waite summoned up all the courage within and left the protective barricade exposing him to the sniper fire, sprinting as fast as possible toward the wounded boy. Keeping as low as he could, he heard the "CLACK," "CLACK," of the sniper fire zeroing in on him as they turned their attention to a new moving target. The bastards were good, he thought. He moved faster, racing toward the boy with a speed he didn't know he still possessed. Diving down beside him, Waite rolled onto the ground and in one sweeping motion, grabbed the boy and flung him across his shoulders in a fireman's carry.

Hesitating only a split-second to regain his balance and get a good grip on the boy, he resumed his run.

"CRACK!" "CRACK!"

The bullets whistled by them.

Maybe luck was with him. Maybe they were meant to live another day. Maybe he didn't care. In a desperate, final lunge, he reached the collapsed storefront and burst through an opening in the courtyard wall. Catching his breath, he gently laid the boy down behind the protection it afforded. The boy gasped in dreadful pain. He had been hit in the left shoulder and chest. Blood oozed through his white T-shirt, draining the life within him. Waite knew he had to stop the bleeding if the boy stood a chance of surviving. He tore apart the boy's shirt and stuffed a piece of it into a gaping hole in the boy's chest applying pressure to it. He was losing a lot of blood fast.

The cloth plug stopped the flow temporarily, but the bleeding was profuse. Waite knew the boy wouldn't last long if he didn't get him to a hospital soon. There was only one thing left to do. The boy opened his eyes and stared at Waite. The boy seemed to recognize him; perhaps he had seen Waite on one of Beirut's many side streets somewhere. The boy uttered something in Arabic pronouncing Waite as his savior. Waite wasn't sure what his mutterings meant as he continued to work feverishly on the boy's wounds. The youth tried to

The Palestine Conspiracy

speak again, but Waite gestured with a hand to his own mouth to quiet him. He must save his strength he told him.

They had to get to a field hospital. Waite knew the PLO had such a place a few blocks away staffed by British doctors and nurses. If they could reach it, the boy just might have a chance.

First, he had to figure out how to get around the sniper. Waite couldn't believe that the Israelis were shooting at old men, women and children. It was the first time he had seen anything like it. He tried holding up a white handkerchief, but the firing continued.

The boy was losing too much blood for him to stay put, and he knew he had to take another chance. Waite crawled along the inside of the stonewall dragging the boy under one arm, then suddenly heard a crackling sound at his back.

He jerked around to see Ahmed and another PLO soldier making their way toward them with a rocket launcher dangling from Ahmed's back clanking against the rubble.

"Jesus! Ahmed! Get down. What the hell are you doing?" he said in a burst of excitement.

"How bad is the boy?" Ahmed asked in a heavy Arab accent.

"Not good," Waite replied eyeing the other soldier armed with a Kalashnikov. "He won't last much longer unless we get him some medical attention. Even then . . . "

"O.K. . . . let's try for our field hospital," Ahmed answered and began setting . up the rocket launcher pointing the barrel of it through a small hole in the collapsed wall.

The Palestine Conspiracy

"First, we must get the Israeli gunners."

Breathing slowly through the side of his mouth, Ahmed carefully rested the launcher on his shoulder and took direct aim at the two Israelis firing from an old blown-out hotel five blocks away.

Waite held the boy closely to him, and put more pressure on the temporary bandage. The bleeding had eased somewhat, but he had lost a lot of blood and was already unconscious. They had to get him out now.

"Hurry," he prodded Ahmed. "But, don't miss."

He saw they only had one rocket.

Ahmed steadied the barrel and sighted the hotel window from where the Israelis were shooting. He held his breath while his companion slid the rocket into the long brown cylinder with a metallic scrape. Ahmed looked straight ahead as the missile locked into the breech with a loud clink. A split-second later, he felt the familiar tap on his helmet, his partner signaling him that the rocket was ready to fire.

Ahmed spoke a silent prayer to himself and slowly tightened his grip on his launcher. His fingers tightened slowly at the trigger mechanism.

Waite swung over and pulled the boy aside to avoid the recoil back blast from the launcher and waited.

Suddenly, the wall shook as Ahmed fired the missile toward its target. They watched through the dust as the rocket headed straight for the third-story window and hit with devastating accuracy, the blast catapulting the two Israelis out of the building and onto the pavement below.

Waite heaved a sigh of relief and slapped Ahmed on the shoulder. He heard the cheers from the Lebanese people who now poured out into the street to celebrate the small victory over the Israeli gunners.

Ahmed and Waite did not get caught up in the euphoria and wasted little time hoisting the boy onto a makeshift stretcher.

"Quickly, to the field hospital," Ahmed yelled.

They lifted the boy between them and made their way several blocks to the hospital, located deep in the basement of a bombed-out church. A doctor and nurse were on duty and immediately began working feverishly on the boy in a race against time. As Waite watched the medical team at work, he couldn't help but wonder if the effort would do any good. He simply stood there in silence watching as the surgical team opened the boy's chest and tried to stop the hemorrhaging.

The nurse started an I.V., and began transfusing him with blood and plasma. His color was now almond white, and his breathing irregular. He was as close to death as anyone could be and still be alive. There was no concern about sterile conditions. They would worry about that later if the boy survived, and there was not the usual attempt to remove Waite from the operating room. They were used to this in Beirut. And, there simply was no time to waste on hospital procedure or lack of it involving sterile conditions when a life hung in the balance. He was fascinated by the way the doctor and nurses worked. Their movements were almost automatic as they sutured the wounds and poured more plasma the boy's veins. Only God could save him now as he watched them finish.

When he could watch no more, Waite left the makeshift operating room, and found himself standing before a woman with a white veil covering her face. She had followed Waite and Ahmed as they brought her son into the hospital through a small doorway at the far end of the hallway. It was the wounded boy's mother. With her was another small boy.

Ahmed, motioned for Waite to stand still, then whispered something to him.

The woman tried to contain her anguish but tears came forth in a rush of grief that only a mother could feel at that moment. A doctor appeared outside the operating room and spoke to her in Arabic, pointing at Ahmed and Waite, explaining that they had brought the boy there. A few more minutes and her son would have had no chance to survive. The wounds had been nearly fatal but they were clean, missing the vital organs. This had spared the boy. But, a few minutes longer, and the boy would have died from loss of blood.

The Lebanese woman touched Waite's arm. She spoke to him in her own language, one he didn't understand. Ahmed translated while Waite listened to her sobbing gestures of gratitude. But, he understood the love of a mother for her son, the same kind of love his mother had for him when he was a boy growing up on the near west side of Cleveland. It was the same kind of universal love that mothers everywhere have for their sons.

"You are an American, yes? I owe my son's life to you. My people are witness to that. I will not forget this day. If my son lives, his name will no longer be Rashid. I will rename him after you. You have breathed new life into a dying boy. His name will be your name. If he dies, he will have died as a Lebanese

The Palestine Conspiracy

on Lebanese soil. In spirit, you are his new father. May Allah always be with you?"

The woman wiped at her tears and left Waite standing there feeling embarrassed and almost ashamed to be an American. She had even kissed his hand, the hand of an American they generally considered the enemy. Waite shrugged his shoulders at Ahmed.

Ahmed finally spoke.

"Not only have you been a good friend today, but you have performed a good deed for the Palestinian people. What the woman said to you, she said out of great respect for you. If you can understand and accept that, then you can understand my people."

As they rested in the shade outside the hospital, Waite told Ahmed how he had tried unsuccessfully to get more information about the secret message. He reassured Ahmed that he had not compromised his security in any way. But, the news that the message was probably a genuine intelligence transcript stirred Ahmed to emotional excitement.

"I knew it," he shrieked. "It must be something of great importance. Akram wouldn't have risked his life unless it had some utmost value."

Waite couldn't have agreed more. In death, Akram had been the real hero of the day.

The Palestine Conspiracy

CHAPTER 7

London: May 5. 3 p.m.

Brian and Geoff chatted in the briefing room at Langehorn finalizing their arrangements for departure.

He and Brian were the advance party for Mrs. Thayer and they would be responsible for executing her itinerary during the historic trip.

Only a few key military officers at ICE, Britain's Intelligence Central Elite, knew the real purpose of the mission.

"When are we scheduled to meet Fasi Etebbe?" Brian inquired.

"We meet him on the 'morrow at a remote village outside Beirut, 60 miles from Damascus."

"Isn't it rather dangerous to be that deep inside PLO-Syrian territory?" Brian questioned.

"I suppose so, chum. But it would be just as dangerous for Fasi if we met him at a spot in Beirut, or in some other heavily populated area where Israel's Mossad is operating," Geoff countered.

"What if we get kidnapped?"

"Don't worry old boy, Fasi's men have already set it up. No one gets kidnapped in-and-around Beirut without his approval, period. We'll be blindfolded for the journey, and we'll have to travel by truck to his desert campsite. Oh . . . by the way, from now on, we'll refer to Fasi by his code name . . . Goliath . . . and Mrs. Thayer's . . . as David.

"David and Goliath? Who came up with that?" Brian quipped.

"They fit rather well, don't you think?" Geoff retorted scarcely hiding the fact that he was the obvious perpetrator of the code names.

"Thayer is taking on a monumental task. If Fasi agrees to end world terrorism in exchange for a Palestinian state, the event will not go unnoticed by any stretch of the imagination. She will have symbolically slain the giant, eh?"

"And, just really who is this giant?" Brian asked.

Geoff stared blankly out the window and finally responded.

"Probably, in this case, Israel. Funny how that's changed. Go figure."

"Come on, let's go. Time for our plane," Geoff interrupted reaching for the secure phone that connected him to flight operations.

He gave some final instructions to a trusted colleague and hung up.

The pair boarded a jeep, which took them to a waiting military cargo aircraft, an Albatross, its doors open wide and engines warmed-up for the mission. Jumping from the jeep, duffel bags in tow, and briefcases chained to their wrists, the two climbed aboard the plane strapping themselves-in for the departure.

The pilot craned his neck to the back and politely informed them that it would be a bit chilly at high altitude and that a portable heater was available if they needed it. But, both were wearing thermal underwear for the occasion, knowing the comfort level from prior experience with Her Majesty's air service.

Flying into Beirut by military cargo plane was the best way to get into Lebanon undetected for the mission. Both Brian and Geoff were wearing RAF military fatigues and had been instructed to say as little as possible to ground crewmen. Once they landed in Cairo, they were to go about unloading cargo and trade places with two other regular RAF crewmen there and board another plane, for the flight into Beirut. The two RAF crewmen would trade places again with them on the return trip.

So far, the trip to Cairo had been uneventful. And, after unloading the cargo, they found themselves cruising at 25,000 feet toward Beirut, a two-hour flight. Everything continued smoothly over the Mediterranean and the pilot skirted wide around the Israeli coast.

It did no good, however, as the RAF pilot came on over the intercom and announced that two Israeli fighters had appeared off their starboard wing. Brian and Geoff peered out the window and into the darkness amazed to see two Jericho F-22's flying in tight formation with their wing lights on approaching their aircraft.

As the F-22's moved in for a closer look at the Albatross C-11, the Israeli fighter pilots established radio contact with them on standard RAF frequency.

The RAF captain was instructed to hold a steady course after he identified himself as a British cargo carrier flying medical supplies into Beirut Airport. The

Israelis radioed the information to Tel Aviv and in a few seconds gave a verbal O.K. for the Albatross to proceed to its destination after an inspection.

"Geoff, what the hell is going on? Why are they intercepting in international airspace?"

"It's something they just started doing. We don't know their exact reason, but I surmise it has to do with arms shipments being smuggled into the PLO," Geoff answered.

"They come up alongside all military aircraft, even commercial flights, and run a surveillance on the plane. Get ready to cover your eyes when they switch off their wing lights."

Brian was nearly speechless.

"Why do we need to cover our eyes," he said breaking the tension.

The RAF pilot came back on the intercom.

"All personnel will shield their eyes for 10 seconds beginning now," the pilot commanded counting backwards from the count of three. Geoff and Brian didn't argue, and immediately put their hands over their faces as their pilot ordered.

Outside the plane, the Israeli pilots turned their fighters slightly away from the C-11 dropping back about 500 yards from them.

The Israeli pilots flipped switches, which sent a burst of laser light shooting across the night sky illuminating the Albatross with a powerful blast of ultra-bright blue-white light.

The plane and its inside were showered with the penetrating light in a search for arms and ammunition. The Albatross had, in effect, been X-rayed by the laser beam. The Israelis had informed foreign governments that the light wasn't damaging to humans as long as no one looked directly into it. The laser had the ability to penetrate and photograph everything inside the plane without harming anyone.

With the inside of the Albatross now lit up for a few seconds, the entire effect was like some giant strobe light at a disco party. Only this was no party. Geoff remarked it resembled the kind of flash of light that was described by scientists who witnessed the first atomic bomb blast over Yucca Flats, but without the radiation.

From the ground, however, the flash of light was almost indiscernible because it had been focused sharply upward and away from any observer.

"I've never seen anything quite like that in my life," Brian said utterly astonished. "Are they absolutely sure that was safe? I could see my bones for a brief second. Bloody hell!"

"No, but we didn't have any choice? It's a lot better than getting shot out of the sky, isn't it?"

After the pilot gave them the all clear, they uncovered their eyes and looked outside the window just in time to see the F-22's fighters' break-off and disappear into the night. By now, the Albatross was 20 miles from Beirut, and the pilot was beginning his descent, which would give them one chance for a final approach. It would be a direct landing without flaps at a higher-than-normal speed.

This would be hard on the pilot and equally as hard on the plane and its passengers because of the angle and impact of the wheels. But, it was the best way into Beirut Airport these days to escape anti-aircraft fire and heat-seeking missiles.

The Palestine Conspiracy

The pilot came on the intercom again.

"Now hold onto your panties ladies, and please . . . refrain from throwing up in your seats. It might get a little rough if we manage to pick up some triple-A from the Shiites or Druse.

Brian had a pissed-off look of trepidation.

The flight had been full of surprises, not at all the way Geoff had briefed him. Geoff laughed acknowledging the mental double-cross.

"O.K. O.K. So a few things have changed since I was here last," he apologized as the pilot dove for the airport.

"Ja . Ja. .Jesus . . ." Brian stuttered. "Bloody hell!"

The maneuver by the pilot caused them to pull about five G's, and when he flared out for the runway, the smoothness of the landing all but surprised even Brian, who was having white-knuckle second-thoughts about taking on the mission.

In all, it was a rather uneventful landing by Beirut standards, and the Albatross gracefully descended into the glare of the runway lights lining the airport. Brian looked out into the darkness as the plane let down with a thud, then another smaller one.

The thumps brought him back to reality as he surveyed the Beirut skyline, now nearly non-existent after twelve years of constant aerial and artillery bombardment. He knew it had once been the financial capital of the Middle East. Even with its recent turbulent history, Beirut was once a proud city with a reputation as a banking center where European and American businessmen could wheel and deal with the Arab community. Twenty-five years ago, it was a place where a businessman could find anything to fulfill his

The Palestine Conspiracy

financial fancy, and then some. It had a unique greatness and capacity for hospitality, amidst splendid accommodations, which had been undiminished throughout time.

Beirut was a place where financial experts could work during the day and unwind in the evening playing until dawn. It was replete with the finest prostitutes money could buy.

But now, Beirut was a burnt-out relic of the recent past, as Arab factions, fought to re-gain control of what was left. It was now only a shell of a city, inhabited by multitudes of tormented people who refused to leave their makeshift homes amidst its rubble, holding onto the stubborn conviction that they would once again live to see self-rule and the city reborn to greatness.

Perhaps they were too idealistic, these Lebanese people.

Or, perhaps, they realized if they continued fighting for whatever it was that they were fighting for, they could construct a new reality, a new dream of peace on their terms with Israel.

Enter the PLO. Enter the countless of other terrorist groups who had their own agendas and who would persist in their dream to drive Israel into the sea.

If miracles could take place through sheer determination, then Beirut indeed did have a chance to survive the bloody onslaught between the Arab and the Jew. Perhaps this same persistence could lead them to make peace with their enemies.

The C-11 taxied to the terminal where the cargo would be unloaded and where Brian and Geoff would melt into the background of Beirut's streets. As the cargo doors swung open, Brian whiffed the fresh salty air blowing in from the Mediterranean.

Suddenly, his thoughts were with Adrienne. He recalled her subtle beauty and her freshness, pure like the ocean breeze. He remembered how he had made love to her in his flat . . . it all seemed so distant now. . . as though it hadn't really happened at all. But, it had. And, he was thankful for that. The night air made him shiver as he stepped down from the plane's ramp and boarded an old ram shackled bus to the city.

So, this was Beirut.

CHAPTER 8

Israel: The Negev Desert: May 8. 8:30 a.m.

At a clandestine base in the Negev Desert, technicians worked feverishly placing an atomic warhead atop a missile with a range of 1,500 miles, easily within reach of all targetable enemy countries in the Middle East. Israel had built its first intermediate-range ballistic missile with nuclear capabilities, and had flight-tested it secretly off the coast of South Africa at the Walvis Ridge Missile Range in the Atlantic Ocean only months earlier. The firings, a total of ten, had been extremely successful, carried out meticulously by project military planners.

Such an operational missile would guarantee that no one would dare attack Israel without paying the ultimate price - complete and total destruction in a matter of minutes. It was an unannounced secret that Israel possessed the atomic bomb and the means to deliver it by warplane. But, nobody had yet realized they were developing a missile comparable to the longer-ranged ones the super powers possessed, capable of carrying bigger and improved warheads. Even longer-range missiles were already on the drawing boards. That, too, was a secret.

At the Negev installation, scientists prepared the first of five missiles, which would be operational within two weeks, safely secured in the underground

98

blast-proof missile silos at Haifa. The silos were comparable to the designs used in the United States, impenetrable and invulnerable to nuclear attack cushioned in hardened silos. Military planners referred to them as "hardened" silos. Even a direct nuclear hit would not impair or deter retaliation.

Israeli Defense Minister Prahoe watched with satisfaction the technicians at work. Even he, a patient and intellectual man, had grave doubts about the project. But he, like every Jew like him in Israel, had convinced himself that Jews must never again be subject to the inhumanity of man wrought by the Germans or anyone in pursuit of annihilation of the Jews. These nuclear-tipped missiles would guarantee that. If ever the time came when Israel couldn't count on the military support of the United States, they could go-it-alone in a full-blown crisis.

Protections built into the system were a fail-safe design. Launch of the missiles could be accomplished only by the designated command of the prime minister in agreement with the Israeli Knesset and the Chief of Staff of the Israeli Armed Forces, unless unilaterally ordered by the prime minister alone to counter a threat during an enemy surprise attack. Only, and only in that situation, could the prime minister make the decision to launch nuclear weapons without any consultation. Prahoe inspected the security codes and reassured himself that he had made the correct decision in allowing the missiles to be deployed. His mental justification was his sworn duty to Israel. He was a Jew first by birth and by principle. And, the one principle all Jews adhered to first was survival - survival by any means. Prahoe, whether he was a politician, an intellectual, a teacher, or a rabbi, was no different in his thinking on the matter. They all thought that way.

CHAPTER 9

Damascus: May 8. 10:00 a.m.

Fasi Etebbe's soldiers huddled near the campfire at the desert stronghold.

Their commander was preparing for the usual morning prayers just outside Fasi's Bedouin tent when an aide rushed inside.

Fasi issued a sharp command to a guard outside the tent. The guard stepped aside at once. Fasi pulled the canvas out of the way and stepped into the morning sunlight, wiping away beads of perspiration from his sun-darkened face.

"My general," the aide said. "The British intelligence agents are making their way across the Gideon Plain as we speak. They will arrive within the next hour with our guides."

"Excellent. Prepare to receive them. One hour after they arrive, bring them to my tent as guests," he said.

"Yes, oh great one," the aide obeyed.

Already with Fasi was a tall thin, mustached man who nodded approvingly at Fasi's every word. His black, cropped, oily hair befitted his five-and-a-half foot wiry frame. Wearing a white tropical suit and hat, he appeared almost comical, as though misplaced from an old Humphrey Bogart movie. The be-speckled man spoke with a distinct Peter Lorrie accent directing much attention to him, occasionally brushing the desert sand from his suit while wiping his forehead with a cloth he held in his right hand.

"My dear Fasi, what in the world would you do with it, even if I could get my government to deliver one to you?" the man said incredulously. "And, you are asking for two!"

"What would I do with it?" Fasi quizzed him like a schoolboy who should know better than to ask. "I would use it at the right time and under the right circumstances. But I need two. One without the other cannot guarantee annihilation. The deal must be for two."

"If my government refuses?" came the olive-skinned man's rebuttal.

"Then I shall look elsewhere. But, surely for 10 billion dollars, and the promise of an alliance against India," Fasi explained, "even the most stubborn holdouts can see the wisdom of such an arrangement."

"Perhaps so. But, what if the plan fails?"

"Palestine has been Palestine for more than 5000 years, and 1000 years before that. We have not failed yet."

"What if talks with the British collapse for some unknown reason?"

"So, you're afraid that no British follow-through could doom the pact worldwide?"

"Yes, that's so."

"But, don't you see. It was Mrs. Thayer who first proposed the solution for the Middle East. If the English parliament refuses at the last moment to approve the agreement, Iraq will be free to continue to terrorize Europe, perhaps even attack Saudi Arabia for control of the oil interests in the region. And, if that happens, the United States would be drawn into a battle with Iraq at last. Eventually, Britain would be forced to commit its military resources, too. I think Mrs. Thayer is too clever to allow that to happen. She'll agree to it." Fasi continued.

"At any rate, Iraq is becoming too threatening in the region for the good of the rest of the Arab countries. Someone will eventually have to deal with her," Fasi said.

"You see, no one really wants to do it, except the United States. Even I am no fool when it comes to taking on the United States. They will not trifle with Iraq anymore. Iraq's leaders are being overly militant and stupid."

"Now, back to the business at hand. Delivery of the equipment must be timed perfectly," Fasi told the man from Pakistan. "The material must be shipped over water and by the overland route I have formulated to avoid suspicion and detection from spy satellites."

Fasi outlined the route for the Pakistani. The shipment would proceed across the Gulf of Oman, originating from the Pakistani capital, Karachi, then across the Trucial Coast into the Rub Al Khali Desert by means of Bedouin caravan passing near Riyadh, then northward again to the Syrian Desert, crossing into Syria and finally into Palestine.

Then the remainder of the plan, the signing of the pact, could proceed on schedule.

The Palestine Conspiracy

Palestine would be formed by the agreement, signed by Britain and contributing Arab countries. The plan would then be taken to the United Nations and voted upon by the general assembly, and once passed, the U.N. Security Council would guarantee the creation and establishment of the State of Palestine. The entire plan would be announced to the world at the same time.

World pressure would be brought to bear by Britain and the U.S., and perhaps even by Russia. Once in motion, these forces would be difficult to hold back. World opinion would be crystallized in favor of creation of a Palestinian state. The world would look on with great disfavor if Israel refused to go along with the peace plan.

The plan was indeed workable from the Pakistani's point-of-view. It was all perfectly feasible. The nuclear devices would provide security from Israel if the peace initiative failed, and in case Israel ever tried to attack Syria, Jordan and the new Palestinian homeland.

Fasi felt he would be justified in using the weapons to save his people from annihilation at the hands of Israeli soldiers. And, if Iraq felt pressured to attack the Saudis, it too would have to think twice knowing that the United States would block an Iraqi advance down through Kuwait and into the heart of Saudi Arabia.

The man from Pakistan smiled and nodded his head in agreement with Fasi's logic.

It was true.

Iraq was becoming too powerful on the Asian continent. Pakistan had already felt the military pressure from the Russian war in Afghanistan, and they didn't need a new threat by an antagonistic Iraq or Iran. In short, pressure on its borders from a paranoid Iranian leadership was intolerable. Pakistan had more than its share of problems with India impinging upon its territory and disputed lands in Kashmir.

Speaking directly, "Of course, our government will deny the very existence of this conversation and my meeting with you or anyone else connected with the nuclear devices. I say this now so that we understand each other clearly. It is a necessary precaution so that we will not be attacked by one of the super powers or Israel who would oppose delivery of such a weapons system. Do I make myself absolutely clear on that point, my dear Fasi?"

Fasi nodded.

He knew that Pakistan would not deliver the nuclear warheads if there were even the small risk of an attack by another country in retaliation for its policies. They were too careful to let that happen over a mere realignment of political causes.

"Naturally, " Fasi added. "We, in no way, will jeopardize your government's security by placing Pakistan in a difficult position for its having supplied us with our military needs."

The reassurance by Fasi to the Pakistani intelligence operative was necessary. He was a nervous little man. And, the reassurance pushed the Pakistani to make a favorable decision for Fasi. The diminutive character shook hands and promised to be in contact with him again in a few days to finalize the arrangements.

The overland odyssey would begin in a week, originating from Sehwan then to Karachi.

The Palestine Conspiracy

Fasi estimated it would take five weeks to travel the entire route. It wasn't an efficient plan, but it was simple and workable, one he could control and trust.

It was time for the Pakistani to leave, escorted by his own security team he had brought to the meeting. Meanwhile, the PLO security squad protecting Fasi carefully monitored the Pakistani's boarding of the helicopter and lift-off from the desert camp. In a whirl of desert sand, the Pakistani was back on his way to Islamabad.

Hours later, when things calmed again, Fasi's attention was diverted to a commotion near the front of the encampment. Standing in the shadow of his Bedouin tent, he watched the arrival of the two intelligence agents from ICE - Brian Smith and Geoffrey Frase. He was glad the three men – the departing Pakistani and the Brits – had not crossed paths.

That would have been difficult to explain. Now, he could finalize the details for Mrs. Thayer's secret visit.

* * *   * * *

Coincidentally, Ahmed had arrived simultaneously in the PLO camp.

He hadn't told Waite about his journey to the camp; he didn't need to know.

A small contingent of PLO soldiers had accompanied Ahmed to the camp for a stint of rest and relaxation from the front lines. He and his men were to be quartered in a tent near Fasi's after walking most of the four-day journey, a distance of some 65 miles.

106

The Palestine Conspiracy

They were exhausted from the journey. Ahmed unpacked his gear and spread his bedroll on the sand preparing a makeshift pillow with his extra clothes. He rested his head on it and immediately fell asleep.

After sleeping for nearly two hours, he was awakened by the sound of warplanes in the distance, somewhere, closing in on an unseen enemy. They were either Syrian or Israeli. It didn't matter at the moment. He was so tired he just wanted to sleep. The war seemed to have no end. It had been a long, complex one, and had gone on for decades and decades. The war had been a part of him since childhood; he had grown up with it, as did thousands like him who lived in Beirut. Middle East countries sided with one another, and then changed political sides according to each own's interests, realigning with another and so on and so on in a desperate struggle to gain the upper hand. Everyone had a different political stake and a different political role.

Power!

That was it!

Combined with greed, it was a deadly aphrodisiac, as it had been since the beginning of time.

Thousands of years later, the Middle East was still fighting the same old stereotypes, battles and issues, each side fighting for its own identity in a modern world which had left the region behind a long time ago threatening to leave their differences in a policy of suicidal idiocy.

Who was he to change it?

Could the Middle East ever change?

The Palestine Conspiracy

Could it ever progress as a civilized people with the mixing of the Arabs and Jews?

Could they ever agree?

Perhaps in time they could.

But, Ahmed couldn't think clearly anymore as he drifted into a much-needed sleep. As warplanes flew into the distant night sky in search of enemies to fight, Ahmed dreamt instead.

CHAPTER 10

London: May 19. 9:30 a.m.

It had been nearly two weeks since Brian's departure. Adrienne had sunk into a mild depression during his absence.

She missed him terribly.

Funny.

Here she was, a 27-year-old, unmarried, successful career woman.

By British societal standards, she was getting off the mark a bit late.

She had dreamed of marrying at a decent age when she was a young schoolgirl. But, now a decade later, she was still fantasizing about the right man for her.

She indulged herself from time to time when she would meet her whimsical prince charming. But, the flaw in that kind of thinking had got many of her friends into an early marriage, pregnant, and divorce, not necessarily in that order.

Perhaps there would never be a prince charming that would sweep her off her feet. It would be even more difficult for Adrienne because she demanded so much of her men. Still, she had the right to fantasize if she wanted to, as long as it didn't interfere with her real sense of life as she lived it.

Her thoughts ended quite abruptly when she nearly missed her stop at the London Times.

Adrienne jumped from her seat on the double-decker with such abruptness; she alarmed several of the passengers sitting next to her.

No apologies necessary, as she hurried through the exit. Jumping from the bus and over puddles, she flopped open her umbrella to shield herself from the drizzle and traffic spray which dampened her long hair. She welcomed the fresh beads of moisture striking the contour of her olive-skinned face.

Stepping briskly into the office, a woman of purposeful confidence, she cheerily announced her arrival to her co-workers seated along a neat row of desks in the editorial room. She brushed the rainwater from her trench coat and spun her umbrella 'round twice before propping it up in a corner of her cubicle.

She sat down in her swivel chair and reached for the telephone to tell her editor she had arrived, but before she could lift the receiver, it rang.

Damn, he had beaten her to it. He sounded irate on the other end of the line. Worse yet, he wanted to see her immediately.

God, how she hated that. Not even time for a first cup of coffee.

Patiently listening to his tirade on arriving late, Adrienne could feel her blood boiling as she hung up the receiver wondering what all the commotion was in his voice. She set off for his office. Maybe something really big had finally come up. An interesting assignment perhaps, anything to deliver her from the unending boredom that had descended upon the newsroom.

She approached Pete's office in an aggressive mood. She was a tough journalist, and would not cower under his hostility today. She would be his match. She pushed open the door and closed it firmly behind her.

"Well, it's about time you got here!" he started in on her where he had left off. "You know we do start work around here at 8 o'clock a.m., not p.m. Just where in the hell have you been all morning?"

Anticipating his insult, Adrienne countered with a neutral remark, which only angered him further.

"It couldn't be helped," she said.

"Couldn't be helped!" he shot back. "What do you think we pay people like you here for? To sit on that ass of yours?"

She wasn't sure whether she had just been insulted or not, but gave him a nonplussed stare at his pathetic behavior.

After a few seconds, Pete cooled down enough to get down to business, dropping his dressing-down behavior in favor of a softer, less intimidating approach.

"Look, I'm sorry, O.K.? Would you like some coffee?"

"You mean a peace offering?"

"Something like that. I know they don't serve coffee on the bus."

It was a peace offering she wouldn't refuse.

Pete knew Adrienne's background as a competent, tough-minded Journalist, and was familiar with her award winning investigative skills. Plus, she could write like hell when pressed at deadline. In short, she could be one single-minded reporter when she wanted to be. What's more, deep down, he respected her talents, even when she was in one of her combative moods. He liked that about her. She wasn't a pushover. It was purely her style that attracted her to him as a writer, and his inescapable part of his being an editor.

The Palestine Conspiracy

Newspaper editors were like that. Most of them simply couldn't control their tempers when they knew what they wanted in print. But, he nearly always forgave her while he could never forgive himself. He drank away all his own forgiveness's at the local pub every night. He was the ultimate loner; a drunkard of a loner.

Pete gestured for her to sit down, and told her why he was so worked up.

Leaning toward her and fixing his gaze straight at her, he said matter-of-factly, "We're sending you to the Middle East."

The sentence hit her like she hadn't heard it.

"Where?"

"Beirut!"

"Beirut!" she gasped incredulously.

"Yes, Goddamnit. Beirut. That's what I wanted to tell you two hours ago."

She looked at him in disbelief. She knew Brian was already there.

"But, there's hardly anyone left over there anymore," she started. "It's dangerous as hell . . . what's going on?"

Before she could continue, he cut-her-off.

"That's what we want you to find out. We really want to know what's going on over there. You're the best investigative reporter we've got. We both know that," he said, soothing over the morning argument knowing that he must now negotiate terms with her.

Adrienne drew in a deep breath.

"Flattery never did get you anywhere with me, and it won't this time, either. And, not on this assignment. Are you trying to get me killed?"

112

The Palestine Conspiracy

"Wait . . . "

"I've never done any international reporting before."

"I know, I know, but you are the best we've got, and besides, I know you can do the job. Now, hear me out on this. Let me tell you what we've got, then I'll let you decide."

"What kind of foreign correspondents are left over there?" she asked.

"Nobody, except a few hack reporters from UPI who need better jobs."

"Oh, great! So what you're really doing is throwing me in all alone on this one," she said hardening her position.

"Now hold on. Before you get up a head of steam, let me finish."

From his tone, it must be a rough assignment, and in the Middle East to boot. Dangerous as hell, but it would probably make for one damned good story if she could handle it.

"How soon would I have to leave?"

"Right away," he said, sounding as though Adrienne had already accepted it. "Here's the skinny. We got a tip from one of those splinter peace groups two days ago. The caller wouldn't identify himself, but he said something significant was up in the Middle East. He didn't say what, so we don't have any details or what motivated him to call us. The guy just phoned in to one of our reporters Tuesday and began talking about a covert operation by British Intelligence, oil interests and Mrs. Thayer.

"He said he didn't know anymore than that but that's all we'd need to get started. That's all he said, and hung up," Pete continued.

"Well, we get so many of these damned calls anymore, we didn't take it seriously at first. Then one of our reporters, covering the Thayer re-election campaign, noticed a change in her itinerary corresponding to a date the caller gave to the reporter for a so-called big event in the Middle East.

"July 24.

"Now, it could still be a crank call, or there might really be something to it. We'd like you to check it out further. Also, Thayer has cancelled her campaign stop in Yorkshire this weekend to attend an international oil conference in Saudi Arabia. Again, it may just be coincidence, but we don't want to miss something big over there. We'll keep on top of it here; we need you over there covering our ass in case there's something to it."

"What about communications?" Adrienne asked him, now tuned-in fully to his explanation.

"We'll set up everything you need to operate undercover as a volunteer Red Cross worker when you get there. You'll meet Rick Waite, one of the American United Press International reporters, at the airport. He's originally from Cleveland, Ohio. He'll be with another Red Cross worker to authenticate the look.

"UPI, huh? You mean those are the only guys left in Beirut? Terrific. You really know how to stick it to someone, don't you?" rolling her eyes.

"Any idea who your deep throat is?"

"No. He hasn't resurfaced. We doubt that he will. These guys usually pass on a tip and leave it to the media to do the dirty work."

114

"All right," she said clearly piqued. "You've got me. I can't refuse. I'll finish up what I'm doing this afternoon and start packing."

"Uh, uh. You won't have time. Your old assignments are already handed-off. Just get ready. You're already ticketed through Heathrow and, by the way, your cover story has already been worked out with a friend of mine at the International Red Cross. Sort it out when you meet her at the airport, but as far as you're concerned, from now on you're a worker helping war victims in Lebanon, Red Cross armband and all.

"You'll meet up with Waite at Beirut Airport. He's well known there, and because of his duration, as a reporter, any terrorists watching you, won't suspect you're on his staff working undercover. Just keep it together and let him guide you.

"I'll bet you didn't know the assignment carried an apprenticeship in acting, did you?" he grinned. "This could be your big break."

As she prepared to leave Pete's office, he said, "Oh, one more thing."

"What?" she turned.

"Don't get yourself killed."

Adrienne flashed the dirty little smile she had saved up. Pete could be something else. But, she was thankful for the deliverance from boredom. At least things weren't going to be dull for the next few months. But, what the hell was she going to tell Brian when he called. The last thing she wanted to do was blow his cover and her own. The thought of even mentioning her trip to Beirut bothered her. His intelligence-conditioned mind would go into overdrive.

No. She had a better idea. If he called her from the

The Palestine Conspiracy

Middle East, she would use an answering machine to avoid the inevitable questions. Also, she would have to devise a message that would make Brian think she was out of the country and unreachable - somewhere perhaps in Europe on a rolling assignment. She had even mentioned that possibility, even though it was wishful thinking at the time, to Brian the day before saying she would jump at the chance to do news coverage from there. It would be the perfect cover for her cover.

The phone system in Paris was so awful, she could easily alibi out of any suspicions Brian might have by telling him that she never got the message.

She took a cab to Brian's flat to pick up her belongings and then to record the outgoing message on her answering machine at the flat. When she got there, she talked calmly into the microphone.

"Hello, this is Adrienne. I'm sorry I missed your call, but I'm out of the country covering a news assignment in Paris, and cannot be reached for the next three to four weeks. If you need to get a message to me, contact my editor, Peter Rowan at the London Times. He will see that I get it. Terrah!"

After playing back the message, she was reassured that Pete would not give Brian any information to blow her cover. He knew Brian worked for British Intelligence. But, she'd better clue him in anyway.

Satisfied that the answering machine was set up, she put down the phone and got undressed. She turned on the shower to hot. The bathroom steamed as she lay on the bed relaxing a few minutes thinking about her assignment. Her plane was due to depart at 7 o'clock that evening. It was already 4 p.m.

Maybe, she'd better call Pete now to confirm the

departure time. But, she knew better. If Pete said he had made all the arrangements, why bother. He was always so damned meticulous about detail. She could wait and call him from Beirut. For now, it was a chance to rest for a few minutes.

The Israeli wire-tapper sat up in his chair when he heard Adrienne record her message on the answering machine, but he thought nothing unusual about it so why bother Moshe. It sounded like business as usual for a news reporter off on a regular assignment. He readjusted the volume on his headset and could hear more sounds coming from another microphone hidden in the headboard of the bed. He leaned forward to catch every sound and whispered to Moshe. The sounds became more intense, and a smile crossed his face as he and Moshe looked at each other in disbelief.

They listened as Adrienne worked her hand over the inside of her thighs. She had become aroused just thinking about Brian. If he couldn't be there, then the next best thing would be to fantasize that he was.

She reached across to the nightstand for a small hand-held vibrator and began working it up over her stomach down to her thighs. The soft, warm vibrations aroused a pleasure deep within her. When Brian had first used it on her, she had objected, but finally relented on his insistence that she would like it. It had given her one of the most pleasurable orgasms she could ever remember. It had been a memorable lovemaking session, the vibrator deep inside her, and Brian teasing her bottom. She brought the vibrator up along her sensitive spot, and slowly ran it back and forth across her clitoris. She let out a girlish giggle recalling how Brian would go down on her. Her smile grew more intense as she inserted the vibrator and moved it in and out. She began filling with passion. A tingling sensation gradually crept over her entire body as a new intensity overcame her. She pushed it in deeper yielding to her insatiable craving for more pleasure. She let out a tiny squeal as her body grabbed at the vibrator. The thrusts at last led to an uncontrollable rush of pleasure.

Moshe and Nooka were glued to their headsets as they listened to her reach climax.

When she finished, she lay back underneath the covers for a moment to catch her breath. Moshe and Nooka exchanged knowing glances. Adrienne closed her eyes, when the telephone rang twice. She picked up the receiver.

"Adrienne, this is Pete."

"Pete, I'm just getting into the shower. What's up," she said trying to recover.

The two Israeli eavesdroppers listened intently to the conversation.

"How about getting over to the airport an hour earlier? I want you to meet that friend of mine I was telling you about before you board the plane. Her name is Katherine. She'll meet you at the ticket counter. O.K.?"

She agreed to the moved up timetable and hung up. But she had forgot to tell him about the cover message on the answering machine. Damn. It wasn't like her to forget things like that. No matter. She'd call him later and stepped into the hot steamy bathroom. The shower would feel good.

Showering, she decided what she would need in

The Palestine Conspiracy

Beirut. She figured on some extra clothes, but not too many. Red Cross workers weren't supposed to be the most fashionable dressers in the world, and she needed only enough to launder for a week. She might need a miniature camera, too. That was about it besides her personal travel kit, makeup and toothbrush. Anything more would create suspicion.

She would keep the camera concealed in her bra. The camera was plastic and would not be detected by Lebanese customs as they scanned for handguns and bombs. Well, if necessary, that's the way it had to be. She was amused by it all. No Arab man would ever search her. What a reporter wouldn't do for a story.

Finishing up, she dressed comfortably for the flight and left her flat making absolutely sure she had pressed the answering machine to ON before leaving.

She was a little disappointed that Brian hadn't called before she left. It meant they would be out of touch for at least a full month. Carrying her bags to the front of the apartment building, she flagged down a cab . . . "Taxi". . ."Taxi". . . and left for Heathrow.

CHAPTER 11

Karachi, Pakistan. May 25. 7:00 p.m.

The PT boat captain looked at his watch, reset the elapsed time stop mechanism, and locked the gyrocompass to a heading of 275 degrees northwest across the Gulf of Oman to the port city of Muscat.

From there, the secret cargo would be transported by truck out of Oman to a waiting caravan of camels, which would cross the Rub Al Khali Desert beginning that same evening.

The journey across the gulf would take 48 hours but they would have to make the crossing undetected from the American naval units operating in the area. An aircraft carrier battle group consisting of six destroyers, four frigates, two guided missile cruisers, and two nuclear attack submarines continually patrolled the route. It was a formidable fighting group that could bring immense firepower into play against an enemy anywhere within range of its 12-inch guns, cruise missiles, and warplanes.

The PT captain signaled to his crew that everything was ready for their departure. The engines of the speedy craft roared to life for the night crossing. The PT boat would have to maintain strict radio silence and move at a deliberate sailing speed to fool American naval radar and sonar. It was fitted with special rigging to resemble a double masted schooner, silhouetted at night against a full moon, moving at about

120

14 knots. It would fool a sleepy lookout or sonar watchman of another vessel.

The PT boat eased from its moorings as the crew cast off her lines. Inside her belly, lay a mysterious cargo destined for the PLO. On each side lay two missile warheads lashed down with camouflaged canvas. The boat moved slowly from the harbor entrance, the captain being careful to avoid all incoming boat traffic.

When they cleared harbor, the captain ordered the craft's running lights turned off to conceal their presence, and they melted into the darkness of the Gulf of Oman.

Thirty-six hours passed. It was night again, and the voyage had been uneventful so far. The PT boat captain reckoned by his gyrocompass that he was about 12 hours from Muscat. Once there, representatives of the PLO would meet him and other terrorists from Oman dedicated to the same cause.

They would remove the cargo and load the trucks. It would become very dangerous once they reached port. The port city was crawling with CIA operatives and they would have to move silently and efficiently so as not to arouse suspicion. Most of the dockworkers had been bribed to stay away that night.

The PT boat, even though Pakistani in origin, was unmarked. The crew carried no kind of identification, which could link them to their own government in case the unthinkable happened and they were caught.

The propellers churned the water effortlessly and the sleek craft blended in perfectly with the black gulf waters. The captain glanced at the depth finder and read the ocean bottom at only 20 fathoms. Everything

The Palestine Conspiracy

was going precisely the way it was planned.

Three miles away lurking beneath the Gulf of Oman, an American nuclear attack submarine, the Thresher II, cruised at periscope depth, just beneath the gentle stillness of the moonlit surface.

Its captain was asleep in his quarters while the submarine crew kept the nightly vigil. Red lights reflected eerily through the narrow passageways while the sub's sonar traced schools of fish feeding near the ocean bottom. The crew had rigged for silent running at 6 knots.

As the sonar man yawned under the onset of fatigue, he occasionally adjusted his headset to the ocean sounds straining to pay attention to every irregular sound pulsating through his earphones, listening for some unfamiliar noise that would tell him he had made contact with an unknown vessel.

When he heard the first "ping" echo through his headset, he leaned forward to make sure he had actually heard it.

Instinctively, he switched off the night-light and concentrated his gaze on the sonar scope that had a range of 80 miles. He flipped another switch, which activated the close-in scope and saw that the object was only 17 miles away and running at the relatively slow speed of 14 knots. It appeared to be a small surface going vessel about the size of a sailing vessel.

Just to make sure, he brought it to the attention of his chief petty officer to take a look at. The chief petty officer decided to close the range to 1,500 yards to get a more precise look visually through the periscope.

"Left full rudder. Bring about to two-eight-seven. All ahead one-third."

The Palestine Conspiracy

"Aye, aye, sir," the main helmsman responded and moved the steering control arm slowly to the left, turning the sub in a widening arc bringing her to a course which would interdict the surface target slicing through the surface water.

The captain asleep in his quarters, felt the sub roll slightly but didn't awaken.   Five minutes passed. Then ten.

The petty officer gave another order.

"Up periscope."

The periscope, a giant piston moving under immense hydraulic pressure, came up with grace-like ease.   The periscope could identify the intruder, popping through the surface to leave a slight telltale wake as the submarine cruised forward picking up speed at 15 knots.

"All ahead, two thirds."

The petty officer peered through the periscope as the sub closed the distance between it and the target. His eyes widened at what he saw. He barked another command.

"Sound general quarters!"

That, the sub captain heard.   The clanging bells jolted him to life, and he jumped feet-first from his bunk wondering what the hell was going on. Pulling on a green T-shirt, and exiting his quarters at the same time, his quick strides soon got him to the conning tower scrambling up the scuttle hole ladder. Now fully awake, he saw the petty officer gazing intently through the night periscope.

"What the hell are you looking at?" the captain charged onto the scene. I'm not sure. We made contact with this boat a half-hour ago, and I thought we'd better take a visual."

"What is it?"

"Looks like some kind of sailing vessel by the sonar configuration. We're switching to night scope to get a better look at the silhouette. Want to have a look?"

"I thought you'd never ask. You know me, I always like to see what's sailing out of Iraq or Pakistan these days."

The captain peered through the night scope and saw what looked like a double-masted schooner sailing through the moonlit waters toward the coast of Oman.

"Looks O.K. to me. But, he's making pretty good speed with his auxiliary diesel, isn't he?" the captain observed.

He turned to the weather duty officer, and asked him to check the surface wind speed.

"Slight breeze blowing seven knots, southwesterly," he answered crisply.

Odd, the captain thought.

Most small schooners carry a small diesel auxiliary engine and used it only in emergency. At best, the most they can do under full power is about 8 knots. This one was moving at nearly 14 knots, nearly twice that, and against a slight headwind.

"Sonar man, what type of engine do you make that out to be?"

"Don't know for sure, sir. But it sure sounds like a Bledsoe-Harris J25?"

"Are you familiar with the type of vessel they're configured with?" the captain pressed him.

"Yes sir."

"And . . . what is that?"

"Normally, a PT boat, sir."

"Christ, that's a powerful engine. What the hell is a schooner doing with a signature like that here in the Gulf of Oman?"

The captain looked more intently into the night periscope, but could only see a schooner's silhouette.

"What's the range?" he snapped.

"1,800 yards, moving away," the sonar man replied.

"Close the range to 700 yards for an attack sequence."

The chief petty officer yelled a new command.

"All ahead two-thirds, attack speed."

It was risky. If the boat had any kind of adequate sonar aboard, it would probably discover their presence. But, the captain was curious now, and he had to have a better view.

Onboard the PT boat, the Pakistani captain's lookout saw nothing unusual. The helmsman steered a course straight for the Port of Muscat, now only about 30 miles out. Another few hours, and the cargo would be safely in port, and unloaded. His job would be done.

The Pakistani captain continued a direct course for the Port of Muscat, and he looked out into the distant blackness knowing he would soon see the city's lights appear on the horizon.

But, his musing was suddenly cut short when the sonar's alarm went off with a strong intermittent, whelp breaking the smooth hum of the PT engines. He swung around and looked at the surprised helmsman.

"What is it?" the captain asked.

"It looks like a submarine, probably American," the helmsman responded.

The Palestine Conspiracy

"Damnable luck," the captain muttered nervously. "And, we're almost to port."

He'd seen them only occasionally as they patrolled the Gulf of Oman, but none of them had ever stalked him. Would the sub surface to have a better look? He realized they'd have to dump the cargo overboard if they were stopped and inspected. But, at this point, he wasn't sure if the submarine's captain suspected they were nothing other than a schooner. The wooden cutouts they had constructed and nailed onto the sides of the PT boat in the shape of a schooner had done the job so far. They reminded him of what the British had done during World War I, disguising destroyers as innocent looking, defenseless freighters, then dropping the wooden sides down to unveil their guns and blasting the attacking German U-boats to pieces.

He decided to proceed normally for the time being, until the sub committed itself one way or the other.

"Yes, it's probably American," the helmsman shouted.

American, the captain thought.

He had an idea and ordered the crew to ready signal flares for launching. He would make the submarine captain think they were a "party" vessel with its occupants having some sort of celebration on the high seas. It was their only chance to avoid discovery and to keep the sub from surfacing.

"Launch the flares. Different colors at five second intervals, two at a time," he ordered the crew.

Two flares were launched into the darkness . . . a red and a blue one.

Below, on the sub, through the night periscope, it

looked like the Fourth of July. The sub captain saw two white flares follow, and then two green ones in succession. The crew of the PT boat was using Veri guns to fire others into the night sky at random.

"What the fuck are they doing up there?" the sub captain asked motioning the petty officer to have a look.

The petty officer leaned into the periscope.

"Christ, almighty. Looks like some kind of celebration going on up there. Maybe it's some kind of Islamic holiday or something. It's too early for Ramadan."

"Yeah. Can you identify that schooner?" the captain asked.

"Uh, uh," the petty officer shook his head. But, it looks like they're having one helluva good time!"

The PT boat captain ordered the helmsman to switch on the ship's radio to a station broadcasting Western style music out of Karachi.

"Turn up the volume as loud as you can," he ordered. "And make a lot of noise, quickly!"

Below, the sub captain closed to within 700 yards and stopped.

"Christ, captain, it sounds like their having some kind of party up there music and all," the sonar man responded.

The sub captain laughed, reassured that what he was looking at was merely a private chartered fishing boat returning to port after a weeklong jaunt in the Gulf of Oman, and nothing more. They certainly were a common sight in these waters. They'd often passed similar vessels as they cruised along the various ports of India, Pakistan and the Arabian coast.

The Palestine Conspiracy

"Looks O.K. to me," he said. "All ahead, one third, and bring her about to port. Down periscope. Set a heading for six-five degrees at 200 feet. Resume patrol. Maintain a steady six knots. Bill, take over. I'm going back to sleep."

The PT captain breathed a sigh of relief as he watched the sonar blip start to move away from his vessel.

The ploy had worked.

He had fooled the American sub captain . . . this time. He checked the compass heading and knew that he would be inside the 12-mile territorial limit within fifteen minutes. His crew had performed admirably as they readied the boat for entrance into Muscat harbor.

When they crossed the 12-mile limit, the captain switched on the running lights again, and studied the coastal lights in the distance.

He relaxed a bit more as the boat churned its way slowly through the harbor waters avoiding the marker buoys bobbing up in the waves.

A few more minutes, and they would be ashore unloading their precious cargo. They had done their job. It was now up to the PLO to do theirs for the rest of the journey.

He was safe.

His crew was safe.

And, his government was safe.

CHAPTER 12

Riyadh. May 29. 7:14 a.m.

General Necomis awakened with a start.

The air raid siren wailed in the distance. He instinctively picked up the red telephone and called Sarti Air Defense. He looked out the window and saw two F-16 interceptors streaking off into the distance with their afterburners on.

"This is General Necomis. What is the meaning of the alert?"

The Sarti commander told the general he didn't know, but they were in the process of finding out. Two more jet fighters scrambled into the clear morning skies. The American built F- 16's could fly in any weather, day or night. General Necomis knew the plane's capabilities very well. An enemy intruder was no match for it in the hands of a skilled pilot.

The phone rang.

"Yes," the general answered.

"Sir, Iraqi warplanes on AWACs radar showing offensive movements at low altitude over the Persian Gulf."

"What do you think they're up to?" the general questioned.

"We're not sure, my commander. We have eight of them on AWACs. It may be only that they are testing our air defense systems along the coast. They are approximately 150 miles out and closing at 600 miles per hour."

Necomis ordered more interceptors into the air from coastal air bases, but instructed them not to attack the Iraqi fighters.

"Observe them within attack range, but make no move against them until I give the order."

Necomis had a definite combat method. Let the Iraqis know that the Saudis were aware of their presence, and that they could destroy them whenever they wished. The eight Iraqi Mig-23 Fishbeds closed to within 25 miles of Dhahran, the Saudi's largest oil loading facility. Necomis quickly got dressed and went over to the air operations room the king had built underneath the palace, where if he wished, he could monitor air defense with his military consultants. Necomis entered the situation room where thirty military personnel were tracking the Migs.

Again, the AWACs had picked up the potential enemy, this time at only 500 feet above the gulf. They had avoided the coastal radar stations, but they couldn't avoid the AWACs.

Necomis watched the Migs closing in on Dhahran, and noted precisely where the F-16's were in proximity waiting to attack on his orders. The Migs refused to come no closer than 25 miles. They were good. The formations were tight, controlled and they moved as a rigid unit back-and-forth across the gulf, skirting the waves.

The general watched his fighter planes track them from a higher altitude in the sun, closing the attack distance to ten miles. The Iraqi's were good, but the Saudi's were better. Necomis knew the Migs spotted the F-16's, when they abruptly changed course ninety degrees and began a steep climb away from the Saudi's, and back in the direction of Iraq. It was obvious they wanted no confrontation with the F16's this time.

Necomis flashed a wide smile.

They were flying outdated Mig-23's, a formidable warplane, but certainly no match for the F-16's. The eight F-16's Necomis had sent up, relaxed their hold on the Migs giving them wide maneuvering room as they streaked toward their own coastline.

The Saudi's broke off the engagement and flew in formation over the Dhahran installation waggling their wings to the air defense stations below. The Arabians cheered and waved with wild enthusiasm.

It had been a test of their coastal defenses. General Necomis telephoned the king.

"Excellent General Necomis. You have performed well. I want you to lodge a formal protest with the United Nations if the Iraqis are found to have violated the 12-mile international limit."

The American press would make it the lead news story if the Iraqi's did that.

"Alert the news agencies so the whole world knows what the Iraqis are doing," the king requested.

King Fasaid was an excellent tactician, and he knew what would make the evening news broadcasts in the United States. The Saudi king was also strong politically in the Middle East. And, his contacts among his brother Arabs were legendary. He usually got what he wanted. What he wanted was security for his country. What Iraq wanted was anyone's guess. But, he didn't know how far the Iraqi's would take the threat, or if the threat was designed to be real or just to make the Saudi's uneasy. He could not take the incident lightly.

Always, in his thoughts, his humble beginnings were a nagging reminder of his origins and of his people, and a constant reminder of those values instilled in him as a young boy growing up as a Bedouin among the family of nomads in the desert.

For he was the son of a Bedouin chieftain and raised in the Rub Al Khali Desert where life was barren and hard, hot under the searing sun by day, and by night, cold enough to see one's breath. There, alone among the dunes, he had lived a life of practical hardship and habitual prayer, with his family in the desolate terrain which was the most unforgiving on the face of the earth.

His father had taught him to breed and sell camels to the trader caravans in the northern cities of Tebuk and Jubba. And, from there he would travel back-and-forth and over and over again to his father's campsite, constantly wary of the bands of thieves who would rob and plunder his herds.

Young Fasaid also traveled occasionally from Jubba, south to Medina and Mecca where he visited the holy cities to offer Allah prayers for his personal safety on the most dangerous journeys. Those prayers had been answered only once, but it was as though the hand of Allah had reached down and plucked him from harm's way when he was attacked and nearly killed by a group of rival chieftains. Only by the will of Allah, had a passing caravan with whom he had done business only months earlier intervened to save him. His father, upon hearing the news, offered his daughter to the friendly chieftain in gratitude for saving young Fasaid's life. It was a day of both joy and pain. Young Fasaid was happy to be alive, but he knew deep within that he would never see his sister again. He kissed her good-bye and watched her journey into the desert with a man she didn't love and a man she never knew. Now, according to Bedouin law, he was her husband and master.

And, so after that, young Fasaid remained in the desert, and upon his father's death, he vowed to his mother that he would find his sister some day and return with her to reunite them. As the years passed, and the trips across the desert became less frequent, Fasaid built considerable wealth buying up as much land as possible with his considerable earnings. He had indeed remembered what his father had instructed him to do. His father too had loved the desert, and like he, Fasaid, too was dedicated to its way of life - the love of the sands and the soul of a Bedouin.

Was it an omen that his father had instructed him to never part with this desert land long before anyone knew of its huge oil deposits that lay just beneath the sands? He often wondered about the answer to this, yet, somehow, he knew the unmistakable wisdom in it. He had often asked himself how it was that an uneducated leader of a nomadic Bedouin tribe could know that a wealth of oil existed below the desert sands in uncharted geological rock formations in that region of the world?

Indeed, perhaps it was Allah who had blessed his father and shown him a vision. For soon, young Fasaid had accumulated a hidden treasure of oil, to later be discovered by the British and Americans during the 1920's and 1930's. It was not to be squandered. Young Fasaid had inherited these lands containing this oil wealth to continue the family's good fortune and hard work.

His father had often wandered with him among the sand dunes teaching him the ways of the desert, and how it could kill a man who took it for granted. He taught young Fasaid how to survive weeks at a time, eating and drinking only what the desert had to offer. They would meditate in the evening hours atop the sand dunes overlooking their campsite below, kneeling in the sand, ever eastward toward Mecca and Medina in Bedouin prayer. They shared meals with each other, eating roast lamb, rice flavored "ghee", a purified butter, dates and unleavened bread baked in round loaves, from a single, large communal platter. During such meals, the Bedouins curled one leg underneath and the other knee raised to rest an arm upon. The true Bedouin ate only with his right hand. The main meal was often supplemented with camel milk or yogurt. In the morning, as a gesture of hospitality to guests, young Fasaid might offer a stranger of the desert a drink of sweet tea served in a small brightly colored cup, a sign of Bedouin hospitality. The tea was brewed by boiling the tea, sugar and water at the same time to obtain the correct sweetness. Such was the law of the desert.

A quiet bitterness swept over him during those years.

He had seen his two older brothers venture off to find their fortunes among the coastal fishing villages along the Red Sea. A third, oldest brother, Fasi, in near despair at his many misfortunes of life, had made his way to Syria in search of adventure and some semblance of stability and success. Fasi, young Fasaid, knew him as a revolutionary, one who would rather fight and take

The Palestine Conspiracy

his reward without regard for those he took it from. He was the forgotten one of the family.

In time, when young Fasaid married and had a family of his own, like his father, he would often take his own sons into the desert to help carry the water from the well to the camel herds they owned.

He made them do this in spite of his wealth, because it was necessary to be able to earn a living in the eyes of another Arab if the wealth suddenly disappeared like a mirage in the desert.

One of the brothers, Dawoud died early from diphtheria, caught from one of the nearby nomadic tribes. And, Talal, the middle brother, finally returned home in despair to care for his ailing mother.

Young Fasaid often wondered if the poverty of the Bedouins would ever end. Perhaps all his people were cursed with poverty, pain and continual sacrifice. Perhaps it would never change. And, if war came to this land of the Bedouin, it would be its final destruction. Now, as the king of Saudi Arabia, he had made much progress to improve the standard of living for those living in the most populated areas. He had built schools, mosques, and had given his people a minimum monthly per capita income from the immense oil revenues.

With the oil money constantly flowing in, he built many hospitals with staffs of highly trained doctors and nurses educated in the United States. He had given these select Saudis everything humanly possible, including the technology to wage war, if necessary. His generosity, which he had inherited from his Bedouin upbringing, had made him a popular king.

The Palestine Conspiracy

But, if the Iraqis did launch an attack, all this good fortune and planning could be changed in an instant.

There was an unwritten law practiced among all Bedouins. And, it was this. All Bedouins must comply with the unselfish act of extending hospitality to any beleaguered stranger arriving at a Bedouin camp, even if he were an enemy but in need of food and drink. The Bedouin must receive him for at least three days and three nights, and even protect him from other enemies while traveling with their caravan. After the hospitality, he was free to go in peace. Such was the way of the Bedouin. The name itself in Arabic meant, "people who become visible," and it stood for courage, generosity and cunning. The tribes in the desert had been the neglected ones. But, because of the many political factions that existed among them, the constant bickering had made it virtually impossible to reach agreements on the disposition of lands held among them.

And for more than fifty years, the endless squabbles had nearly exhausted him as king. As he now approached old age, King Fasaid still harbored a sense of guilt for not having done more to resolve the problems of the Bedouins nomadic existence.

"General, you will be my guest for dinner and evening prayers, " he ordered Necomis.

"Thank you, your majesty. I will welcome the opportunity to spend more time with you. Have you anything else you want of me today?" Necomis asked.

"No, my general. I only wish to pray to Allah for his guidance in the days ahead. Surely, he will have more answers than either you or I have. Is not that so?"

"That is so, your majesty."

The Palestine Conspiracy

Both the king and general were pleased with each other.

CHAPTER 13

**Abou Sentre.   Inside Syria, 40 miles from
Damascus. May 15. 9:35 a.m.**

Brian and Geoff had been inside their tent for more
than an hour sipping Bedouin morning tea.

Suddenly, through the tent flap, came rushing in a
PLO aide who had been forwarded by Fasi to attend to
their personal needs.

The morning sun burned through the tent opening
and warmed the air inside. The black Bedouin canvas,
which formed the ceiling of the tent, billowed out as the
desert breeze whooshed- in.   The two Brits readied
themselves for the meeting with PLO Chief Fasi.

It had been a tedious week of planning. The two
Brits had observed with great interest exactly how the
PLO functioned - formality mixed with informality,
orders being issued and remanded, customs and
loyalties being obeyed without question.

It was odd that in any organization, whether it was
British, German, Russian, or American or whatever, the
first and foremost duty was always obedience without
question. It was incongruous to logic, but that's the way
a military or paramilitary functioned most efficiently;
when the moving parts, humans included, all moved
together as one. The military
structure seemed to enhance, then overrule the concept
of human conscience. Brian had found that element a
disturbing fact throughout history of civilization that all

armies, from Alexander the Great to Caesar to Napoleon to Stalin to Hitler, mobilized around its leaders and obeyed commands down to the minutest detail, even when those orders seemed irrational. Even when faced with certain defeat, subordinates followed those orders to the utmost. Orders simply had to be obeyed for an army to function. It was the way any efficient organization survived. It had been that way since foot soldiers learned how to organize and wage war in the early years of civilization. It would probably never change.

The PLO aide instructed Brian and Geoff that Fasi was ready to receive them.

Brian pushed aside the flap and stepped into the hot, arid desert air. Suddenly, without warning, he was stunned by a sight he would never forget.

Thousands of Bedouins lay face down in the desert kneeling toward the East reciting a Muslim prayer. The sight and sound of it was almost too much for him to comprehend. It was simply amazing.

The Arab nations had been squabbling with each other constantly; yet, here they were, representatives from all Arab states, gathered together, praying to the same God for an identical purpose.

Geoff straightened through the tent opening putting on his pith helmet to block the sun from his forehead. When the prayers had concluded, a bugle sounded in the distance and the thousands of tents were dismantled and dissolved into the surrounding sand dunes, and the Bedouins becoming nearly invisible.

The scene was surrealistic, like a mirage. He was witnessing the entire thing, but he wasn't quite sure it was really there. Geoff wiped his eyes.

The Palestine Conspiracy

"Bedouin," Geoff said aloud.

"What did you say?" Brian asked.

"Bedouin," Geoff repeated.

"Badawiyan," he said again, but in an Arab accent he had been trained to duplicate.

"These are Bedouin soldiers. Take a close look at them. And, don't forget what you see here today. They are among the most cunning, fierce fighters ever known to mankind. Don't ever under-estimate them."

Brian recognized the long caravan, the Bedouin garb, and even a few had the British Enfield relics, a throwback in time of lone, sentry figure atop camels, while the others had slung over their shoulders or raised in the air, Russian-made AK-47 Kalashnikov rifles, a more efficient, deadly weapon.

Even the Enfield served its purpose. It could hit a target with deadly accuracy at a half-mile in the hands of a marksman.

Geoff imagined he was looking at Omar Sharif himself as he watched the sentry balance himself in perfect rhythm to the punishing gait of the camel's gallop. He was reminded of the movie Lawrence of Arabia he saw as a little boy, with thousands of them charging at full gallop in a thundering formation through the desert in full regalia for the attack. It was as though he had stepped through a portal of time some seventy years ago.

He clearly recognized the reality of it all. His senses could feel the rhythm of it now - the baying of the camels, the chanting of the Bedouins, Syrians and the PLO banded together for a common cause.

He knew there was a change in the wind, a change stirring in this desert stronghold.

The Palestine Conspiracy

"When's the last time you saw 27,000 Bedouins at one time?" Geoff marveled.

"I never have before. And, I probably never will again," Brian answered while taking it all in.

"I wonder what it all means?"

"Yes, I, too?"

Then, Fasi emerged from his Bedouin tent, and inexplicitly a chorus of shouts rose from the multitudes assembled on the dunes. Some had waited all night for a glimpse of Chairman Fasi and the British envoys.

The Bedouins had seemingly shown up from nowhere. The evening before, the camp had been nearly empty, and Geoff and Brian had heard nothing but the high-pitched howl of the desert wind.

Fasi acknowledged the cheering throng with a wave of his arm in a triumphant gesture.

In turn, they raised their rifles into the air, as the crescendo grew so loud that Brian remarked he couldn't hear himself think. The "yipping" sound made with a stuttering of the tongue on the roof of the mouth, pierced the air like a soldier's saber.

"My two friends, the Arab nations have sent Bedouin soldiers from seven nations to observe what we have done here this past week. It is a sendoff for you, a tribute and a sign of respect for what you will attempt to do for Palestine. They have been sworn to secrecy under the oath of death by their own nations not to reveal what they have seen here. They know in five weeks, a new Palestine will be born, and it is why they have gathered here at its birthplace," Fasi said.

The Brits were awestruck by the notion.

"Tell Prime Minister Thayer that the nation of Palestine will be founded at this very spot on July 24.

The Palestine Conspiracy

We will forever be indebted to her majesty, Queen Elizabeth. We will welcome England's influence in this region once again." Fasi spoke.

Geoff, acting as translator for the two, thanked Fasi for his assurances that in exchange for Britain's support in the United Nations and the absolute halt in world terrorism, a new Palestine would be created.

An agreement had been reached.

It was now up to the representatives of the respective countries to carry out the plan to its logical conclusion.

Fasi entered the tent with the two men and sat down on the soft Bedouin rug completed for him by his mother. He invited Geoff and Brian to join him for breakfast.

"Most Westerners would like to own a rug such as this, eh?" Fasi asked. "They would like to own them because they think of them as a luxury. But, for us, such a rug is looked upon only as a necessity, a simple cloth to rest one's weary body upon, regardless of its beauty. And, then, for others, it is something only to be walked upon, is it not?"

Geoff and Brian understood what Fasi was getting at.

"Mr. Etebbe, the English have always regarded anything created by the Arab people to be cared for with the utmost respect, that includes your religious beliefs and cultural values. I would venture to say that it would indeed include any Bedouin rugs, which we may have in our homes. They are there because of the dignity, beauty and value we place on them. The same can be said about our feelings toward the Arab people."

Fasi smiled. He was appreciative of the polite

sincerity of Geoff's answer. And, Brian was literally spellbound by the ability of Geoff to bullshit his way through any situation.

Fasi offered the two some morning tea pouring it himself, playing the gracious host and giving a lesson in Bedouin hospitality, using a brightly colored teapot and teacups, traditional among Bedouin tribes.

"If Mrs. Thayer agrees to this principle of a free and independent Palestine, my people will be forever grateful. In return, I am prepared to end the 20-year reign of terror in the Middle East and Europe."

Brian listened intently as he explained the PLO's role in world terrorism, how it was coordinated with other Arab nations, how it was financed and how it was all meant to deceive. It was by design, Fasi explained, that one Arab country would bicker with another for control of certain geographical areas in the Mediterranean, including oil interests. But foremost, their interests as an aggregate force came first politically as a people. The same strategy had worked well for the oil cartel. And, it had worked extremely well in world terrorism. The Arabs were united as a brotherhood the way families were united by blood despite the many large and small differences among them.

Brian and Geoff were impressed with the way Fasi had presented his ideas. Here was a man who had brought a rabble army together and welded seven Middle East countries together to create a massive terrorist organization, which stretched beyond continents, one the likes of which the world had never seen before or would want to see again.

It, like the oil cartel, had literally made the western

nations stop and take notice of the Palestinian issue like never before. The interruption of world trade alone had been devastating. But, did killing have to be an element of it?

Brian felt the man could be a genius, terrorism aside, if he could bring this anger under control and push his goals to a loftier aim.

Fasi could foresee the inevitability of a Palestinian state for that part of the world to return to stability. His people must have the right to co-exist with Israel, and the right of return to their homes, no matter where they were.

And, Israel would have to come to that conclusion sooner or later. There were already diplomatic signs that this was occurring.

In a newfound role, England could once again be a chief influence in the region. Britain could again be the dominant military and political force, catering to the needs of the Arab nations, while receiving in exchange, a peaceful Europe and access to all the oil it needed.

Fasi was no idealist. He was a pragmatist. With stability brought to the region once again, the Arabs could educate, rebuild and modernize their countries. The Arabs could then irrigate and update their agricultural methods, turning arid wasteland into productive farmland.

Brian and Geoff knew that Fasi was no dreamer. Put in the proper perspective, Fasi could put the agreement in force throughout the Middle East.

Fasi knew such a Palestinian State was possible, except for Israel. Fasi knew he could not let Israel stand in his way. No, Fasi was not the kind of man who would allow that to happen. He was too fanatical for

144

that.

That bothered both the Brits. Brian knew that Fasi must hold some kind of trump card he could use - a card he would play when he was ready.

Perhaps, the 27,000 Bedouins gathered in the dunes were a clue? Why were they really here?

As Geoff listened to Fasi continue, he knew that in another war with Israel, Fasi could count on the full support of Syria, Lebanon, Jordan, Saudi Arabia, Libya, Algeria, Tunisia, Oman and even Egypt if they pressed President Musrak.

But, they knew Fasi could not count on two nations in the region - Iraq and Iran. Iran had no further military resources left, and Iraq was a paranoid, isolated wild card, which might turn against Saudi Arabia in a power struggle.

"My plan is to ask Jordan, Lebanon, Syria and Saudi Arabia to each present specific geographical areas totaling 2,500 square miles of land from which the State of Palestine would be formed. Palestine would have five borders, one adjoining Israel. Palestine would thus be born, and formalized by United Nations ratification of a charter and eventually become a member nation.

"The new state of Palestine would be prepared to announce world neutrality for the next 100 years.

Imagine," Fasi gestured with his open hands, "if you can, Palestine as a Switzerland of the Middle East."

Brian sat speechless as he heard the plan to its conclusion. He sat motionless. It was a brilliant piece of strategy - one that could serve the needs of the entire world. Perhaps, even Israel might agree to the long-term benefits.

But, could Israel agree to such a creation? Israel

was indeed the wild card in the entire process. They, too, were a country born of a dream in 1948. But, why not a free and independent Palestine? Why not?

It would take a lot of convincing; literally a world campaign on behalf of the Palestinian people, but it could be done.

Possibly, Mrs. Thayer and Fasi were on the right track.

The Brits finished their tea, brushed themselves off and shook hands with Fasi. The agreement was now sealed.

Mrs. Thayer would announce her conditions beside Fasi at a formal signing ceremony with the
political leaders of seven Arab countries and the world witnessing the event by media.

Israel could agree to it at a special meeting of the United Nations.

As they exited Fasi's tent, PLO soldiers placed their luggage aboard the old battle worn army truck they had arrived in.

As they departed, a lone Bedouin soldier raised his rifle in a triumphant gesture and screamed in Arabic, "Let there be a Palestine. Long live Palestine!"

Twenty-seven thousand Bedouin soldiers signaled their approval by firing rifle volleys into the air as a farewell salute to the British envoys.

Fasi smiled broadly.

Fasi had arranged the salute for their attendance at the Bedouin stronghold.

To the Bedouins and the Palestinian people, the Brits being there symbolized freedom for their people at last, and in the end, a homeland of their own.

CHAPTER 14

Muscat, Oman. May 25. 11:00 p.m.

The port city slept peacefully in the obscurity of a moonless night.

Neat rows of fishing vessels lay abandoned by their workers, biding a time in place until the next day. The boats, in point of fact, created an artificial reef behind which Muscat fishermen could repair their nets when they gathered in the early morning hours. All was tranquil except for the occasional shout of a dockworker's voice trailing off in the distance echoing off the wooden hulls.

The sun had set hours before and the chill of the sea breeze gently brushed against the moist foreheads of the PT crew as they approached the landing.

An old army truck rolled up, its brakes screeching it to a halt as the PT captain steered his boat into mooring carefully. The crew quickly removed the dual mastheads and hurriedly dumped them over the sides as the boat swished to a stop thumping against the wooden docks. The boat was now flying the Pakistani flag, signaling to anybody who was interested that it was tucked safely in Oman Harbor.

At nearly 11:30 p.m., when all was clear on the docks, the truck pulled alongside the PT boat and the crew began unloading the precious cargo.   Amal, the driver of the truck, signaled the captain that all was well.

"We will be in the desert within a few hours. We travel caravan by day and rest by night," he shouted to the captain.

The captain signaled back that he understood. It would be a difficult, hot journey with temperatures reaching more than 120 degrees Fahrenheit at the height of day and 30 degrees at night.

Amal signaled to his brother, Atar, to proceed to the edge of the city where the caravan waited. The PT captain re-boarded his craft, waved good-bye to them, and started his engines for the return across the gulf. This time, he would use all four engines and would make the run at a brisk 40 knots. If there were any American submarines still trailing them in the murky waters, he would easily outrun them.

The boat shuddered as the four diesels caught fire and roared to life. He had only used one engine on the crossing to Oman. It was the only way he could maintain his slow pace. Without the silhouetted disguises, the crew cast-off the mooring lines and the PT rumbled from its berth toward the open sea. Half-a-mile into the bay, the captain gunned the engines to harbor speed and cruised out past the same marker lights that had guided him on the way in.

The Muscat official who had greeted him earlier and who had been successfully bribed not to inspect the cargo, turned away as he watched the craft leave the harbor. He could only imagine what might be inside the large brown crates they had unloaded. Even the captain didn't know for sure. He had been warned not to inspect the cargo unless they were about to be stopped by U. S. patrol boats. The captain obeyed his orders as a faithful Muslim, but knowing where the cargo had originated. He had a suspicion of what might be inside.

"Warheads," he whispered to himself as they left the harbor. "Nuclear warheads."

A sense of foreboding welled up in him as he strained to see the horizon for the way home to Karachi.

* * *   * * *

12:30 a.m. On the outskirts of Muscat.

The truck rumbled along the dusty road and pulled to a stop near a grove of trees five miles outside the city.

Waiting for them was Yemet, one of Fasi's sons.

Amal and Atar, both cousins, broke into wide smiles when they saw Yemet come into view. Atar was driving like a madman and almost lost control of the vehicle as he braked to a halt.

They jumped from the truck and quickly ordered the other PLO soldiers to unload the crates.

"Quickly . . . move . . . we must hurry . . . " Yemet implored them.

Fasi had instructed him and had meticulously rehearsed the planned journey over and over again until Yemet could recount it in his sleep.

Yemet was to take no chances. Fasi's orders were to be followed in detail as outlined. The camels were to be rested during the night with most of the travel done by day. Everything, which the caravan leaders normally did, had to be adhered to. There would be no change in the travel route the caravan would take, not the slightest deviation. They would follow the same route, which had been used for hundreds of years by Bedouin tribesmen. If a passing caravan greeted them, they would reciprocate with the traditional centuries-old Bedouin hospitality of sharing drink, food and a campfire. To observe this ancient tradition, a Bedouin must not refuse traveler hospitality or help in the desert – the imperative unwritten law that all Arab nomads innately agreed to in principle.

Fasi could have flown the equipment in by helicopter, but it would have been too dangerous, passing over Syrian territory. The Israelis were monitoring everything that flew in-and-out of Damascus and the laser X-ray the United States had given them would enable them to detect the warheads when they intercepted the planes. Plus, United States satellites were photographing everything in the Middle East on a daily basis.

Satellites could detect every type of armament shipment known to military experts, especially radioactive materials. Fasi's best chance to avoid detection was to use the desert caravan routes with lead shielding covering the warheads. The "hot spots" created by the radioactive elements could be hidden, in the broiling heat the desert, and would throw off the infra-red cameras hovering high in synchronous orbit some 23,000 miles in space. The lower orbiting satellites with their superior detection systems would also be fooled by equipment moving by caravan, an unlikely source of supply for such modern weapons. The two missile warheads would probably go undetected even if the satellites spotted the caravan.

The Palestine Conspiracy

The radioactive warheads had to be protected by specially lined leaded canvas material. The warhead itself was encased in a lead apparatus, which had been carefully tested by the Muslims for radiation leakage. The caravan carried Geiger counters to monitor the escape of any slight radiation release, which might be picked up by intelligence satellites.

The secret cargo looked innocent enough when broken down into its components. The launchers were already at Fasi's campsite. Together, they would complete the attack unit.

Yemet continued to supervise the loading of the camels. It went so smoothly, that they embarked into the desert an hour earlier than scheduled, using a dead-reckoning method of navigation and Yemet's vast knowledge of the desert terrain. Yemet knew how to navigate the desert, as did his father and his uncle, King Fasaid. All Bedouins knew the desert for its life-sustaining elements. From these parched desert sands, evolved a different kind of existence. Living conditions were rugged and served those well that knew how to utilize the sparse resources.

It was not a comfortable way of life, but it was, in spite of everything, life - a Bedouin way of life suitable only for a Bedouin.

Indeed, Yemet, his cousins and uncles were the best of Bedouins.

* * *   * * *

Sarti Air Base. Saudi Arabia. 6:00 p.m.

The Palestine Conspiracy

General Necomis readied the airbase for more surprise attacks from either the Iraqis or Israelis.

Most probable was an attack from the Iraqis since their recent test of the coastal defenses near Dhahran and Daha had given them fresh intelligence data on the Saudi defenses. The AWACs were now flying around the clock in 8-hour shifts circling high above in a 25-mile arc over central Saudi Arabia.

Necomis had radar surveillance of 250 miles in all directions reaching far into the Persian Gulf, part of Iraq, Iraq, Jordan, Lebanon, Israel and the Mediterranean. It was the most technically advanced defense system ever deployed by their armed forces, one that now became indispensable to them.

Necomis had already secured the base against Iraqi sapper squads or other terrorists. He had surrounded the base with 20,000 Saudi marines, similar to the ones deployed at the palace in Riyadh protecting the royal family.

He was confident his troops could repel any attackers. Complementing the ground units was radar guided anti-aircraft batteries and Hawk anti-aircraft missiles with a kill ratio of nearly 100 percent. They were the same missiles that had taken out the Israeli reconnaissance planes. Saudi Arabia could not afford to be without them. Replacement missiles had already been made battle-ready, and re-supply came from American ships stationed in the Persian Gulf. Necomis also had three squads of anti-tank weapons at the ready.

Now, if an attack came, the Saudi's would be at full strength.

Necomis had thought of everything.

And, now his thoughts turned to the king, once

again.

* * *   * * *

The king was preparing to address the United Nations General Assembly in New York the following day with Great Britain. It could not occur a day too soon. The recent reconnaissance mission by the Israelis would be aired publicly and questioning of Israel by U.N. delegates would most likely take place before a worldwide television audience. Saudi Arabia was beginning to put political pressure on Israel to own up to the mission and explain to the world why it had made an incursion into Saudi Arabian airspace.

King Fasaid was a master politician in the world arena. It would be high drama. He would make the world understand. He would make his own people understand, and he would make the Israeli's apologize for the intrusion.

Gen. Necomis knew this would be a performance worth remembering.

CHAPTER 15

Somewhere over the Mediterranean: May 20. 2:11 a.m.

They departed Heathrow on schedule at 7 p.m.

Adrienne met Katherine from the Red Cross as planned and discussed what was to be her role.

She was to enter Lebanon under a passport of her own name, but listing her identification as a Red Cross volunteer from England. Rick Waite, the American UPI reporter, would meet both at the airport. After that, her fate would be in the hands of Waite and his intimate knowledge of the city.

"I suppose you get so used to flying, it becomes second nature to you," the Red Cross worker, Katherine remarked to Adrienne.

Adrienne fidgeted in her seat.

"Uhhh! I don't mind flying. Actually, the take-offs aren't so bad. It's the landings that get to me a little," she said.

Adrienne was lying.

If the flight got bumpy, Adrienne would experience a case of white-knuckle nerves. During those few tense moments before landing, little glimpses of her past would emerge from her subconscious. The more she tried to suppress her fear during such landings, the more she learned about herself and the crash in Cyprus. To take her mind off it, she resorted to working crossword puzzles to force her to think

The Palestine Conspiracy

straight.

"Do you play cards?" she asked Katherine.

The tension rose in her as the plane over-flew Nicosia, the same airport where she had crashed eight years earlier.

"Yes," Katherine responded reaching into her purse for a deck of cards the flight attendant had given them earlier.

"I'll deal," Adrienne said stretching to reach the cards when she felt a slight shudder of the aircraft's fuselage.

A split-second of terror pierced her heart like a dagger.

She fought to regain her composure. Then, a split second later, another shudder went rolling through the aircraft.

The captain's came on the intercom.

"Good evening. This is the captain. Some of you may have noticed in looking out your starboard window, that's the right window, that we are being escorted by two Israeli military fighter jets. We are in contact with them on our civilian frequency and we have been advised that they will shine a laser beacon on our aircraft as a method of inspecting our baggage compartments for any armaments being shipped into the Middle East. This has been a regular practice by the Israelis for several months now, and although it is a minor inconvenience, it poses no threat to you or the aircraft and will cause no delay to your destination.

"All passengers are requested at this time to pull down the shades of each window and to shield your eyes from the laser light which should last no longer than 10 seconds. When I count down from 5 seconds to

155

zero, close your eyes and cover your face. Do not look outside the aircraft windows," he repeated emphatically. "The laser beam is very powerful and any direct sighting by the retina could cause permanent blindness. I will begin my count now."

The captain's tone re-assured them that everything would be all right as long as these instructions were followed.

"Five, four, three . . . two . . . one . . . zero . . . shield your eyes now!"   The beam of laser light illuminated the Boeing 767 streaming from the lead Israeli F-22, perpendicular to it and from below. Inside the 767, a white light diffused through the cabin for an instant then quickly faded. The passengers kept their eyes closed, some covered their faces. In a few seconds, it was all over, and an audible murmur swept through them. The captain was right. It was painless.

But, Adrienne was visibly shaken.

Katherine, who had been through it before on an earlier trip to the Middle East, was unperturbed.

"I didn't warn you about it for a reason," she said. "I wanted to see you react under pressure."

Adrienne looked at her dumbfounded. She had come close to real panic when the pilot had rolled the aircraft slightly to adjust his course to the jet fighters. Now, she wondered just who Katherine was?

"You did O.K.," Katherine said firmly. "Not bad for someone who survived a major air crash?"

The comment caught Adrienne off guard.

"How did you know that?"

"You told me."

"I told you?"

"Sure. People who've either had close calls or

survived plane crashes all act the same way. You took the first open seat in the rear of the plane near the aisle, and you didn't ask me where I cared to sit," Katherine observed.

"Then, you removed your shoes upon being seated. It was a little too noticeable. And, you looked for all the emergency exits and strapped yourself into your seat before we left the terminal."

Adrienne forgot her fear and thought how ridiculous she must have looked.

The captain came on the intercom again and announced landing preparations.

Adrienne relaxed.

Odd. They were on final approach, and for the first time, she wasn't nervous anymore. Perhaps Katherine's analysis of her behavior had been the therapy she needed.

The plane's air speed dropped. They were descending. Adrienne could feel the air brakes pop-up into place and hear the landing gear drop down from the plane's undercarriage causing the plane to vibrate a bit more. The huge plane shuddered from side-to-side slightly, but Adrienne disregarded it now as normal landing noise. As the 767 bumped to a smooth landing, Adrienne's grip   relaxed on the seat handles,
as she felt the reverse thrusters of the big jet take hold and jerk them slightly forward. Her breathing returned to normal as the plane exited the runway and taxied to the Beirut Air Terminal.

The landing incident seemed peculiar to Adrienne. She was not afraid anymore. Katherine had been just the right therapy for her.

Adrienne knew she had arrived at last.

CHAPTER 16

New York: May 21. 10:02 a.m.

The U. N. delegates milled all over the general assembly room in confusion as reporters from national and international wire services and television crews set up equipment readying to broadcast live via satellite.

Word had it that the meeting would be the most important event since the Cuban Missile Crisis of 1962 when Adlai Stevenson and Nikita Khrushchev squared-off with the latter pounding his shoe on his desk in the assembly room. Stevenson had shouted back in an exchange of accusations that he'd wait until "hell freezes over if necessary" for the appropriate response from the Soviet chairman. It was not a pretty sight, but it made for great broadcast journalism.

There was the same air of anticipation that today's events would produce something equally as controversial.

Israel had only days to prepare its defense. But, Saudi Arabia had gathered extensive evidence of the downed planes over its territory. The case would be difficult for Israel to refute.

The news media had given the incident worldwide attention. The entire world knew exactly what had happened. What they now waited to learn was what had motivated Israel to act in such a manner toward a nation with which they were not at war. It would be one of the most interesting dialogues at the U.N. in a long time.

Network crews rehearsed the anchormen. Special network news analysts had bolstered news correspondents with up-to-the-minute information. The Today Show would broadcast live from the balcony of the assembly room floor, as would their rival stations. The atmosphere took on the appearance of a national political convention. Indeed, it was equivalent to a world convention where a vote would be taken to sanction Israel for its actions.

There was no denying the incident held serious consequences regarding world public opinion. The discussion would be important to the geo-political world. Even a delegation from Borneo had arrived that morning.

The noise in the hall abated as the speaker approached the rostrum. Delegates scrambled from the aisles to their respective seats, and everyone held their breaths as cameras clicked on and photographers warmed up their battery packs. The whirring could be heard throughout the hall as the gathered hushed and delegates began posturing when cameras were aimed at them.

Again, the mood in the assembly hall tightened down to total silence. Speaker Hans Vensberg, Secretary-General of the United Nations and a native diplomat from Switzerland, opened the conference with a few brief remarks directed at the delegates.

"Member delegates, we are gathered here this morning out of necessity to address a question which has been the focus of world-wide attention for the past several weeks; namely, the incursion by Israeli armed reconnaissance planes over the sovereign territory of

The Palestine Conspiracy

Saudi Arabia.

"We will debate the question of whether the incursion was accidental or deliberate, and what amends the Israeli government must make to Saudi Arabia for its actions."

Delegates in the audience listened intently through headsets as interpreters in the back rooms of the U.N. translated the remarks for them. Everyone was now seated, and the two prominent delegations, the Saudis and the Israelis, were very evident as cameramen focused on their every movement. Anchormen, high above the auditorium in soundproof cubicles, described the proceedings pausing only long enough to catch important information as it was spoken. Some anchormen finally stopped to let their audiences listen for themselves.

Minutes ticked away as delegates listened to the evidence presented by the Saudi spokesman. Film and documented tapes were shown of the downed Israeli aircraft, even the bodies of the pilots, identified by foreign news crews who visited the crash scene.

The evidence was incontrovertible. It was clear, direct and accusatory. Military communications of the downed pilots were re-played for the delegates to hear, along with the retaliatory radio transmissions, which took place between General Necomis and King Fasaid as their armed forces launched the Hawk missiles.

The drama heightened as the U.N. delegates heard the king of Saudi Arabia give the order to shoot down the Israeli planes. Then, as the Saudi speaker was about to finish, the scene took a dramatic turn.

"Representatives of the United Nations, I will now make way for the concluding speaker from the Saudi delegation.   Distinguished delegates, I present to you King Fasaid Etebbe, his royal highness, the sovereign king of Saudi Arabia."

Stunned by the announcement, the U.N. delegates stood to applaud the king as he strode to the lectern. The room filled with excitement. Israel wasn't prepared for this.   They had sent no delegate of higher stature than their top ranking U.N. diplomat.   Whatever explanation they made to the representative this day would not disprove the already stated facts.   The emotional tide had already clearly swung to the Saudis before Israel could respond.   The Israeli delegation, obviously in total disarray, would have to act fast or lose credibility.

A U. S. senator rushed over to consult with them wanting to know what was going on? Had they known the king was going to appear?   The Israeli representative shrugged his shoulders. He hadn't known.

As King Fasaid reached the speaker's lectern, a silence fell over the auditorium.   Speaking in English but with a heavy, Arabian accent, the king recounted the events for everyone.

"With the kind of evidence before you, we will ask the United Nations Security Council to vote for condemnation of the Israeli actions for this blatant attack against us."

The U.N. delegates leaned forward anticipating the next statement.

"We are a peace loving nation. We take no further retaliatory action against Israel or its armed forces. We seek no military victory over Israel. We simply want to live as Arabs at peace in an area that should, and must remain stable for the good of the entire world.

"Therefore, the only question we want answered to satisfy ourselves and interested world opinion is the reason why the over flight was ordered. We seek only an apology by the Israeli government in this public forum for its actions. We seek no reparations for damages. Monetary gestures are meaningless to us in a land where pride and courage are far more valuable."

The U.N. delegates were amazed at the king's superb performance. By the time he finished, delegates were on their feet applauding with such vigor that the network anchors were flabbergasted. They scrambled to get the best shots of King Fasaid waving in political victory. Fasaid left the podium knowing he had already won his case.

His speech has been an unprecedented historic success. It was the first time that a king from Saudi Arabia had addressed the United Nations. The circumstances were unique. The message had unified the Arab delegations even before Israel could make its afternoon address. Who would they send to the rostrum?

Israel was clearly on the defensive, and they had to do the impossible - turn the perception in the assembly hall around. The Israeli ambassador to the United States left immediately for his U.N. office. He had to telephone the Prime Minister who was watching the morning's events on Israeli television. The significance of what had just occurred was politically remarkable. He knew Israel had just taken a political and moral beating. At best, they would have to concede their actions and put on the best possible face, or just plain concede the point.

It looked as though Israel would finally lose a battle to the Arabs.

CHAPTER 17

Beirut: May 21. 8:00 a.m.

Adrienne awakened with a start.

Mortar rounds were thumping the city from the west.

Waite burst into her room and yelled for her to get downstairs in a hurry.

"Move it! Quickly," he ordered. "That one was close. The next one will have our names on it!"

Adrienne shouted the alarm to the next room, and jumped out of bed with only her underwear on; Katherine, the Red Cross worker, was right on her heels as they bolted through an open doorway toward the basement. The shells were closer now, and the building shook like it was caught in the throes of an earthquake.

"Christ, where is the fucking basement?" Adrienne blurted out staying as close to Waite as possible.

"Right over here!" he yelled plowing his way through the open doorway and almost diving headfirst down the stairs.

"For God's sake," said Adrienne. "Is it like this every morning in Beirut?"

"Luv, welcome to the city that never sleeps. The coffee's bad, most of the women are nothing special to look at, but the wake-up service is fantastic!" Waite echoed sardonically.

Adrienne and Katherine had little time to laugh and even less time to be afraid as another mortar hit the building. It shook the bones of the old hotel's foundation; an old stone church built some 1500 years before.

"Who in the hell is doing the shelling?" Adrienne shouted, feeling a little embarrassed for being scared half out of her wits.

Waite was cowering under an old card table discarded in the dingy basement while the girls hid underneath some old wicker furniture leftover from the previous owner.

"How in the hell should I know from down here? My guess is that it's the Israelis. They sound like standard 120-mm issue. The A-rabs don't use that kind. They use the superior 140mm Russian-made Katusha's."

Adrienne more frightened now than at any time since her arrival in Beirut, subconsciously moved closer to Waite for protection. She could feel a subtle pressure on her backside and turned to find his hand neatly pressed against her.

He caught her look and quickly removed it.

"Sorry! I didn't realize that was you."

"Not to worry. But, how long is this going to go on?"

"As long as it takes for them to run out of ammunition."

Adrienne looked at him blankly. Couldn't he ever give her a straight answer?

"You know . . . as soon as they finish waking everybody up. It happens all the time here. Keeps you honest, off the streets, and down on your ass. There's a method to it you know. It keeps the terrorists from wandering around too much."

The Palestine Conspiracy

Flattened out on the other side of the wicker chair lay Katherine waiting patiently for the bombardment to stop.

She wanted no further explanations from Waite.

"Of all the damned places to get stuck, sleeping in an old bombed-out hotel that the Red Cross is using as its headquarters," she complained. "Of course, there isn't a whole helluva lot to choose from in Beirut these days because there isn't much of anything left standing."

Adrienne laughed because she realized Katherine was right.

And, she wondered how the Israelis could mistake the Red Cross building for a military target.

"Can't the Israelis see our flag on the front of the building?"

"That's the problem," Waite answered. "The flag is on the front, and they're shooting from the rear."

It was not a joke. That's what was happening.

"We need more God-damned Red Cross flags. One on each side of the damned building. Any kind of flags. Israeli, French, British, surrender flags, anything," Waite shouted over the din of the mortars pounding in.

Another round hit the building, collapsing another exterior wall.

"It's like a living hell. How do you stand it every day?" Adrienne yelled reacting to the direct hits.

"You don't. You kinda get used to it. You learn to tolerate it. But, you never, never, learn to accept it. Nobody can. Nobody in their right mind, anyway."

Four more rounds hit the old hotel shaking its foundations. The south wall collapsed taking more than

166

twelve rooms with it. Vroom! Vroom! Vroom! Vroom!

"Well, there goes the honeymoon suite. They must be Israelis? How can you tell they're 120mm's?" Adrienne wanted to know.

Waite knew this was her baptism under fire. It was the beginning of her learning experience in Beirut. There were some things you couldn't explain but had to experience, like the Vietnam veterans, who knew the buzz of an AK-47 bullet, the familiar clack, clack of it in close-quarter-combat, and the whistling sound of the 120's.

"You can hear them as they come in," he explained. "Listen for the high-pitch rushing sound. Hear it? That's when you know they're 120's. The 140's make a sound more like a freight train crashing in. They're bigger and deadlier. That's the difference, understand?"

"When will I hear one of those?" she asked now huddling under the same table as Waite. He looked as though he hadn't heard the question. God, she could be irritating.

"I hope you never do. But, if you do, don't take too much time looking around for a place to take cover. They don't give you as much warning. By the time you hear it, you have only about two or three seconds to get under something."

Waite sounded like a typical male chauvinist at times like this. But, he wasn't. In tense situations, it really helped him keep control of his own sense of fear. Adrienne sensed it and understood it. It helped control hers, too.

After a few minutes, the mortar rounds began

tapering off, and in another few seconds, it was finally over.

"Thank God we're all right," Adrienne sighed wiping away the beads of perspiration from her forehead.

"God!" Waite let out a gasp.

He knew one of these times his luck was going to run out. He'd been over here for three years, much too long for a reporter to still be alive. Most of his colleagues had been either killed off or left Beirut months ago.

"How come you haven't been killed or taken hostage?" she asked. "You're an American reporter."

"Because whether the PLO likes it or not, even though I'm an American, they know I'm their only link with the outside news organizations that give them credibility. What I report here everyday gets fed to the major newspapers, wire services and TV networks. Especially, the TV networks. I tell the PLO side of the story. I tell it like it's happening. Good or bad."

"But, aren't you more valuable to them as a hostage?"

"Are you kidding? Me? Look at me. I'm just another dime-a-day reporter doing his job like every other civilian in Beirut, trying to stay alive. Right now, I'm more valuable to them alive. But, if and when that changes, I'd better be the first one to know about it, or my life won't be worth the ink on my passport."

Adrienne believed him. She was a reporter, too. Albeit one who had won a Pulitzer. Nevertheless, she was cast in the same mold. And, that meant getting the story at any cost. Write the story. Move the story. And, make headlines with it. She understood that. She understood the intrinsic value in it. It's what made her tick, too. And, as long as the PLO was getting headlines in Beirut and elsewhere in the world, she knew Waite would survive. They would make sure he'd survive.

She liked him. She felt herself drawn to him in an odd sort-of-way above and beyond their journalistic communion. His matter-of-fact, cavalier attitude. His know-it-all style. Even his chauvinistic attitude appealed to her.

Sometimes, women liked that, especially when they were in danger. It had been no time to be a devout feminist. Waite and she could get along in spite of all that. They could work together, and perhaps even have fun together. But where did anyone have fun in Beirut? Was there a quiet place in Beirut to relax?

As they dusted-off and clambered up the basement stairs, Adrienne knew she could trust him.

The trio made their way to the hotel lobby, and after Katherine left to inspect the Red Cross operations room, the pair went up to her room and talked about what had just happened. They stood in front of a window giving a full view of downtown Beirut. Fires were burning everywhere the eye could see. Black, thick smoke billowed in the air. It wasn't a beautiful sight. It was typical of Beirut - death and destruction everywhere to be suffered by all.

They brewed and poured some fresh tea, and during the interlude, Rick built up the nerve to ask her why The Times had sent her to Beirut. It was now or never he sensed. He was right about her. Adrienne let down her guard.

"We got tipped-off that something big was on the verge of happening in the middle east, something specifically involving Beirut and the Palestine Liberation Organization."

Rick pursed his lips, pissed at the thought that after three years in Beirut as a reporter, a young hot-shot Pulitzer Prize winner from The Times somehow got the inside lead on a big story involving his international beat. Could it be the same lead he was working on with Ahmed?

"Interesting. Do you know who your tipster is?"

"My editor thinks it's from the PLO or one of the political factions working in London for the terrorists. We don't really know any more than that because our deep throat didn't call us back. It might be something; it might be nothing? We don't know?"

Waite wasn't about to trust her with the information from Ahmed just yet, and he didn't want to tip his hand. But, he had to try to get her to be more specific.

"Look, I've got something that might be related. I can't make heads or tails of it, yet. But, maybe you can."

He showed her the message and waited for any reaction.

"A friend of mine got that for me. I can't tell you how, but it's written on Israeli military intelligence paper. It may be nothing, but I have a hunch there's something more to it. David and Goliath?"

It was the real test as far as he was concerned.

Adrienne analyzed the message with the steely eyes

of a poker player. She didn't have to study it very long. It hit her like a thunderbolt!

David. Brian. Code name. Mrs. Thayer. My God! She tried to conceal her thoughts, but her eyes betrayed her.

She didn't know if she could trust him? Maybe she could chance it. But, if Brian found out about the slip-of- the-tongue, it could jeopardize the whole British mission.

But, as a reporter, she just had to know. Her investigative reporter mind went into overtime.

What could be so important about the message? The July 24 date? What did the intercept mean? Who wrote the intelligence message? Was it really Israeli in origin? Did the Israelis already know about the secret meeting? Her immediate reaction was that she had to contact Brian and warn him, but that seemed impossible now. He was in-and-around Beirut somewhere, but how could she contact him without putting him in danger? And, how could she go about finding him without making her presence known to the PLO or Israeli agents as to what she was really up to? She had no real choice but to hide her compulsion. So for now, she simply had to take a chance on this lowly UPI reporter.

"O.K., Rick. You win. I've got one of the biggest secrets in the world in my English-educated brain. But, it's not from my newspaper editor. In fact, I don't really know if it has anything to do with our deep throat or not, but anything's possible at this juncture."

He watched her with the curiosity of a scientist performing an experiment on something, which some new light was about to be shed.

"Well, I confess. I've got a secret of my own, too,"

he started. "I don't know if you want to trust me with yours, or mine with you."

Adrienne responded, "Mine could be life or death to two world leaders . . . eventually to thousands, perhaps millions of people in the Middle East. I do know this. It has something to do with great historical importance, perhaps the greatest event in the last half-century. But, I can't tell you unless I have your absolute word as a journalist that you won't divulge the story or print it before I find out more."

She studied him for any sign of hesitancy.

"Boy, you Pulitzer people certainly play in the big leagues," he replied. "This doesn't sound like any two-bit lead."

"All right, then, how big is your secret?" she asked like a school kid playing show-and-tell.

"Pretty much the same stuff. It could mean life or death."

They both remained silent for a moment mulling over their options. It was the moment of truth.

"Damnit," Waite began. "You've got to trust somebody sometime, and so help me God, this is probably one of those damned times. I'm probably going to do something stupid, but here goes."

She had him.

He started in . . . "A friend of mine, Ahmed, gave the message to me. He's a member of the Palestinian Liberation Organization and a regular in their army. His brother was killed trying to deliver this message to the PLO commander in the west sector. Nobody else but you knows about the message. Ahmed hid it and brought it to me to see if I could decipher it. He doesn't know what it means, either.

"I tried a translation by one of our embassy staffers without divulging where I got it, but he couldn't come with anything more than we already know, which is pretty much nothing. I don't know where else to go with it. I don't want to involve American intelligence because it's the last I'll ever see of it. I'm completely stopped," he explained.

Adrienne was impressed. He was being sincere. She usually read people pretty well; she felt comfortable with his story. What's more, she didn't feel like he was using her in an attempt to pry away her own secret.

But, now it was her turn.

"This might be important. It involves ICE, British Intelligence. A few weeks ago, I was spending the night at a friend's who is in British Intelligence, at his apartment, and he casually mentioned to me that a historic meeting was going to take place in the Middle East, somewhere near Beirut. He was making arrangements for the British government and all that. It's funny, he never talks about his work, but on this particular night, I don't know if it was because of the singular importance of the mission or what, but he referred to the British prime minister by code name," she recounted.

Rick's interest grew with the added details. He focused his attention completely on her.

"You don't mean that . . . "

"Yes . . . one of the names in the message. It might only be a coincidence," she started to say, but Rick broke her off in mid-sentence.

"Which name did he use?"

The Palestine Conspiracy

She paused a second to think it over one last time, but couldn't stop herself.

"David," she said.

The realization had the impact of a sledgehammer.

"Well, I'll be damned!" he uttered in complete astonishment.

A deal was in the making his instinct told him? But, a deal for what and with whom? The questions went racing through his head.

"How much more do you know?" he asked her trying not to stampede her thoughts.

"A little," she said. "I couldn't even tell my editors because I didn't know if the story I was sent here for had any connection."

Rick knew it damned well did.

"Whoever tipped-off The Times over the phone tried to get some important information to you about the meeting. Whoever is your deep throat doesn't want the meeting to take place," he said. "Does that sound plausible?" She nodded with a yes.

If there was a connection, she didn't have any choice now but to follow through on the plan with the help of Waite. They were both in it up to their necks now.

"We'll have to work together, but my paper will want joint release on the story. If we by-line it together and release it through UPI London, my editor might go for it," she spoke quickly hoping to get him to agree.

It sounded good. It might work for both of them that way.

"O.K.," Waite agreed. "If we release it on a joint basis, my people should go for it, too - your being a

Pulitzer Prize winner and all. It'll give it more throw-weight in New York, make it more believable."

"Good," she said. "If my editor balks, I'll tell him it's this way or no fucking story."

Waite laughed. He liked her style. She was gutsy. It was like something he would do, deliver an ultimatum. Kind of like please get fucked if you don't agree.

"What's the rest of it?" he asked. "Who's the meeting with from over here?"

"Fasi," she answered firmly.

"Fasi! Holy shit! He must be Goliath!"

Rick jumped to his feet in an attempt to control his excitement.

"Easy," said Adrienne. "Brian could be in a lot of trouble if any of what I've told you can be traced through me and back to him in London. We've got to pin down the rest of the story before we do anything, and when we release it, we've got to make everyone believe we stumbled onto it while doing our regular assignments. What about your friend?"

"If the Israelis ever find out that Ahmed knew about the plan to intercept Thayer and Fasi, they'd kill him in a heartbeat, and before he could alert the PLO or anyone else. His life is in real danger. I promised to tell no one. And, now I have. He trusted me completely. His life is in my hands."

"Who is this Ahmed? And, why is he so important to you?" she asked. "Well, it was just a journalist's hunch. You know, I was trying to get an interview with Fasi who was using the most brutal terrorist tactics the world had ever seen to make his point about the Palestinian issue three years ago. There was no way I could even get close to him . . . until I met Ahmed," Waite explained.

"I met him on the outskirts of Beirut. He had been wounded by Druse sniper-fire, and had been pinned down with me and about a dozen of his soldiers. It was a terrible day, hot and dry, and we'd been in there for about three hours, with no help on the way. We couldn't move forward or backward because of the heavy sniper fire.

"Well, Ahmed just kept staring at the sky exhausted and bleeding badly from a head wound, repeating over and over again some kind of Islamic prayer I didn't understand. One of his soldier's leaned over to me and whispered that it was a Bedouin prayer, but he himself had no idea of its meaning, either. Ahmed was almost unconscious from the loss of blood and was talking deliriously . . . saying that I should take him to his uncle in the desert. To calm him, I told him I didn't know his uncle, but that I would do what I could to find him. I thought Ahmed was Jordanian, like his fellow soldiers, but in his delirium he insisted that I could find this uncle in the Arabian Desert near Jubba. The other soldiers thought he was out of his head, too, except that he kept chanting that strange Bedouin prayer over and over again. It was really spooky. Anyway to appease him, I promised that I would take his remains to his uncle in Jubba for a Muslim burial. He wouldn't let go of my arm until I promised," Waite recounted shifting his weight to his other foot and crouching down near the floor.

"It wasn't until much later, when help finally arrived and we got out of the ambush, that I visited him in the PLO field hospital and he apologized to me for being so much trouble. He couldn't remember anything of his ramblings, but he thanked me for saving his life. Perhaps, the other soldiers told him what he had said to me. He said he would make it up to me someday. Well, he did.

"It was Ahmed who set up the Fasi interview after I had exhausted all attempts through regular PLO channels. Ahmed had intervened in my behalf and Fasi agreed to the interview, the first given to a western journalist detailing the life of a PLO terrorist. It was a breakthrough in international reporting.

"When I walked into Fasi's tent for the interview with Ahmed, it was like going back 1,000 years into time. I'll never forget that. Both wore the traditional Bedouin loose flowing clothing, covered from head to foot in a long cotton gown. They spoke to each other in the traditional Bedouin greeting. Each wore a small white cap covered by a loose red-and-white head cloth called a Keffiyeh held in place by a black cord called an agal. I'll never forget it."

"Neither will I," Adrienne said admiringly. "I read your piece. It was fantastic journalism. No one before had ever understood the Palestinian cause and what they were fighting for, until after that . . . after that story. . . their cause took on a new dimension worldwide. It probably saved his people from annihilation. Up to that point, the Israelis had it all their way. The interview changed the direction of public opinion. You should have got the Pulitzer instead of me that year."

Waite interrupted her.

"There was something else, too. As Ahmed lay there in a semi-conscious state, he kept saying that his

177

uncle was a very important man, and that respect and dignity must be accorded him. I still don't know who that uncle is. But, I finally did learn the identity of a brother . . . the one who was killed delivering the message. Ahmed felt terrible anguish about that. I still don't think he's fully recovered from the shock of it yet."

"Go on," Adrienne implored.

"Well, right after that, he came to me with the message and made me promise not to reveal its contents to anyone. So, here we are," Rick said.

She was still a bit puzzled.

A man accidentally kills his own brother and inadvertently discovers a secret document seemingly connected with Israeli intelligence. Why didn't Ahmed deliver the message to PLO headquarters himself? Who was this uncle that Ahmed referred to in his delirium?

"If he's that important, then we must know him," Adrienne said. "How do we go about finding Ahmed? He has the information we need to solve this riddle."

Waite shifted nervously considering whether or not to bring her into this any further.

"The meeting is set for July 24th. Now, why in the hell would the Israelis want to intercept them? And, if that's the case, how are they going to intercept David and Goliath? Does that mean . . . they are going to kill them. . . or does it mean they are going to break up the meeting through some other means?" Waite speculated.

Their eyes met the instant he had said it, in immediate recognition of the deep, dark secret the world knew nothing about. Waite had blurted it out inadvertently.

That was it. Someone was going to be killed. The prime minister. Fasi. Or both.

The Palestine Conspiracy

"Do you think the Israelis would do it?" Adrienne asked.

"Are you kidding? They'll do what they have to do for Israel," his answer chastised her for not knowing better.

"But, we don't know for certain it is the Israelis? It could be done through any dozen of splinter terrorist groups, including the Shiite's or a dissident member of the PLO? Christ, it could be any one with a cause over here," Waite correctly assessed. "It could even be you."

They both had their work cut out for them. And, it would be a race against time, but with a different sort of deadline. They had just eight weeks to piece everything together and prevent someone from getting assassinated. Eight lousy weeks to gather enough evidence and go public with the story, and more importantly, to prevent a full-blown Middle East war. If something happened to Fasi, war would surely break out on a large scale the likes the world had never seen in the region. Arab nations would unite on all fronts against Israel. How far would Israel go to defend itself? Would she use the nuclear weapons she possessed? Would it involve the United States, the Soviet Union, Great Britain . . . Britain would be in it up to her teeth because of Thayer. Those were the hard, cold, inescapable conclusions.

"Come on, we've got a lot to do. I'll take you over to the bureau and show you around so you can get the feel of it."

"I think I already got the feel of it this morning," Adrienne said remembering how Waite had touched her earlier in the day.

At least she was developing a sense of humor, something she lacked back in London. Rick's face reddened at the remark.

"C'mon. Put on your armband. Remember, you're a Red Cross volunteer from England. Don't ask too many questions, just observe. Even my own people won't know who you are. Let's keep it that way for the time being."

They left the Red Cross building and went out into the plaza, carefully side-stepping their way through the rubble from the morning's shelling.

It was already 9 o'clock, and an uneasy quiet settled over Beirut.

CHAPTER 18

Haifa: May 21. 10:45 p.m.

A pair of Jericho fighters stood poised on the flight line manned by two crack Israeli pilots.

It had become a routine mission.

Intercept and inspect two planes flying from Tunisia via Libya bypassing Egypt to its final destination, Beirut.

Since Israel had imposed a military quarantine around Lebanon both at sea and in the air, all ships and planes had been intercepted and inspected by laser penetration radar, LPR.

Israel had not announced this unusual step publicly, but every pilot who flew into the region knew it was going on in retaliation for the taking of American hostages and the killing of Israeli prisoners of war. Seven Americans were being held hostage and several hundred Israeli prisoners were behind Lebanese lines and being threatened with death. Negotiations had continued for the safe release of them but no negotiating team - American, Israeli or PLO - had set any conditions. Israel was still refusing to talk with the PLO.

The Israeli navy operating out of Haifa did the stopping of sea traffic easily. But stopping the flow of secret arms shipments into Lebanon by air was a different matter and much more difficult challenge.

The Palestine Conspiracy

The Israelis had secretly developed a technically advanced system using a laser device outfitted on fighter planes, which could shoot a beam of light through any airplane, focusing its X-ray capability along the beam of light using the intensity to photograph the contents inside. It was a relatively safe procedure, but in some cases blindness could result if anyone inadvertently looked directly into the light's brilliant ray for more than a split-second. To remove that danger, all aircraft were contacted on standard radio frequency used by civilian, commercial and military planes.

Instructions were then given to the pilots and their passengers to take precautions to protect themselves from any danger. The X-rays were low- level and posed no harm to individual passengers if these precautions were met.

The Jericho's rolled to the edge of the runway, their blue-and-red strobe lights flashing brightly like holiday twinkle lights. The hydraulically operated canopies smoothly clamped down over the pilots helmets while they chatted with flight operations.

"Jerr Haifa One and two, ready for takeoff."

"Roger. Targets at 45 degrees west, four five, runway three clear for takeoff," the instant reply came.

"Affirmative."

The pilots pushed the throttles forward.

The two planes pounced from the take-off line and began their roll down the 10,000-foot runway, eating up the distance in a matter of seconds.

170 knots. 180 knots. 190 knots.

The Jericho's reached takeoff speed in tandem.

215 knots. 225 knots.

"Rotate," the lead pilot calmly spoke into his

mouthpiece. At the same precise second, the pilots pulled back slightly on their sticks and kicked in their afterburners on the twin-engine fighters beginning a steep climb-out into the night sky toward their intended target.

"Jericho Haifa One climbing at 425 knots and accelerating to 900 at a vertical intercept of 30."

"Roger," came the reply from flight operations.

Two minutes later the fighters were at 24,000 feet and climbing at an intercept speed of 915 knots, the sonic booms echoing through the night sky as the planes continued their long arc, which would position them slightly above and behind their targets.

"Intercept estimate two minutes," radioed the lead pilot.

"Affirmative. Switch to night tactics," flight operations ordered.

"Roger."

The pilots shut down their wing lights and flipped the cockpit lights to infrared, which only the pilots could see through their helmet lenses. Then they switched on a computerized targeting system, which silently sent out a signal bounced back to the fighters giving them a constant mille-second positioning of their aircraft in relation to their targets.

It also told the Jericho pilots the most advantageous angle of attack and the most threatening target. Their defense system would then automatically pre-select a fire control sequence to destroy those selected threats. The Israeli pilots knew the value of their superior technology. The lead pilot looked at his radar screen for any identification and the nationality of the targets they would be intercepting. But, it didn't really matter.

He'd seen just about everything they could throw up in the air during his seven years as a fighter pilot in the Israeli Air Force. For him, it was just another routine mission, a job to do, part of the air quarantine that his country had ordered three months ago.

They had encountered no real threats during this time and had not discovered any secret shipments despite Israeli intelligence warnings of such impending traffic.

"Haifa One, do you read me?"

"Affirmative!"

"One minute to intercept. No visual yet. Have them on holographic radar."

"Roger. Verify when visual."

The fighters bore down on their targets like a fox closing in on its prey. 1,200 knots and closing. Ten more seconds. Five. Suddenly, they were there, dead ahead. Right where they were supposed to be. The two fighters flashed by the two C-47 vintage aircraft which looked like leftovers from World War II, flying with no visual markings or running beacons and painted dark brown.

"Haifa One to base. We have them in sight about one-half mile coming up behind them from below?"

"Describe them."

"They're American C-47's. Look like CIA-type aircraft. What are our instructions?"

"Make your presence known to them!"

With that, the fighters ranged in toward the cargo planes to only a few hundred feet on a parallel course. Flying alongside the cockpit of the C-47's, they switched on their running and landing lights. The action jolted the C-47 pilots awake as the Jericho's flashed

The Palestine Conspiracy

alongside.

"Jericho red calling C-47 flight leader. Do you read me?" the Israeli pilot radioed on civilian frequency used by non-military aircraft.

There was no answer.

The Israeli waited a few seconds then tried again. He maneuvered his fighter near the C-47 cockpit and tried again.

Again, no response.

The Israeli pilot knew they had surprised the C-47 pilots. Both looked surprised as they wiped away the condensation from the inside of the cockpit windows.

"Haifa One to cargo plane. I repeat, do you acknowledge?"

"This is C-47. What do you want? Identify yourself?"

Haifa One transmitted to Haifa that radio contact had been established on the 10,000 Mghz. frequency.

Haifa dialed to the frequency and listened.

"We are Israeli fighters ordered to intercept and inspect your cargo. What are you carrying?"

The C-47 pilot, sounding very much American, answered that he was carrying medical supplies bound for Beirut.

"Medical supplies, plasma, blood and food from the International Red Cross," he radioed back.

"Why are your planes unmarked? Red Cross planes use their own insignia?" the lead pilot asked.

Flight operations ordered the Jericho pilots to X-ray the cargo.

"Instruct the C-47's to hold their present course for the laser ray."

"Roger."

The Palestine Conspiracy

"Haifa One to C-47. We are going to inspect your cargo using laser light. When I give the order, hold your course steady for approximately 10 seconds. Instruct all crewmembers aboard to shield their eyes and do not look directly into the light. No harm will come to you if you follow these instructions. Do you understand, over?"

There was no immediate answer.

After a short delay, the lead C-47 pilot radioed compliance.

One Jericho fighter dropped back from the formation at an oblique angle. Re-establishing radio contact, he ordered the pilot to hold his course steady.

"Roger," the C-47 acknowledged more rapidly now.

The Jericho switched on the laser light and began photographing the freighters contents. The X-rays were immediately transmitted back to Haifa for analysis.

"C-47. X-rays completed," the Jericho fighter pilot radioed.

"Affirmative," came the reply.

Intelligence experts poured over the computer-enhanced digital photos being transmitted from the fighter. The two intelligence officers could hardly believe what they saw even though they were staring at them.

Inside both planes were detonators. Not the common detonators used in conventional bombs, but the kind used in nuclear warheads.

"Haifa base calling Haifa One and Two. Acknowledge."

"This is Haifa One!"

"Nuclear detonators on board both C-47's. Advise you request they follow you to Haifa."

The Israeli captain's adrenaline kicked-in.

"Roger," he replied flipping on the arming mechanism to his sparrow missiles. Haifa Two followed suit.

"Haifa One to C-47 flight commander. I have instructions for you to follow me to Haifa on a setting for a direct landing. I repeat, you are being forced down. Do you understand?"

There was no reply.

"Haifa One to C-47. I have been instructed to escort you to Haifa where you will land immediately. Is that clear? Do you acknowledge?"

Again, silence from the cargo planes.

Suddenly, the lead C-47 veered from formation and began a long, slow descent into the darkness toward the ocean some 23,000 feet below. The other C-47 held a steady course.

The lead C-47 was trying to get away. The Israeli fighter commander, not expecting the sudden maneuver, lost sight of the evading C-47. He ordered Haifa Two to maintain its vigil on the other C-47 and to shoot it down if it failed to obey the command to fly to Haifa.

Haifa One rolled into a tight turn and nosed toward the fleeing target visible now only on his radar targeting system. His eyes focused on the night scope. He knew the C-47 was out there somewhere and below them, but he didn't know exactly where. It would be the radar's job to find it.

The C-47 was now in a steep dive trying to get close to the water so the fighter's radar would be

187

useless, bouncing back its radar signal and overloading the targeting computer. As the C-47 pitched violently downward, its cargo door swung open and two crewmen fired Sidewinder heat-seeking missiles from inside the plane.

The co-pilot in the attacking Jericho saw them on his radarscope immediately.

"Captain, two sidewinders closing from 10 degrees at 2 o'clock. Ten seconds to impact. Circling to our tail."

"I'm releasing flares," the captain responded automatically.

"Captain, they're still with us. Evade! Evade!" the co-pilot shouted, his voice shaking in urgency to get the words out quickly.

The radar man began his countdown.

The Israeli captain looked over his right shoulder and could see the two sidewinders streaking toward his aircraft's tail where the exhaust was white hot. He could hear the radar-man's count in his headset as he concentrated to break off the attack at the correct precise second.

"Three . . . two . . . one."

In the next instant, the pilot pushed the stick hard over to the left, pressed his foot down for left rudder, and kicked in the jet's afterburner. The Jericho's nose swung sharply and it rolled immediately to a new heading. The missiles flashed by the exhaust of the Jericho just missing the plane by inches, tracking themselves into oblivion.

The co-pilot breathed a sigh of relief.

"Damned, Ariel, that was close!"

"Yeah, uhhh! Where is that C-47 now?" the Israeli

commander repeated urgently.

"Come around right 27 degrees and line him up in the unit. We can hit him with the sparrow on the way down. Range five miles," the co-pilot spoke now in control of himself once more.

"Lining him up. Switching on the target illuminator. Got him close in. Have him . . . steady . . .range 5 miles . . . 4 miles . . . increasing velocity . . . to 1,000 knots . . . closing . . . closing . . . 3 miles . . . missiles armed and locked . . . firing 1 and 2 . . . NOW!"

Whoosh! Whoosh!

The sparrows flared and leapt from underneath the wingtips of the F-22 streaking toward its nearly invisible target below them. The missiles homed-in on the target C-47. Flight operations watched on their tracking radar.

"Two seconds to impact," the Israeli co-pilot said.

Both pilots saw the blip disappear from their radarscope spotting the flash of two explosions in the night below them as the C-47 went up in a bright ball of fire.

Two direct hits.

The F-22 closed-in on the burning craft and the Israeli captain watched with satisfaction as the debris crashed into the sea below churning up the water in a shower of white sea spray.

The other C-47 wanted no part in tangling with the far- superior Jericho's.

"Base operations to Haifa One. Return to base?"

"Roger," came the businesslike reply.

Haifa One circled the ocean crash site one more time, then broke off and climbed back to 23,000 feet and set a course for Haifa. They would be there in 7 minutes. They landed without further incident.

The Israeli government knew it had something big. It sent out naval units to recover the wreckage, but it wasn't necessary.

Indeed, they had captured the detonators that were being smuggled in the C-47's. They had recovered everything they wanted for now. The Israeli prime minister was notified that the C-47 crew was American after it landed.

CHAPTER 19

Muscat: May 21. 11:00 p.m.

Illuminated by the moonlit sky, the caravan was now about ten miles outside the port of Muscat. The string of twenty camels looked like the ancient caravans some 2,000 years ago plodding in the awkward gaits that they always had.

The wind blew the desert sand across the paths of the camels, continually erasing their tracks as the shadowy riders covered themselves to keep the sand granules from biting their faces.

They had more than 2,000 miles to travel, and they would pass other caravans whose destination was the port city where they had just departed. The trade routes had not changed or the method of navigating the ancient deserts since the Birth of Christ. Despite all the money from the Arab oil wealth, there had been no attempt to build modern highways to facilitate travel by motor vehicle. Perhaps it was the Bedouin rulers and the significance of the old customs, which made this final modernizaton impossible. Indeed, it was the ultimate change that would end a way of life, which they held so sacred since Biblical time.

The Bedouins had fought in many wars and had taken immense casualties from the Turks in World War I before finally defeating them. They had survived hundreds of years of fighting against armed invaders who had tried to wrest control of the desert lands from them. All the attempts ended unsuccessfully for the attackers.

In the end, it was the desert that won – the desert, which dictated who the winner, would be. And, in an indirect way, the victor was the Bedouin, because he had long ago adapted to the ways of desert life. It was the Bedouin surviving the invasion of his enemies because it was the Bedouin who alone simply knew how to take the losses, retreat, and live to fight another day. In short, the Bedouin soldier knew how to adapt there and fight, and win in the long run. The defeat of the Turks had been the high point of an enemy's failure to gain control over the elusive desert landscape.

A favorite Bedouin tale describes a Turkish army unit in World War I, which had all but annihilated a group of some 400 Bedouin soldiers and their camels. The Turks had surrounded them and would wait until daybreak to begin their final assault figuring on an easy mopping up operation. But, when dawn came, the Turkish army colonel awoke to the realization that during the night the desert winds had shifted the dunes in such a way that they now found themselves surrounded instead of the other way around. The Bedouins pinned the Turks down during the heat of the day - for eight hours, then ten hours, then 12 hours – forcing them to surrender or die of thirst. Hundreds of them died.

When the commander did finally surrender, the Bedouins told them they could go free, if they could find their way out of the desert. So, they gave the Turks enough water for three days, but killed their horses. Legend has it the Turks walked for two days until their water ran out, and then died on the third. In the end, it was the desert, which killed them.

The Bedouins knew that if the Turks escaped they would always think they could venture into the desert anytime they pleased. They knew that if the Turks were to be victorious, they had to conquer the desert first, but only a Bedouin could do that. They had sent a brutal message to the Turks. Two weeks later, the Turks withdrew all their units from Saudi Arabia.

This is the reason the Bedouin reveres the desert as a holy place, a place to be cherished out of necessity.

It is his desert.

It is for no one else.

The caravan moved onward. The camels would not take on water for several more days until they reached the next oasis, a group of wells near Al Hadida.

Their trek would take them 100 miles east of Riyadh to avoid detection, then northward toward Jubba, then Sakaka to the Syrian Desert, and finally into the border region of Iraq and Jordan before their final destination of Latakia, near the Lebanon-Syria
border where the equipment was to be delivered at Fasi's campsite.

It would require another three weeks to complete.

To the Bedouins, this was merely a short journey among the countless ones taken by the many generations of Bedouins who preceded them.

They were merely repeating the route their ancestors had taken millions of times before; it had become a processional of protection for their people.

Even the camels seemed to sense that as they plied deliberately through the sands.

The Palestine Conspiracy

CHAPTER 20

The United Nations: New York: May 21. 1:35 p.m.

The delegations filed back into the assembly room from the reception areas, which had been set up for the press and visiting dignitaries.

Delegates were astonished at the king's speech that morning. More importantly, it had captured the attention of the average American on the street.

On-the-street interviews with people who had heard the speech, described it as unique and surprising. They sensed a shifting of sentiment. In a matter of a few hours, old stereotypes and even older historic attitudes had been re-awakened.

The U.S. relationship with the Arab world was changing. Europe was transfixed. The anticipation in Paris was beyond doubt. And, in London, people were indeed mystified by Israel's actions. The Soviet-bloc countries announced full support for the king and wanted an immediate explanation from Israel. In effect, the entire world was demanding an admission of guilt from Israel.

King Fasaid had made his point.

He had proved he was a major world leader, one who had to be dealt with.

The Israeli delegation paraded into the assembly room and began preparations for its presentation to the member nations, deciding who would deliver the response to the Saudi charges.

A delegate turned to the floor aide in charge of communicating with the general secretary and frantically scribbled a note and sent him off with it. The aide went to the podium and delivered it to General Secretary Hans Vensberg. Vensberg opened the folded note, read it carefully then tucked it inside his vest pocket.

At that very moment, the Saudi delegation entered the hall led by King Fasaid himself. Upon being recognized by the member nations, applause broke out until it grew to a thunderous ovation. The king responded with a simple gesture smiling broadly, and then took his seat with his delegation at their assigned table. The sergeant-at-arms called for quiet bringing the hall to order.

After a brief moment, Vensberg stood before the podium and announced. . .

"Member nations . . . delegates from the State of Israel will at this time respond to the statements made by King Fasaid Etebbe of Saudi Arabia earlier this day. I have been informed by the Israeli delegation that Defense Secretary Shali Prahoe will make a statement at this time. Thank you."

Onto the stage strode a purposeful Prahoe. He could be a formidable opponent when pressed, and today he would have to prove as much if he was going to change the minds of an already decidedly pro-Arab general assembly. He was an articulate man, this part of his character not a weakness, but rather a genuine strength to get accurate, truthful information into the hands of world opinion leaders. Prahoe had been instructed by the Prime Minister not to dispute the set of facts offered by the Saudis.

That part was inarguable and already well established by growing public evidence. What lay ahead was the kind of explanation which could now placate negative public opinion, and explain the reason for the incursion.

The delegates remained riveted to their seats as millions of television viewers from all over the world watched the events unfold by satellite.

Prahoe approached the microphone, impassively searching the floor to locate the key delegations that would support him. He made eye contact with several groups.

The United States. Great Britain. France. Germany. Italy. Perhaps China. Maybe Spain. His eyes skipped past Poland, Czechoslovakia, Romania, the Soviet Union, and other Eastern bloc countries.

Finally, after several seconds, he began . . .

"Mr. Secretary-General . . . member nations . . . distinguished delegates . . . members of the international press corps . . . non-member countries . . . representatives in the gallery . . . and all friends of Israel. I stand before you as a representative of the State of Israel, which was established in the year 1948 and recognized, by this very own body of delegates that same year as a sovereign state.

"Israel has always been a nation that has abided by the rules set forth by this world organization and by the rules of international law which recognizes civilized principles.

"Upon hearing the testimony by the very able and distinguished King Fasaid Etebbe of Saudi Arabia, and after consultation with my prime minister who was not available to make this presentation himself, and after consulting with our allies and past supporters of the policies of Israel for many years as well as other nations, we have concluded that to even think of trying to evade the issue in this incident would be a grave mistake and would do great injustice to the integrity and members of this world body of nations.

"It would indeed be a disgrace to consider that what Israel did two weeks ago over the skies of Saudi Arabia was justifiable from any standpoint of international law. To say that the flight was unintentional would be a serious breach of Israel's principle of honesty and integrity to the free world, which, by now knows otherwise. And so, we have concluded that the best course of action in all this is to openly admit with forthrightness that our actions on May 3rd were indeed a serious violation of international airspace over a sovereign country.

"Israel stands guilty of an act of provocation against Saudi Arabia," the defense minister stated flatly.

A murmur swept through the delegations huddled intently while listening through their earpieces to translators keeping pace with the defense minister's statements. TV anchors now turned their full attention to the defense minister while cameras recorded his every gesture hoping to catch some unusual movement manifesting itself under stress by a wave or a turning of the hand as Prahoe spoke with a sense of subdued confidence.

"Israel apologizes to Saudi Arabia at this time. It apologizes to all countries of the world, which respect international law and order. In deference to his majesty, King Fasaid, the Prime Minister of Israel respectfully sends a direct apology to the people of Saudi Arabia.

"By no means did Israel intend to or plan in any way to attack Saudi Arabia. The actions Israel took in penetrating Saudi airspace were purely defensive in nature . . . I will explain."

The gallery stirred.

They had expected the apology because world leaders were demanding one. But, Israel was about to give a rationale for its actions. This had never happened before. It was an exciting moment.

"It has come to the attention of the Israeli government through certain intelligence sources outside the State of Israel that certain components necessary for the construction of a nuclear device were being delivered through Saudi Arabia for eventual delivery to Lebanon by a country which is yet unidentified. If such a delivery had been successful, the balance of power in the region would change from an Israeli defense standpoint, politically and militarily."

By now the delegates were enraptured. Defense Minister Prahoe was going public with sensitive intelligence data not heard before in the general assembly hall since the Cuban Missile Crisis. A pall hung over the assembly room as everyone waited for Prahoe to continue. Newscasters could scarcely believe what they were hearing.

It was a bombshell announcement - an announcement that would make the world take notice of Israel's position.

It was an attempt at an explanation that might take the pressure off Israel. Indeed, it was a huge gamble to explain such a motive, but it could pay high dividends if it could be proved.

Prahoe went on.

"Israel has further reason to believe, through these same intelligence sources, that a delivery of nuclear warheads and detonators are already inside Saudi Arabian territory or are in the process of being delivered to the PLO. Needless to say, these detonators are invaluable to anyone desiring to construct a nuclear bomb for whatever ultimate objective they may have.

"Without a detonator, an atomic bomb is useless. The State of Israel learned three months ago that these detonators were to be transported either by civilian aircraft or sea-going vessels. Beginning last February, Israel began an unannounced surveillance of all routine civilian flights into and out of Beirut in an effort to discover and stop this delivery from being made into the hands of known terrorists operating inside Lebanon."

Prahoe continued.

"It is the desire of the Israeli government to bring these facts to the attention of the world so that it fully understands what Israel has been up against. We are a peace-loving nation whose sole objective is to co-exist with all Arab nations in the Middle East region. We believe this is possible only if the surrounding Arab states recognize Israel's basic right to exist. If such an agreement is recognized, it could lead to full cooperation on many matters including trade and mutual economic development. Such has been the case since Israel and Egypt signed a peace accord in 1979.

"Member delegates, Israel cannot let go unchallenged a significant shift in the balance of power. If the PLO obtains such weapons for offensive purposes, then Israel must respond accordingly. Our prime minister, once again, sends his personal apologies to his majesty's government. Unfortunately, when such intelligence was received, Israel felt

compelled to act and authorized the reconnaissance flights. Thank you."

Prahoe had finished with the inclusion of that simple fact.

It clearly stated that, in reality, regardless of any apologies issued by the Israeli government, Israel would take whatever action necessary to protect the balance of power in its favor in the Middle East.

The delegates were awestruck by the statement though the reaction was muted.

The explanation seemed to satisfy everyone except for the end part of Prahoe's speech. He made it crystal clear that Israel would take the initiative to protect itself. The comment didn't sit well with many of the pro-Arab delegations. And, it didn't play well to news analysts covering the speech.

But, it wasn't meant to. It was designed as a warning from Israel to its neighbors that it was prepared to strike first if confronted with a nuclear threat. It was also a message to all delegates in the general assembly hall that Israel wanted exclusive membership in the Middle East nuclear club, and that it would not allow others to exist with that same technology, no matter what.

Confusion swept over the special session as questions to the Israeli delegation were queried back-and-forth across the assembly-room floor. Delegates huddled to prepare strategies for the upcoming question-and-answer session, which would involve both representatives from Saudi Arabia and Israel. As Prahoe prepared to leave the podium, a member rushing to his side from the Israeli delegation suddenly interrupted him. He whispered something urgently as they paused in front of the audience. A hush fell over the member delegates as their attention once again focused on Prahoe. His face was somber, almost ashen. Something had occurred. Everyone sensed it. News anchors turned their full attention to the podium as Prahoe returned to the microphone to make another announcement.

Prahoe called the assembly to order once again.

"May I have your attention, please? Please! May I have your attention? I have just been informed by my government in Tel Aviv, that precisely fifteen minutes ago at approximately ll:00 p.m., Tel Aviv time, Israeli jet fighters intercepted and shot down an unmarked, unidentified cargo plane carrying nuclear components, destination Beirut.

"A second plane, also carrying nuclear detonators, was forced to fly to the Israeli port city of Haifa where the nuclear detonators were confiscated. International news teams have been summoned to the site to verify the announcement by film and show the captured devices, which the Israeli government will offer as evidence to this world organization.

"The aircraft were of unknown origin but are believed to have originated from Tunisia. The crew has been taken into custody by the Israeli government. I am sorry to say that the plane was intercepted over the Mediterranean in international airspace, but that's the price we have to pay as a small nation protecting its borders. The crew has been identified as . . . as . . . American."

That revelation just about blew everybody out of

their seats, as though a bomb had hit the place.

Delegates exploded from their tables and stampeded toward the American delegation whose chairman was frantically insisting he knew nothing about such a flight. They demanded to know what was going on?

The secretary- general of the United Nations took the podium in an unsuccessful attempt to restore calm.

In complete frustration, he adjourned the meeting until that evening and declared an emergency session of the United Nations Security Council.

It had been a stunning day for the world organization. News teams had so many big stories they hardly knew where to begin.

Not only had the day been historic, but now everyone knew a crisis was brewing.

The world was in grave peril.

And, America was involved once again.

CHAPTER 21

Beirut: May 22. 7:30 a.m.

Adrienne scarcely stirred as her alarm clock went off. She was exhausted from the day before and had slept for 12 hours straight. But, she dragged herself out of bed, washed, brushed her teeth and quickly got dressed. She was in a hurry to meet Rick downstairs in the hotel lobby. From there, they were to meet Ahmed at the field hospital where he was checking on the wounded boy. Rick had wanted to ask Ahmed more questions about the coded intercept. They had watched the fascinating events at the U.N. on television most of the night and wondered if there was any connection between it and Ahmed's coded message.

When Adrienne got downstairs, Rick spoke hurriedly as they entered what used to be the main lobby of the Beirut Hotel. Adrienne looked out the window and into the morning daylight. The sun's rays draped her in a natural brightness. She turned, smiled and brushed her hair back like a young schoolgirl flirting with a schoolboy.

"Did you sleep well?"

"Yes, thanks. It was nice to wake up to silence instead of the usual shelling."

Waite nodded. "It's a bit unnerving if you're not used to it. Come to think of it, it still is even if you're used to it."

Adrienne laughed.

The Palestine Conspiracy

"Would you like breakfast?" he asked.

Ahhh. . . yes, I could use that," she replied. "This assignment is turning into a constant search for food. What do you suggest?"

Waite shrugged his shoulders apologetically for the fact that he had brought it up. "C'mon, we'll manage something. I know a few places still left in Beirut where they still serve hot food."

He knew she was vulnerable, searching for that little bit of security like everyone else in the world. But, in Beirut, the people searched for it constantly. And, in Beirut, there just wasn't a lot of security. So, you got used to it. Most just took what came day-by-day. And, now it was that way all over the Middle East.

Back home, in the States, it was different.

The world had changed, and the men and women who ran it had changed, too.

Security. It was an elusive quantity to find, and, equally as difficult to hold onto.

He would find out more about her at breakfast having anticipated it all night long, lying in bed thinking about her. It would be nice to exchange words with a member of the opposite sex in Beirut, an English girl at that. They might even be able to talk about life in general instead of the world's problems. It would make for an interesting day. They walked out into the street to an old cobblestone plaza exactly where Waite promised they'd be hot food, a wonderfully, quaint, tiny restaurant right in the heart of the rubble of downtown Beirut.

It was hard to believe it was still open, but there it was, pleasant enough, and a private spot where they would be as safe as anywhere else, at least until the bombardment started again.

Oh, it would start again. It always did.

Day after day after day. He paused to look at her.

He realized she was simply beautiful. He studied her closely as the restaurateur led them to their table. As they neared the tiny wooden table, Rick awkwardly reached behind her for the chair using all the skilled grace he could muster. He had helped seat her like a gentleman, and the old reporter was proud of it. He was still civilized in an uncivilized place. The social grace he had just executed caught Adrienne by surprise.

"Oh, my!" she offered. "You don't need to do that."

Here was a woman he could relate to. Intelligent. Witty. Good looking. Wonderful figure. And, gutsy. She had to be. Anybody who would volunteer for such a bullshit assignment had to be. He respected that in anybody, man or woman.

When the waiter brought the platter of pieces of lamb and unleavened bread, they ate, drank an inexpensive wine and discussed their respective lives.

Rick had majored in journalism at Kent State University during the lean years following the Kent State shooting, while at about the same time, Adrienne had attended school in London. Rick started as a copywriter for the Cleveland Plain Dealer, worked the police beat for two years before getting bored with it, then finally applied for the UPI Beirut post as a foreign correspondent. It was a last-ditch effort to get an overseas assignment where he could make a name for himself. If he didn't succeed, he'd be dead professionally. Either way, he had nothing to lose, and it was better than starving. Most of the beat journalists didn't want the post because of the enormous danger involved, an almost unwritten guarantee that eventually they would be kidnapped or killed. But, Waite jumped at the chance to do something noble, for himself and for others. He truly felt he could accomplish something in the Middle East.

He soon learned about the people of Lebanon and developed a special relationship with them in the city, an almost instant rapport with the differing factions, including an unspoken assumption that they would let him do his work untouched - all of them, the Druse, Shiites, the PLO, the Christians and the other extremist groups like Hezbollah and Hamas.

During his three years there, he had become a legend in his own right and embraced by the local populace as an impartial, fair-minded journalist with an exceptional willingness to tell the story on the Palestinian question and just report what was happening.

He didn't fully understand why they trusted him, or the full implication as to why each faction was fighting one another, but then again, who did? He respected their right of self-determination and their wish for a homeland of their own – a place for the Palestinian people.

It was an issue, that before his arrival, few people in the world fully understood. Here was a chance not only to do something for himself, but also to take on an honorable task for the Palestinian people to whom he had come to respect and admire. He understood them.

There wasn't a person in Beirut who hadn't heard of his exploits to get the true facts about any story or any skirmish throughout Palestine. The Palestinians needed a man like Waite. He was a person long overdue for them. They understood that and accepted him on that basis.

"You mentioned that you weren't born in England," he asked, taking note of her dark, brown hair. "Where, then?"

She made eye contact with him.

"I don't know. I was adopted when I was 14 years old after surviving a plane crash in Nicosia on a flight from Riyadh. I don't remember anything about myself before then. I only know I was one of seven people who survived that crash. The last thing I remember was holding onto the hand of a man sitting next to me. He was a Turk, killed in the crash. It was horrible," she recounted, visibly upset again of having to recount the disaster.

Rick hadn't realized she was Arab, but her clear, olive-skin made him look at her again more closely, looking for distinct physical attributes. Smooth skin, dark complexion, brown dominant eyes, brown hair and a subtle sexuality.

"I think I was probably born somewhere in Saudi Arabia. But I have no idea who my real family is? Someday, I would like to return and look for them. Have you ever wondered about something that has been kept secret from you all your life? Something in your past? You cannot imagine how difficult it has been for me all these years not knowing who I really am?"

Waite acknowledged, "Perhaps a psychiatrist can help you remember?"

"I've been through all that. Even hypnosis. It didn't work, so the only way I'll probably remember is to go back and retrace some of my ancestral steps.

Maybe, in that way I'll be able to remember something . . . anything that I can build on," she sighed searching his face for solace.

Maybe Waite could help her with his experience of the region once this assignment was over. He knew the mid-east like the back of his hand, and perhaps he could help her remember something about her past.

"Look, if you ever need someone . . . and don't take this wrong; I mean when this is over, maybe I can help you," he told her. "I have a lot of connections over here, and maybe we can find something out."

"That would be very generous of you," she said accepting the offer. "Yes, I would like that."

They finished breakfast and drank some more coffee, making plans as they discussed the situation in Beirut during the remainder of the morning. Events were breaking rapidly now. If there was a connection with the Israeli shoot-downs, some kind of clue might still remain with Ahmed.

"I've got to find Ahmed and ask him about the prayer he uttered when he was delirious. He kept repeating it over and over again. Something to the effect that an uncle was an important power figure in the Middle East. The Bedouin chant he was saying might prove that. We've got to find out who that uncle is. Ahmed must have a hidden past."

Adrienne suddenly stopped eating.

"What kind of chant was it?"

"I don't remember it. I need to find him and ask," Rick said getting up out of his chair with a renewed urgency.

"C'mon, we'll head over to the field hospital, then double back to the UPI office where I'll introduce you to my staff. Put on that Red Cross armband."

Waite paid the waiter and left on two bicycles Rick had borrowed from a local Lebanese family, promising to return them by the end of the day. They took off in the direction of the field hospital.

Adrienne's journalist mind absorbed the utter carnage and chaos of Beirut as they biked along. It was strange. She had never been to the city before. Here, she was twenty-seven years old, and couldn't remember any films of Beirut as Beirut. She could only remember scenes of death and destruction on the daily newscasts, a city filled with smoke, rubble and innocent people being slaughtered and maimed. But, she could remember the appalling condition of its children.

They were always the true victims of any brutal war. It seemed to be that way in every war that was ever fought. New leaders would teach the children how to kill and then the vicious cycle would begin all over again.

After a short ride, they arrived at the field hospital.

"Is Ahmed here?" Waite asked the British nurse on duty. "He might be visiting the boy we brought in a few days ago?"

"He's been here already and gone."

"Gone? Gone where?"

"I told you. He's gone off. I don't keep track of visitors. I just let them visit, and leave," she said testily, bothered by Waite's questioning.

"All right. But, did he mention anything to you that might give me a clue to where he was going?" Waite tried.

"Look, you're a very nice chap, but I've got a busy

schedule and lots of patients to look after. I wish I could be more helpful, but I'm afraid I can't. He just left without saying anything to me or the doctors."

The nurse shrugged.

"Now, if you'll excuse me."

"Yes, thank you. Oh, just one more thing. How's the boy doing?"

"He's going to live. I understand you were the one who saved his life?"

Waite hadn't expected that and it caught him off guard.

"Uhhh. Well . . . it was more because of Ahmed than me. We were able to get him here," Waite said not knowing what else to say.

Adrienne knew he was trying to play down his efforts, and she admired that in him.

"Let's go, we've got to find him," she interrupted.

She was interested in what Ahmed had to say about the Bedouin prayer.

They left the hospital and headed for the UPI bureau. Biking had been a good idea because they could cover a lot more ground that way, and it was safer. They blended in with the local populace.

After a few miles, they arrived at the burned-out UPI headquarters and climbed the stairs by the alleyway entrance.

Waite's two helpers were already setting up the news wire for transmitting.

"Where the hell have you been!" everyone said at the same time as Waite and Adrienne entered the room past a lone security guard.

The UPI men's eyes gaped open at the sight of Adrienne.

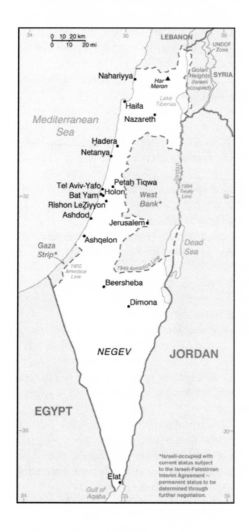

"Hello, to you, too!" one of them said at the first sight of a woman walking into the bureau. "Now, how in the hell did you find someone like her in Beirut?"

"Yeah," the other one said. "Where have you been keeping her?"

"All to myself," Waite kidded hoping not to offend Adrienne with the remark.

"Oh, hell. All right! I can't lie to you guys. She's from the Red Cross. I met her yesterday at the airport coming in to do volunteer work from England," he said trying not to show his guilt at the telling of an obvious lie.

"You mean you're a Brit?" one of the men quizzed her.

"Jolly right! she said. "And one that likes safe working conditions. That's why I volunteered to come to Beirut. Nothing unsafe about this place they told me."

Everyone in the room burst into laughter. It loosened things up a bit, and she was immediately accepted by them.

"Ted, we're looking for Ahmed. Has he been by today? We thought . . . " Ted cut him off in mid-sentence.

"No one's been here since we arrived to set up."

"Shit. We've got to find him. It's really damned important."

"What's going on?"

"He has some information we need to verify a story. Nothing too exciting,

I'm afraid, but I need it to corroborate something," he said still lying to his friend.

"He's the direct source."

212

The Palestine Conspiracy

"Oh," Ted acknowledged nonchalantly ignoring the fact that he knew Waite was lying to him.

"Look, I can't come clean on this yet," Waite apologized, "because we don't know much about it yet, and you guys have enough to worry about. When I do verify the story, we'll all get involved pretty fast, O.K.?"

Waite hated to do that, but it was the safest way to proceed until they got to the bottom of what was going on. And it seemed to satisfy them.

"O.K.," they responded in unison.

They always trusted each other and worked well together, but there really wasn't much to tell anyway, and if he told them what he already knew, it could leak out to other foreign correspondents and blow the lid off the whole thing.

It was in everyone's best interest for now to keep the whole thing as quiet as possible from a journalistic standpoint.

"Look, we've got to leave here now. We're due back at the hotel. If Ahmed comes by, tell him to meet us at the hotel at 7 o'clock tonight. Got it?"

"Gotcha," Ted responded with a thumbs-up sign.

Adrienne and Waite left the bureau and bicycled past several checkpoints manned by Shiite militiamen. The Israelis advance had ground to a halt because of the events unfolding at the U.N.

Civilians once again came out into the open. It was hard to believe that there were still so many people left in Beirut. Rick was amazed at where they all lived. There was at least three million of them living under the worst possible conditions.

"Let's get back to the hotel and wait for him. He's bound to show up sooner or later. He could be anywhere," Waite said.

Adrienne thought it was a good idea, feeling a growing attachment to Rick as they now worked the streets as a team. When they got back, they went up to his room and watched the evening newscast via satellite and began the long vigil for Ahmed.

Waite poured them both drinks. It was 6 o'clock. They sipped at their drinks while waiting for the news to come on. The couch they were sitting on reminded Adrienne of the one she had in her London flat. But, this one had been salvaged from the lobby downstairs.

"All the amenities of home, eh?" she kidded.

"Just like where I grew up," he quipped back.

He moved closer to her on the couch and took a long swig of scotch. They were both tired, in the mood for something exciting, but they didn't know what would happen next – until it did.

Adrienne moved comfortably closer to him. She liked his confident, take-charge attitude. And, he was attracted to her easy personality. Adrienne had a subtle quality that made most men feel like they were special when they were near her. After a few moments, he rested his hand on her shoulder and put down his drink, and without saying a word, leaned over and kissed her. Adrienne accepted the kiss without apprehension. Her lips met his with a tenderness she hadn't felt in a long time. After a few seconds, she backed off, then without saying another word, kissed him back with a gentle, but longer caress. She didn't want to disappoint him. She kissed him with an urgency he understood.

Rick pulled her to him so quickly; it nearly took her breath away. Her drink slipped from her hand and dropped to the floor shattering the glass into fragments. But, he couldn't be bothered by that now. Their sexual desires overtook their self-control. They embraced and slid down on the couch kissing with an even more arduous passion. His hands moved above her waist to the top of her blouse and slowly uncovered her breasts. He was gentle to the touch. Her breasts grew firm as his fingertips soothed them. He bent down and caressed them. She reached down and unbuckled his belts, and felt his erection. She held him in her hand and worked it back and forth until she sensed he was progressing too rapidly. He raised her skirt to her waist and pulled her nylon pantyhose down to her ankles and then off altogether.

Waite brought his hand up along the inside of her thigh until he could feel the warmth and moistness between her legs. She pushed forcefully against it with her hips and began kissing him harder as he inserted his finger into her. His movements increased her erotic desire to have him with more strength than she knew, while she continued to caress him in return.

She suddenly pushed him away, sat upright, removed her skirt and climbed on top of him. He was large. How lucky could she be? Falling in love with him, his rugged, good looks, his attitude, his intelligence, his protective nature, and now this, too. They spent the entire evening like that, not wanting to be interrupted, hoping that Ahmed would not return that night. They did it twice more during the night until they finally fell asleep.

They slept until morning.

Ahmed did not show up. It was what they had wished for.

CHAPTER 22

London: May 23. 8:00 a.m.

Brian and Geoff flew back to London the same way they had departed, via the Albatross cargo plane, which had ferried them to Cairo, then into Beirut.

Their secret meeting with Fasi had been successful.

They would be in direct communication with a member of the PLO organization stationed in Damascus to finalize the historic meeting between the British prime minister and Fasi. An agreement would be signed by England, and the newly formed State of Palestine, and endorsed by the heads of state of the seven other countries involved in making land available to the Palestinians.

Everyone had already agreed to the signing ceremony, except Israel, not informed by any of the Arab governments involved. Israel would be contacted and informed of the plan just two days before the meeting. Thus, Mrs. Thayer would place immense pressure upon the Israeli government to come on board on short notice. She was determined not to waste any more time on a peace initiative in that region which, in the past, had amounted to nothing more than a string of glaring and successive disappointments for every nation party involved.

This time, the added pressure of a shortened time frame would accelerate the decision-making process by setting an impending deadline.

If the Israelis were sincere and genuinely wanted peace, they would sign. If they refused, Britain would sign the pact anyway and go along with the seven Arab nations, and establish a new military presence in the Mid East. Israel would be forced to rethink its political position and coalesce to the agreement sooner or later as public pressure mounted through the United Nations.

Mrs. Thayer's plan was a safe one which could re-position Britain once again in a leadership role in that part of the world.

Mrs. Thayer was set for her briefing after Brian's return from Beirut.

"When the agreement is signed, I should want television coverage of the entire proceedings, don't you agree?"

"Yes, m'aam," Brian replied, and added. "Most of the details will be worked out ahead of time so that when you inform the Israelis of the action Britain is taking, everything will be in place for the signing ceremony."

"Good," she responded to Brian's penchant for setting down the itinerary to the utmost minutia. She was delighted with the game plan he had set before her.

"If everything goes as planned, the world shall have a free and independent Palestine, a stable Mid East and an end to world terrorism. In addition," she said, "England shall regain her lost influence and renewed stature in a region far too valuable for her to ignore anymore."

"Yes, m'aam," Brian agreed as Geoff stepped into the room.

"Notify MI-6 of my itinerary so they can work out

217

the rest of the times, destinations, people to meet, etc.," she calmly ordered befitting her conservative nature. She would leave no stone unturned for slip-ups or errors in political logistics. Thayer was a wily one.

When she was candid, it was a pure lesson in firmness. It earned her the nickname, the "Iron Lady." The description fit her aptly in both appearance and attitude. She was a strong-willed woman, whose immensely sturdy character had served her well in many political battles, especially during the war in the Falklands. She had established early on with an unforgiving nature and a reputation among world leaders as a tough, savvy leader who would take the highest percentage risk for the gain of the greatest good, in keeping with the bulldog mentality made legendary by Winston Churchill.

When she said something, she meant it. Argentina had come to realize that too late. Those who didn't recognize that fact, soon became disquieted of what they were up against. England had waited a long time for such a leader. During the ordeal, they had discovered a female version of Winston Churchill.

Brian and Geoff left Number 10 Downing Street that morning with important papers in hand. Brian told Geoff he'd meet him at Langhorne later that afternoon, after he'd telephoned Adrienne at her flat and spent a few hours with her.

"Blimey . . . always in a hurry to get with her, eh?"

"Go on, it's really none of your business, is it? Anyway, see you later this afternoon, right?"

It had been three weeks since Brian had seen or talked with her. He left the cab and waved Geoff off, then entered a nearby pub for a well-deserved Guinness and asked the bartender for change. Hastily swizzling down the warm beer, he entered a phone booth and dialed Adrienne's number.

The phone rang twice. On the third ring, he heard a barely audible click and the message Adrienne had recorded. As he listened to it, his upbeat mood changed to disappointment.

"Damn," he muttered to himself. "Of all the times to be out of the country."

Dating Adrienne had its drawbacks at times and this was one of them. They both had difficult schedules to keep and their jobs often sent them to far-away destinations keeping them apart for weeks at a time. The worst part of it was trying to know each other's schedule. He had been in Beirut at the same time she was but just didn't know it.

As he was about to hang up, he heard a curious click on the other end of the line. He hadn't heard that kind of noise before or after her messages. It sounded like the electronic wiretaps British Intelligence used. He'd worked with most of the bugging systems foreign agents used and knew most of them.

His suspicion mounted. Maybe he'd better go over to her flat and check it out. A fatalistic hunch told him she was involved in something sinister which could harm her. He returned to the bar, ate a sandwich, and finished his beer without speaking to anyone, a near impossibility inside an English pub. He set off for Adrienne's flat in a taxi.

In what seemed like only a few minutes, the cab pulled up in front of her flat. When he reached it, he let himself in with his key.

No one home. Better check the place out. No telling how long she's been gone.

He walked into the kitchen, opened the refrigerator, opened a cold beer and went into the bedroom. Everything looked normal. He walked back into the living room, sat down on the couch where they had made love so many times and switched on the answering machine. As he sipped the beer, he listened to the messages play back. After each one, he could hear the same tell-tale click, the sound made by an electronic switching device automatically coming on and shutting off activated by voice modulation.

It's bugged. The line is bugged for sure. He wondered by whom and how long? He was careful not to lift the receiver. The bugger would hear him for sure if he did that. No, he wanted to find out where the bugs were located and leave them in place for the time being. But, he had to find out who the perpetrators were and why?

He went back into the bedroom where he and Adrienne spent most of their time. Thankfully, he hadn't made any appreciable noise when he entered the apartment. If anyone was listening to them because he was a British agent, they both could be in danger. He knew there was a bug was in their somewhere. He just had to find it. Suddenly, he froze. Damn. He had mentioned the Middle East meeting to Adrienne in that very bedroom while they were making love a few weeks ago. Shit! He had compromised British security? Was Adrienne herself a foreign agent? Was it possible she was working against him?

"Son-of-a-bitch!" he whispered to himself for being so stupid. How could he have been so careless to talk about it? His fingertips moved to the underside of the nightstand, feeling for a small mercury-like bug placed there by some unknown visitor. Nothing. His mind eased a little as he continued the search silently along the bed frame, his fingers sliding along the edges near the bedposts and around the headboard. His heart stopped as his fingers touched a familiar dime-sized object.

"God-damn-it," he said silently to himself. It was there all right, stuck right smack in the middle of the headboard. There was probably one in the living room, kitchen and maybe even the bathroom.

He'd no time to find them all. But he knew for sure that his conversations with Adrienne had been listened to. He had to tell Geoff about it, but certainly not from her telephone. It had to wait for the time being. First, he had some other things to check out. He must get in touch with Adrienne. For now, he knew he could contact her through her editor. He drank the rest of the beer, put the glass in the sink
without making a sound and penned a brief note to her.

No. He changed his mind and crumpled it, and stuffed it into his pants pocket. He might not be the only visitor to the flat. If whoever was bugging the apartment showed up again, he would read the message meant for Adrienne and know he had been discovered. ICE could perform a counter-intelligence operation on the bugger. Better to talk with her directly from a payphone.

Brian put on his raincoat, re-set the recorder, and left the flat exactly as he had found it.

But, he knew his problems were about to get worse.

CHAPTER 23

Haifa: May 30. 9:00 p.m.

A week had passed since the United Nations assembly listened to the charges and countercharges between Saudi Arabia and Israel.

American military planners were clearly on the defensive by the disclosures of possible CIA involvement in delivering atomic detonators to the PLO. Official statements coming out of Washington stated that the United States had no direct involvement or knowledge of the clandestine flights.

Nor had the White House authorized or sanctioned the CIA or NSA or any other government organization to undertake such a clandestine operation. The denials were fairly convincing, but the fact was that the U.S. had no choice but to make such denials under the presumption of plausible deniability, newly concocted by the previous presidential administration.

Even the Russians, who regularly tried to eavesdrop on CIA conversations, had issued statements confirming that they found it difficult to believe that the U.S. would deliberately arm any Arab nation with nuclear weapons. In fact, there were more questions being created than actual facts discovered, and the new questions were slow in being answered by anyone.

Israeli Defense Minister Prahoe was in Haifa to personally handle the matter himself. He wanted to know first-hand if the captured American crew were

U.S. agents carrying out an unannounced U.S. policy, or if they were privateers who had somehow managed to smuggle the detonators out of the U.S. to the PLO for a price. He arrived at the huge naval base in a gruff mood. As he entered the headquarters where the American crew was being held, he cross-examined the Israeli officer in charge.

"What have you managed to get out of them so far?"

"They are very stubborn, sir," the major said. "They insist they are American CIA, and have shown us identification as such."

"Are the credentials real?"

"No the credentials are falsified, very good, but phony. American NSA sources indicate that their names are correct, but their backgrounds don't check out. They don't match up with anybody at the CIA. They don't really know who they are. One thing is for certain. They are not rogue CIA agents."

"What else do you know about them?"

Leaning toward Prahoe, he spoke in a near whisper.

"We administered truth serum, Plenum 66, a 150 c.c. injection directly into the bloodstream. Each prisoner was interrogated separately. As you know, there is no resistance to Plenum 66. The backgrounds they described check out with the NSA information. They are not CIA. They are members of an elite secret organization, called AFP, operating undetected so far inside the United States not connected with their intelligence services. They belong to an Arab front called Arabs For Palestine. The organization is not generally known around the world. I personally have heard of it only once, and the group was termed non-existent as though it really didn't exist by the intelligence community.

"In any case," he went on, "they are a secret organization of Arab descendents in the U.S. committed to raising arms for the Palestinian cause. They are comprised of members from Arab countries, small cells, but their numbers are kept secret, even to their own members and officers. There are no lists of any kind or a hierarchical ranking to identify any of them publicly as members. Each is sworn to secrecy under the penalty of death."

Prahoe interrupted.

"You mean American intelligence doesn't know the group exists?"

"Yes, sir. That's true."

Prahoe had always prided himself on the Israelis for being well organized. In fact, most of the entire world held the same view. Conversely, the world held the exact opposite view of the Arabs as military incompetents, including their intelligence capabilities.

But clearly now, he was impressed as to the nature of what his own intelligence chief had just told him. The information he had obtained from these Arab-Americans was so convincing that it proved they were indeed well organized, and had penetrated and stolen nuclear weapons to arm the PLO. With this new information, Prahoe realized immediately the impact of what he had just been told. It was now a very dangerous matter for Israel, the United States and the entire world.

"What more information can you get from them?" Prahoe asked.

"We've probably extracted as much information

from them as possible without killing them with the drugs. They are showing detrimental side effects from the Plenum 66, so we stopped administering it hours ago."

"Is there any reason why we shouldn't kill the bastards now?"

"Yes," the intelligence officer responded dutifully. "We might need to parade them before TV cameras as evidence to the world."

"Yes, you're right. Keep them in good physical shape in case we need them to corroborate the details of their ill-fated mission to the news media."

"I consider it my obligation to Israel, sir."

"One more question before I leave for Tel Aviv. Did they give any clue as to who the leader of their organization is?"

"Sir, we asked them that early on in the interrogation. They gave us some kind of code name."

"And, what was that name?"

"Goliath!"

"Goliath?" Prahoe repeated out loud.

"That's correct, sir."

"Goliath," he said pronouncing it again out loud.

"Sir, do you want to see any of them before you depart?"

"No, there's no point in it. You have done excellent work, major. If you find out any additional information you deem important to me, or about the identity of this so-called Goliath, notify me at once?" Prahoe said. He had supreme confidence in his intelligence officer. He had a hunch that Goliath was somebody very important, somebody very special, more than anyone at Israeli intelligence realized.

The Palestine Conspiracy

"Yes, sir. I will notify you immediately of any new developments wherever you are."

Prahoe left the intelligence headquarters and boarded a military jet for Tel Aviv where he would consult with the prime minister on other actions possible with the capture of these Arab-Americans. But, what should be the next move by the Israeli government?

The PLO was up to something, something potentially devastating to Israel and its security.

What was it?

Why would they resort to nuclear weapons?

Were these the weapons of last resort?

Were their no more negotiating positions left? And, most importantly, had Israel's intransigence led to this?

Prahoe wondered if the world had exhausted all its peace efforts?

Had Israel's own inflexibility been a detriment to its very own survival? Palestine would have to be negotiated sooner or later.

These were the unanswered questions he would ask the prime minister.

Meanwhile, the Israeli army was at an ordered stand-in-place in Beirut as a result of the latest mid-east developments.

Justification for the breaking of the cease-fire occurred when the facts about the massacre of 250 Israeli prisoners-of-war took place at the order of the PLO in retaliation for the execution by the Israelis of three captured PLO terrorists who had planted a car-bomb in Jerusalem killing 24 civilians.

The bomb had been placed inside a parked car

outside a busy marketplace in the heart of the holy city. Killed were Muslims, Christians and Jews, an indiscriminate lesson on how terrorism chose its victims at random, making the act more reprehensible. Those who survived the blast accused the PLO as having no moral fiber left whatsoever. The news accounts had been particularly vivid and incited the Israeli government to exact every measure of revenge.

So, it was ironic that whatever had been learned from the Middle East fighting during the past twenty years had not been learned at all.

Violence increased the probability of further escalation. The Israelis would take unilateral action to break the cease-fire agreement between them and the Syrians and Jordanians and occupy Beirut in response to public pressure to the car bombing.

When the Israelis attacked and broke the cease-fire, the PLO had started to systematically massacre the Israeli prisoners.

The prisoners had been held on the outskirts of west Beirut, at an old Muslim mosque where a temporary prison camp had been constructed.

The prisoners had been properly treated until the breaking of the cease-fire. When the Israelis made the decisive move through the city to destroy the PLO army, the massacre was ordered.

The PLO army had re-grouped after a total retreat from the city several years earlier by Fasi via negotiations by the United States.

Even then, Israel had been on the verge of annihilating the 6,000-man strong army. They had been trapped inside the city, and if it had not been for the intervention of the United States, who had negotiated a peaceful withdrawal of the army on condition that it would be dismantled and members transported to Cyprus, the PLO fighting force would have been completely destroyed by the Israeli army.

Now, more than five years later, the double-cross by the PLO was apparent. The United States was furious.

When the Israelis attacked this time, the U.S. State Department said and did nothing to prevent it. The PLO sensed that it meant an all out battle and a fight to the last man.

Knowing they were no match for the crack Israeli units, they methodically lined-up the prisoners-of-war, televising the event to the world, and warned that if the Israeli's crossed the Green Line, the prisoners would be executed.

The Israelis did not take the threat seriously at first, who prior to this had made it official policy never to deal or negotiate with the PLO or their spokesmen.

Instead, they attacked the city with a ferocity not seen since the Yom Kippur War.

The PLO, in response, began massacring the Israelis prisoners without mercy as the Israeli tanks rumbled across the demarcation line.

It was terrible.

And, even more horrible to outside observers who watched it all on television.

After the execution of the first 25 Israeli prisoners by machine-gun fire, another 25 were killed fifteen minutes apart. The prisoners were lined up, and before being shot, the PLO commander announced to the world that the Israeli advance must be stopped or the remainder of the prisoners would be killed in an hour.

The Israelis had no choice but to halt their attack.

It marked the first time the Israelis had ever been forced to deal directly with the PLO. The Israeli public, watching the massacre on TV, had demanded it of their government leaders, and it marked a turning point in the relationship of the two opponents.

A price had been exacted, weighed by the Israeli public, which called upon Prime Minister Yitzak Glaenis to stop the advancing Israelis army. And, by his order, they did.

With the new cease-fire in place, Israel had been forced to accept terms from the Arabs for the first time in history.

The Israeli people were disillusioned. Their army was at a standstill, the three shoot downs had intimidated their air force earlier in the week, and they had been forced to apologize for their intrusion over Saudi Arabia.

Defense Minister Prahoe arrived in Tel Aviv after the thirty-minute flight from Haifa using a special radar-absorbing plane so the Arabs would not be able to detect his movements throughout Israel.

Prahoe had carefully thought out the questions he would put to the prime minister. After his visit to Haifa, he was convinced that something drastic needed to be done by Israel to eliminate any nuclear threat.

His recommendation to the prime minister would be the undertaking of a first-strike attack against the PLO before they could assemble and launch the missiles against them.

Prahoe knew his intelligence officer was good at his job and had extracted as much information as possible from the captured AFP crew. But, he hadn't anticipated they already had the missiles in place and were merely waiting for the arming mechanisms to be delivered.

Israel's own nuclear missiles had already been positioned in underground silos near the port city of Haifa. Two missiles with a range of 1,500 miles had been readied at the edge of the airbase. Everything was ready for them to strike back if Fasi attacked Israel.

The missiles could be launched as a first-strike or in self-defense, instantly using a computerized launch control system, which only he and the prime minister were authorized to use in a national emergency. Both were required to "lock" the arming mechanism by connecting computer code to begin the launch sequence.

Once launched, total flight time to the targets would be less than twelve minutes. But, the preferred method of attack against the PLO campsite where the missiles were located, was to use conventional military weapons as a pre- requisite, and nuclear weapons only as a last resort.

If the nuclear option became necessary would world public opinion stand for it? Israel was already on the defensive. What would the reaction of the U.S. and Russians be?

Even the Russians were alarmed at the growing nuclear power of Israel. Russia might react against Israel even if the attack was limited. Whereas, the United States probably could be counted on to support Israel if enough pressure from American Jews were applied. But, there were no guarantees, and Prahoe knew that. Prahoe also knew that he could not rely entirely on U.S. strategic help in a desperate situation. The U.S. might even stop Israel from taking any action, or even take military action against them to neutralize the threat of becoming involved in a nuclear confrontation with the Russians.

Prahoe didn't know the answer to all these questions, but they wrenched at his intellectual beliefs as he left the plane and headed for the rendezvous with the prime minister and the Knesset leaders.

Maybe they had all the answers in spite of his doubts. He would soon know when he made his own recommendations. Wiping away the perspiration from his forehead, he boarded the camouflaged van, which would transport him to the secret meeting.

Israel was in a horrible predicament. Nonetheless, the three-mile journey through the streets of Tel Aviv was an endurance of beautiful tranquility.

The night was clear.

The moonlight cast long shadows along the obscure side streets enabling him to catch only occasional glimpses of romantic couples walking along the sidewalks, oblivious as to what was going on around them. Mixed among them were the hundreds of worshipers finding their way back home from temple services.

It was a calm and peaceful Saturday evening in Tel Aviv.

Prahoe now wondered how soon Israel should attack?

CHAPTER 24

Beirut: The next day. 8:00 a.m.

Rick and Adrienne spent the night together at the bombed-out hotel.

They again awakened to the regular bombardment by the Israelis.

This time they were not the targets.

Instead, shells were falling into the PLO west Beirut sector, several miles away. The two had become so used to the regular shelling that it hardly roused them from their sleep.

"Are you awake?" Adrienne murmured fighting the urge to open her eyes.

"Shhh," he said. "I'm still asleep."

Adrienne already knew she cared for him. She had known Brian for several years, but she knew instantly there was a difference in her feelings toward Rick. It was the difference of sharing something in common, a shared philosophy, and just simply wanting to be with him. But, she could not risk losing a huge story for love alone. When the noise subsided, she knew they must go out and search for Ahmed instead of waiting for him to eventually show up. Hell, we might not ever see him again Adrienne pleaded with Waite.

"C'mon, wake up!" she begged. "We've got to find Ahmed if he won't find us."

He peered at her from beneath the covers through bloodshot and light-sensitive eyes, and realized she was right. He rolled to a sit-up position, gently putting his hand between her neck and shoulder. She let out a deep sigh. He knew she really liked to be touched. It was as though she had been deprived of that affection as a child. He bent down and kissed her on the lips, tossing the covers on top of her head, bounding out of bed laughing.

"You're absolutely right. If we spend anymore time here, we'll get nothing done."

"Your desire for the impossible overwhelms me," she quipped abandoning the thought of early morning sex with him.

Rick put his clothes on while Adrienne dressed on the opposite side of the room. It was almost like being married to each other.

"Maybe, Ahmed went back to his PLO post?" she said moving toward the window.

"Not a bad place to begin," Waite said. "If he's not there, we can try the bureau again, although they probably would have called me by now."

"Good idea," she said fastening the front of her bra putting on a loose-fitting blouse and her Red Cross armband as they left the hotel room and pedaled toward where the PLO army unit had been last positioned.

When they got there, after being stopped routinely at several PLO checkpoints, Ahmed was nowhere to be found.

They doubled back to the field hospital hoping that Ahmed had gone back there, but with no luck.

As they searched, Red Cross volunteers cared for the women and children who had been wounded in the morning barrage. Civilian losses were mounting steadily. There just was no such thing as safety in Beirut these days.

"Look, I know it's an inconvenience," he asked the Brit nurse, "but could I use your phone to call our news bureau?"

Even though Waite knew that the PLO and Israeli intelligence monitored the lines, he felt he had to risk making the call.

He dialed the number and waited. The phone rang three, four, five, six and seven times.

"Damn it. No answer. They're supposed to be there by 9 a.m. to set up the transmitter to the satellite."

He let it ring six more times.

Still, no answer.

"You don't suppose they were hit by the shelling this morning, do you?" Adrienne asked. "They're in the same sector."

"God, I hope not. The phone could have been knocked out, though."

"Well, it looks like we'll have to pedal for it."

Now that sounded nice to her. A quiet morning bike ride. Her legs were sore from the last excursion, or was it the sex last night that had caused the aching muscles? They had really gone at it.

Speeding through the checkpoints quickly this time, perspiration drenched them as they pressed on with a growing sense of urgency. After a few miles, they skidded to a stop at the familiar alleyway. It had been nearly blown to bits by the rocket blasts. They hid the bikes and hurried past the barriers placed there by Waite and his men to make it look as though the area was impassable. Slowly, they made their way through the debris in the alley, when Waite suddenly stopped dead in his tracks.

"Something's wrong," he whispered to Adrienne close behind. "Whenever we're inside the building, we set a trip-wire which leads to a silent alarm upstairs. It's already been tripped," he told Adrienne.

Waite nervously pulled a gun from inside his shirt. Adrienne's eyes froze on the jet-black 9mm automatic he held in his hand.

"You didn't tell me you had that?" she choked back her words.

"I don't carry one, but for some reason, I thought, what the hell, we might be a little safer with it."

His instincts were right. As they cautiously climbed the stairs in complete silence, moving stealthily past empty beer cans and broken glass without making a sound, they reached the top of the landing looking for some sign of life. Lifting his head just above the floor as he came up to the railing, he could see the transmitter through the doorway lying on the floor in several pieces.

"I think someone's in there," he whispered back to Adrienne, motioning for her not to move.

Slowly, he moved toward the doorway and inched his way along the floor, gripping the 9mm tightly. Adrienne heard the cocking sound as Waite pulled back on the slide and let it slam shut, letting anyone inside know that he was armed and dangerous. He carefully reached around the doorway and felt for the light switch. Tugging down on it, he fully expected a fusillade of gunfire to erupt. When none did, he switched-on the light and in one continuous crouching motion, slid inside the doorway pointing the gun in front of him like he'd seen in the movies. His eyes darted around the room looking for targets.

There weren't any.

There he was, a third-rate reporter, playing agent 007 straight out of a James Bond flick. A sense of relief rushed through him, so he was caught off guard by the sight of what he saw down low behind the desk.

The sight stunned him, and made him sick to his stomach.

Lying in a pool of blood were Ted and Artie, both dead from gunshot wounds to the head.

He stepped back and yelled for Adrienne.

She bolted into the room and covered her mouth. Waite pushed her down to the floor, motioning her to watch the closet door. Her eyes froze on the doorknob. It didn't move. She reached out and pulled the door open with a quick thrust. Waite leveled his 9mm at the opening. It was empty.

The men had been shot through the neck and head. It was an ugly sight, and he held her away from the bodies. There was nothing they could do for them.

"My God. What happened?" Adrienne shrieked when she regained her ability to speak.

"I don't know," Waite said trying not to show his fear. A growing anger welled up inside him. "I don't know."

"Why would they kill them? They didn't know what we were working on," she said.

"Suppose someone thought they did," he replied knowing they had probably been followed earlier.

Adrienne got the message.

"Do you think they know about us?"

The Palestine Conspiracy

"Without a doubt," Waite said as he bent over one of the men and examined the bullet wounds.

"Small caliber. Probably a .22 or .25 cal. It could have been anybody."

As he turned to get up, he reached for the 9mm as a dark shadow passed over the bodies between them and the doorway.

"Don't shoot! Don't shoot! It's me!"

The sight of Ahmed paralyzed him for a second.

"In the name of Allah, Ahmed, you're lucky I didn't kill you. You scared the living hell out of me. Where have you been? Why didn't you meet us at the field hospital like we planned?" the questions gushed forth.

Ahmed motioned toward the bodies.

"That's the reason, my friend."

"I don't understand," Wait replied.

"I tried to warn your men, but I couldn't get through. We think it was an Israeli assassination squad," Ahmed said bitterly. "It's the way they do things, too."

"How can you be sure?"

"A connection I have with Israeli intelligence met me on the way to the hospital and warned me off. They said that I was a target for assassination along with you and your friend," Ahmed said, motioning to Adrienne.

"Uh . . . this is Adrienne," attempting to introduce her. "She's here with the Red Cross from England."

Ahmed smiled at Adrienne.

She smiled in return and looked away.

"My friend, I told you never to lie to me on matters involving our little secret. We must talk. It's too dangerous here, now. We must leave immediately."

The Palestine Conspiracy

"Yes. You're right, of course," Waite agreed. "Look, I'll take care of the bodies. I'll have to notify my people in New York about this. You already know it'll make the evening news in the states," Waite observed matter-of-factly.

"Damn. They didn't have to do this," he said slamming his fist down on the desk. "They didn't know anything. If Israeli intelligence is so damned good, they should have known that."

"Adrienne, you go on with Ahmed. You can trust him. You'll be safe with him. I'll meet both of you back behind the PLO lines."

"O.K.," Ahmed agreed. "We'll meet at my command post in the PLO sector at 2 o'clock."

Waite nodded and began the morbid task of cleaning up the bodies for removal. First, he would notify Beirut authorities of what had happened, and then he would call his home office in New York.

Adrienne and Ahmed were off to the outskirts of Beirut where Ahmed's unit was still operating. Biking their way through the various sectors, Ahmed and Adrienne stopped for a rest and some water from his canteen. Standing next to a fountain, Ahmed refilled his canteen. It was a place where many Beirut families gathered in the evening hours. Adrienne felt apprehensive in the strange surroundings.

Ahmed calmed her and smiled through his tears.

Adrienne was crying, too.

"My dear sister. How long has it been since I've seen you?" reaching to embrace her.

"Fifteen years since I last saw you at father's desert camp," she answered.

Ahmed looked much older to her now as she

studied the wrinkles in his face and the deep scar
across his chin. She hugged him again, both crying in
each other's arms.

"My little Aminah . . . my Adrienne . . . my lost
desert sheep."

"Ahmed . . . it is really you isn't it, after all these
years?"

"Indeed, by the grace of Allah, it is."

Ahmed had finally kept his promise to his mother.
He had found her at last.

"How is father and uncle?" she asked in a surge of
remembrance. The shock of seeing him standing in the
doorway at the UPI office had restored her memory, and
now, a new reality replaced it.

"They are both fine. They fight for the same cause
. . . for the people of Palestine."

Sitting beneath the huge cedar tree, they drank
from the fountain where Ahmed had retreated when
Akram was gunned down on his motorbike.

"This is where I prayed when Akram was killed,"
he told her. "It's peaceful here. This place is a
reminder of death. But, today, with you, it again has the
meaning of life."

"It's good to see you brother. Tell me, what news
do you have for me after so long?"

He hadn't seen his sister since his father had given
her to a Bedouin chieftain at fourteen, and here she was,
now before him, once more. So many events had
transpired. The family had scattered into the desert,
made successful trading ventures in oil and gradually
accumulated great wealth, which had placed them in
powerful positions in Saudi Arabia and other Middle
East countries.

The Palestine Conspiracy

"Leading a double life has been difficult for me," Adrienne said. "There have been times I've been ashamed of the things I've done. But, I hope it has been for the good of our people. I know in the end that Allah will forgive me. How is uncle?"

"Uncle is well. But, he is under constant pressure from factions in Beirut to do something to break the Israeli stranglehold on the Palestinian question. There are some things I know which are to take place soon . . ."

Adrienne interrupted.

"I, too, am aware that something is going on. A man in London, whom I've been having an affair with, works for British intelligence, is helping plan the meeting with uncle and Mrs. Thayer," Adrienne said. "But I sense that something is wrong, that something else has happened. I must know what this is?"

"I don't know anymore than you do. In fact, you may know even more than I do. It is hard to keep everyone quiet on this matter. Secrecy has been very difficult. The Israelis have somehow found out about the meeting and may try to prevent it. We think they may try sabotaging it, perhaps even assassinating them. We are taking all precautions to prevent that, but the Israelis are persistent. They watch our every move.

"The men in the UPI bureau were victims of the Israeli hit squad searching for both you and Rick. They were marked for death because the Israeli's thought they knew something about it.

"Our own intelligence received word from our operatives in London that your man, Brian, discovered listening devices in your apartment - Israeli listening devices. Your telephone had been tapped long ago. So whatever Brian told you, he also told them."

She spat on the ground at the thought of it. The seductive liaisons in the bathrooms and bedrooms, their every word and action had been recorded by the Israelis. The thought repulsed her.

She now understood what they were up against.

"What happens if the Israelis disrupt the meeting?"

"Uncle has pledged to use the missiles against Israel."

"What missiles?"

"I assumed you knew about them," Ahmed said. "Didn't you receive my last coded communication before you left London?"

"No. I've been waiting for information from you for several months. But, I never heard anything."

"The Israelis must have penetrated the mails. No matter now. There are two nuclear warheads with arming detonators being carried across the Syrian Desert by caravan as we speak. One of our trusted cousins, Yemet, is leading the caravan. It was the only way we felt sure we could move the equipment escaping detection by either the Americans or Israelis.

"Since the Israeli air and naval blockade, we felt it was the only way. Do you know about the C-47 cargo planes? We knew the Israelis would take the bait, so we let them intercept us near Beirut. They were merely a diversion for the other ones coming in from Pakistan. The Israelis think they have stopped the shipment."

His explanation sounded like some bizarre plot from a cheap spy novel. Adrienne sucked in a deep breath as if to make sure she had heard it correctly.

She needed to remember all of it.

"If uncle uses the nuclear missiles against Israel,

wouldn't it mean the destruction of our people as well? What would happen to our dream of a homeland?"

"It is written by the prophets that our people will rise up against the zealot and destroy him with a united hand among all tribes. This is what we've been born to do. It is our destiny. If we cannot live in peace with the Jews, then we forsake our children's' birthright forever. The day of reckoning is at hand," Ahmed warned her.

She looked away.

Her thoughts drifted back to a time when they were all happier, for years living as Bedouins. Playing as children, taunting their parents, yielding only when reprimanded, they had all forsaken a desert life for the power and riches of oil.

In an almost barren environment, the desert was the giver and sustainer of life for the Bedouin. That part of the Bedouin culture must remain intact.

"It is a serious risk, Ahmed. If it comes to this, if it comes to a nuclear holocaust, then the entire world is condemned by both Israel and Palestine. May Allah have mercy on us all."

While they spoke, Waite had finished and was hurrying to catch up, when he spotted them near the fountain.

He approached from where they couldn't see him, and caught part of their conversation. Scarcely believing what he heard, the revelations astonished him. The clues had been there the entire time, but he had chosen to ignore them. In short, he had been duped.

The interview with Fasi, his chance meeting with Ahmed, Ahmed's unknown identity, Adrienne's secret past, the coded message, all carefully contrived tricks.

242

And, now two of his closest friends were dead, murdered.

Perhaps, the PLO had done it? Perhaps, Adrienne and Ahmed had planned it?

And, now they were planning a possible nuclear strike against Israel. My God, what had he stumbled onto?

He must get word to the embassy in Beirut before Ahmed and Adrienne discovered he knew. But, before he could make a run for it, a PLO soldier who had approached him from behind struck him a sharp blow to the back of the skull with his rifle butt. Desperately trying to recover his balance, he was hurled toward the stonewall; the PLO soldier struck him again, then again in the face and chest. Everything turned red as Rick fell to the ground while the soldier continued his attack.

"Israelah! Israelah, pig!"

Adrienne and Ahmed leapt up when they heard the commotion from behind the wall.

When they saw it was Rick, Ahmed ordered the soldier to stop at once.

"You fool, he is not an Israeli spy. He is with us. Leave him."

But, it was too late. Waite had been battered into unconsciousness, severely hurt and bleeding from both eyes and nose. At first, Adrienne thought he was dead, but after seeing him flinch when she touched him, she knew he was still alive. Ahmed chastised the soldier and ordered him to return to his army unit.

Adrienne and Ahmed looked at each other in astonishment. Waite was alive, but they knew he had heard something.

How much had he heard?

The Palestine Conspiracy
How much did he know?

CHAPTER 25

Beirut: Later that day.

Waite lay unconscious under a fig tree while Adrienne and Ahmed tried to revive him by means of cold compresses.

He was bleeding profusely from the nose and mouth.   His hair was matted with blood and his breathing came in heavy rasps as Adrienne gently poured water over his forehead.

His eyes fluttered as he fought to regain consciousness, but he couldn't open them. They were swollen shut.   His breathing steadied after a few minutes, while Adrienne furiously wiped him down in an attempt to cool his body. She forced water down his mouth.

". . . ahhgg . . . ahhgg . . . " he coughed up a mixture of blood and saliva, finally coming around. Squinty-eyed, he saw Adrienne in a blur of red.

"Rick, it's Adrienne. Can you hear me? Can you talk?"

Waite rolled his eyes upward but couldn't move his neck. He tried to focus while she held his head upright.

"What happened?" he groaned.

"One of the soldier's thought you were an Israeli spy. We stopped him when we heard the commotion, but you were badly hurt. Try not to talk or move,"

Adrienne comforted him.

"Why were you standing behind the wall?" Ahmed

asked.

Waite mumbled his words as his jaw refused to work properly.

"I finished early at the bureau and came looking for you. When I spotted you over here, I walked toward the wall, and . . . and . . . that' the last thing I remember."

"Did you hear us talking when you approached?"

Waite was afraid to answer that question. If they were who they said they were, his life might depend on a successful lie.

Could he trust them after overhearing their conversation? Had Adrienne double-crossed him? Was she, too, a PLO operative?

His head was spinning.

They had saved his life. But, he wasn't sure if he could trust them. And, if they had any doubts about him, he knew they could kill him right on the spot.

In a state of mental desperation, he remembered what he said to Adrienne at the hotel - you have to trust somebody at sometime.

"I . . . I . . . " he stammered in an attempt to find the right words . . . "I heard what you were talking about, but not all of it."

"How much did you hear?" Ahmed pushed.

"I heard the part about the meeting and . . . the part about the attack on Tel Aviv . . . Ahmed, you're uncle is talking about nuclear annihilation. Is he serious about such an assault?"

"I'm afraid Uncle Fasi understands very clearly what he is doing. It is his final opportunity for the creation of the State of Palestine. If we lose this opportunity, we lose the last chance we shall have in this century for the creation of a homeland for our people," Ahmed said, reciting words like a litany.

"Israel becomes stronger every day, with each passing year. The Egyptians have fought three wars and lost. Others have tried and failed. If we cannot win by conventional means, then we will do it his way. We will destroy Israel and her people."

Waite realized that Ahmed was probably mad like the rest of them, committed to an impossible goal. He tried to concentrate, but he kept drifting in-and-out of consciousness.

"You are not who you say you are," Waite said to Adrienne. "You said you're the daughter of a Bedouin king, and the niece of PLO leader Fasi Etebbe. What am I now to believe? Your real name is Aminah?"

She put her hand over his mouth to silence him . . . "yes, it is true. That is why it has been so difficult for me. I am a Bedouin princess, the daughter of King Fasaid of Saudi Arabia."

Ahmed comforted Waite with a touch to the shoulder.

Ahmed liked Waite because he had been good to the Palestinian people. He wasn't like the others. They had used his people for their own ends. They had used Adrienne, too, because she was young and beautiful.

"What are you going to do now?"

"You must not try to stop us," Ahmed said. "It is my hope that the Fasi-Thayer meeting goes ahead as planned, and that we can defeat Israel in the United Nations. But, if this should not happen . . . "

Waite interrupted.

"You both must see my position. Adrienne, you are still a journalist. This is the most dangerous threat to mankind in the last half-century. It's a chance to achieve genuine peace in the Middle East," he reasoned. "If we do this right, it's entirely possible that the peace initiative might work. I'm not asking either of you to betray your people. I am asking you to help them create a future for themselves. All we need is some time to meet with Fasi before the Thayer summit, and explain how we can put pressure on Israel through the news media. They will have to agree to the plan if other countries accept it. We can make this work in a new way."

Waite was convincing.

"I know the journalist in you," Ahmed said, "and, I know a little about the humanitarian spirit in you regarding my people. But, I also know that you won't sacrifice your ethics by delaying a story for our cause. I know the journalist in you?"

Waite knew Ahmed was damned right about him, to the very core of his existence. But, in order to buy time, he had to convince him otherwise.

"There is one point you haven't considered, Ahmed."

"And, what is that?"

"What if your cause becomes my cause? What if we don't print the story? Then, you run the risk of losing everything for the Palestinian people. Such an assault by Fasi would certainly destroy both Israel and Palestine. Look, I have come to admire and respect the people of Palestine and what they are trying to achieve. I risked my life for that 12-year-old boy in Beirut. Believe me when I say that my cause is the same as yours."

Ahmed wanted to believe him.

The Palestine Conspiracy

"If I must choose between journalism ethics and the destruction of people . . . then, I choose to keep everything secret until we can persuade Fasi to end his nuclear threat against Israel."

Waite had used the word "we" very convincingly.

Ahmed got the subliminal message.

Waite was now one of them by his own choice.

Ahmed and Adrienne hugged.

They would do this together. They would convince Fasi to abandon his nuclear option. They knew it was their only chance to do something to prevent Palestine and Israel from destroying each other.

"What does the message Akram was carrying mean, Ahmed?"

Ahmed stared at Waite.

Would he reveal it?

Waite now knew that Ahmed had known all along what the message contained.

"It was part of our plan to lead you and American intelligence into letting you know that the Israelis were planning something big to stop the Thayer meeting. But, I had not counted on one thing - your fierce independence as a journalist. You were loyal to your sources. You did not divulge anything to the embassy or CIA staff in Beirut. Your integrity ruined that part of my plan, but at least, from that moment on, I knew I could trust you."

"And what of Akram's death," Waite asked.

"That part of the plan was truly tragic. It was an accident that simply occurred by chance. I will have to live with that the rest of my life."

Ahmed explained the rest.

"The Israeli's are desperately trying to prevent the

meeting.   Seven neighboring countries of the new Palestine will be attending the signing ceremony.   We expect the Israelis to try an assassination attempt against Thayer and Fasi.   They will somehow try to prevent this summit."

"Do you know how they will strike?" he asked Ahmed.

"No.   But, our agents are working on it .   We are only weeks away from the meeting.   Time is very critical.   We have the advantage of world public opinion, so we cannot delay what we have already orchestrated.   If we delay, we lose the advantage we have built."

Ahmed wiped perspiration from his face and leaned against the stonewall.

"I don't know if I can stop the nuclear plan if it should be ordered by Fasi.   His plans are in the hands of some very ruthless people.   One of them is a military general under King Fasaid.   It is he who will direct the attack personally if one is to come.   This man is capable of doing it.   Believe me, he will do it, if ordered."

"And who is this general?" Waite asked.

Ahmed looked at Adrienne for the shock that was to come.

"He is Necomis.   General Abdulla Necomis, Adrienne's Bedouin husband from the desert fifteen years ago."

Waite flinched at the thought of it.   The words pierced at his very soul.

Adrienne was married to General Necomis - the man who could very well start World War III?

CHAPTER 26

Somewhere in the Syrian Desert near Jordan: June 15. 9:00 a.m.

Fasi stared at his watch as the Bedouins in the dunes fell to the east in morning prayers.

In two more days, the caravan would arrive with the nuclear warheads necessary to attack Israel if he chose. Fasi looked across the far reaches to the distant desert landscape and contemplated the inescapable conclusion.

If the United Nations did its job, Israel would be sanctioned for its recent hostile acts toward Saudi Arabia. Mrs. Thayer would arrive for the June 24 meeting and a vote would be taken that same week to recognize Palestine as a new nation. If all went well, it could be accomplished within a few days.

Fasi bowed his head toward Mecca, then Medina, and knelt in the sand to pray to the almighty Allah that this could be accomplished. If it could not, he alone would be responsible for its consequences.

In New York, his aides at the U.N. were feverishly organizing the events, which would shake the world - the introduction of Resolution #439 which would seek entry of Palestine into the world of nations.

Israel had been officially sanctioned by the U.N. Security Council which Russia and the United States each held a key veto. Neither had used it in an unprecedented victory for Saudi Arabia.

News teams broadcast the turn of events labeling

them as historic, a signal to Israel that it could no longer dominate the attention and the political affection of the United States as easily as before.

Networks ran story-after-story about Arab culture and the personalities of their leaders, covering every facet of Islam as a religion, its politics, economics and lifestyles as never before.

In America, a hyped-up interest was being exaggerated by the news media, fascinated by the turn of events propelling Arab countries into the living rooms of millions of American television viewers. It was a distinctive change from the usual nightly terrorist acts, which the world had become accustomed to.

For the first time in its history, Israel was being viewed as an aggressor nation while, for the first time in its political history, the Palestinian point-of-view was being felt.

Fasi smiled as he finished his prayers. He asked an aide to bring him the latest newspapers from Damascus. His aide also brought him faxed copies of the New York Times and the London Times, translating the articles to him.

A sense of satisfaction filled him. The camp reminded him vividly of the valley in which he,
Aminah, Ahmed and his brothers would spend hours watching the wind change the shape of the sand dunes. By morning, he was always amazed to see how many of the dunes had shifted, and how many of them had remained the same.

Indeed, the sand dunes were the things that changed, and the wind was the instrument that changed them. But, it was the Bedouin who never changed. Their lives would always be the same. His oldest brother, King Fasaid, had said that the only true change for the Bedouin was in which direction the wind would carry. The Bedouin would say that it was the very force that changed his world. It brought the Bedouin the fresh air, in turn the seed, which sowed the earth; it took away the burning sun from his skin; and it carried the rain to the desert that brought the flowers and plants. Indeed, the wind was the sustainer of life for all eternity. But, it could also be a curse, taking away any life just as quickly.

In the desert, the wind truly was nature's paradox.

Fasi remembered all of this as he looked out across the stretches of endless sand before him. In the distance, he eyed a sandstorm gathering its yellow fury. In a few minutes, the sandstorm would be upon their desert encampment with a ferocity only a Bedouin could comprehend. Such sandstorms were an experience to remember, the canvas tents flapping in the powerful wind, the camels baying at their tie-downs, while everyone scurried to secure them.

Keffiyeh's protected the Bedouins from the wind's sandblasting effects on the face and neck as they bent down to tie the camels hooves to the stakes and calm them. The camels knelt down and buried their heads backward into their forelegs. These were all the natural elements that the Bedouin understood in his day-to-day world. If an outsider was caught in one of these sandstorms, he was destined to a certain death unless he could find shelter in a Bedouin camp. The Bedouins knew how to survive using their years of experience in the desert and their camels for protection. The camel was the Bedouin's desert horse. He used it for transport and shelter. He protected it with all his

courage and might; for without it, he knew he would die. Sometimes, if a Bedouin was trapped in the desert without his camel, he could still survive if he had the sheer will. The tenacity of the Bedouin could be amazing. He could live for weeks with little or no water by digging deep into the sand and tapping the root of the Papyrus plant, which contained a sprig of water. The plant itself was a tribute to all that didn't grow in the desert. The Papyrus could live throughout the entire dry season, and it enabled the Bedouin to live. The Bedouin could live with the desert creatures during the day or night, too. He would use the crawling insects, the rodents, and the snakes for food if necessary. He could walk for days without any appreciable supply of water in the hot, burning sun having been taught to do this from boyhood as a test of
manhood. It was a test he either passed or failed with his life.

So, it had been written for centuries, and passed down to generation upon generation.

Now, Fasi's thoughts indeed were very real.

If he failed, he no longer would be able to walk among his Bedouin brothers. It would cost him his very life. This, he understood, very clearly.

* * *　　* * *

Sakaka:　In the Syrian Desert near Amman, Jordan.

The caravan moved slowly as the sure-footed camels plodded quietly through the granules, their hooves pushing deeper into the sand with each awkward step. But, the camel could walk for days without taking on any food or water, storing enough fat in its hump to live for weeks at a time. A common misconception was that the hump contained the water; when in fact, most of the water stored was in the camel's stomach. The camel could walk four to six weeks without water during the winter months, and during the hot, summer months, it could travel for a week to 10 days, drinking 25 gallons of water at a time when finally reaching an oasis.

In Arabic, camel meant the literal translation for beautiful, taken from the word Jamal. There were more than 600,000 camels in Saudi Arabia alone, most of them the single-humped kind. But, the reason the camel could go for so long in the desert without water was because that its rate of consumption was less than one-third of the average mammal. Below temperatures of 105 degrees Fahrenheit, the camel didn't perspire. And the average camel could gallop at 12 mph for hours at a time. They can travel 90 to 100 miles a day for several days when pushed to their limit. Is it any wonder why the Bedouins relied so much on the creature as its chief source of transportation, milk and meat?

The camel was the Bedouin's lifeblood, and it was a traditional fact that the Bedouin who bred such camels was considered to be of noble descent, and it was these same families who organized the merchant caravans from ancient times to the present-day.

Truly, the close relationship between the Bedouin and the camel was no historical accident. The camel meant the difference between life and death in the desert.

The Palestine Conspiracy

* * *   * * *

The caravan was now some 200 miles from its rendezvous point with Fasi. The warheads, strapped to the camels, had been camouflaged. Bedouin soldiers walked beside the camels guiding them along the desert trails they knew by heart from childhood.

Beneath the canvas, lead-lined containers protected the delicate cargo so that spy satellites focused on that part of the world could not detect radioactivity. Any leakage could jeopardize the entire mission.

Suddenly . . . a baying camel alerted one of the caravan leaders who spotted movement in the sand dunes several hundred yards ahead. The leader shouted to the Bedouin soldiers.

Several armed with rifles hurried to the front of the caravan and took up defensive positions halting the caravan's forward progress. They pushed their heads down into the sand and listened for the hoof beats.

Then, without warning, one of the Bedouins cocked his rifle. He could hear the sounds of hundreds of hoof beats pounding along the desert floor somewhere beyond the sand dunes. They tightened their defensive circle around the caravan to protect its precious cargo, guns pointed toward a yet unseen enemy. Others calmed the camels, forcing them down in the sand, as everyone lay in wait for the horsemen to show themselves.

Suddenly, from behind the farthest dune, a line of horsemen with rifles pointed in the air, riding into the wind, were spotted by the Bedouins now flattened-out in the sand. It was a raiding party, one of the many nomad groups, which roamed the desert, searching for hapless caravans to rob. By the hundreds, the raiders descended from the dunes toward them, shrieking epithets in Arabic.

The Bedouins in the caravan numbered only 20, but they held formidable weapons - AK47's, grenade launchers, rocket launchers and mortars. Even though they were outnumbered, they would still be a formidable fighting force against the raiders.

Yemet wanted a peaceful way out if possible. He could not afford to lose any camels or equipment in a fierce battle. The only chance that Yemet had would be to negotiate with their leader. It would be the symbolic way, and the most reasonable alternative instead of force.

The raiders galloped toward them slowing their gait a bit and spreading their ranks into a long, thin line, and finally slowing their charge to a halt precisely 100 yards from the caravan.

The lead rider cocked a British Enfield and rode his Arabian mount toward Yemet at a trot, his rifle pointed directly at him.

"We are raiders of the desert!" he shouted. "What precious cargoes do you bring to Amman?"

Yemet yelled back, "Friend of the desert, we are not bound for Amman, and we have nothing which might interest you. We carry no gems or metals which can make you rich. Only weapons for our brothers at war with the Jew."

The raider, who had closed the distance between him and Yemet to within 25 yards, eyed him skeptically.

"We shall see for ourselves."

With that, he raised his rifle high into the air and fired a volley. Yemet ordered his men to hold their fire, knowing the shot was merely a signal to the raiders to post position. Ten riders broke rank and galloped toward the front to join their leader.

"Inspect the cargo," the raider ordered.

Yemet let them do so.

The raiders dismounted and searched the camels. When they had finished, they told the raider chieftain what they had found.

"What will you do with these weapons?" he demanded to know.

"My Bedouin brother, we will kill more Jews so that we can once again return to our homelands," he said moving his hands to a prayer-like fold near his face and bowing slightly toward the raider.

"We fight not only for ourselves, but for the benefit of all Arab brothers, so your way of life can continue. If we fail in our sacred mission, the Jew will find and destroy you. Better that we find him first and destroy him before he finds you and does the same. After all, we are both Bedouins. Do you not agree?"

The chieftain remained silent, his Arabian mount snorting at the wind. Suddenly, he motioned with a wave of his rifle and shouted.

"Leave them. Leave them with their precious cargo. It is better to kill the Jew than to kill brother Arabs."

The chief slapped at one of the lead camels with a small whip to turn his Arabian, then straightened to face the other bandits who awaited his orders.

One of the camels, bucked furiously to the raider's

slap, bolting loose from one of the guides. The straps holding the atomic detonators broke under the strain and one of the containers fell to the ground breaking open, exposing the device.

The Bedouins froze.

The equipment was delicate, and Yemet's men scrambled to pick it up and pack it back into the protective lead-lined case. Yemet shouted frantically for them to load the cargo onto the camel and secure it again.

CHAPTER 27

Langley, CIA Headquarters, 7 p. m. June 15.

Overhead, some 25,000 miles in synchronous orbit, an American intelligence satellite, programmed to search for radioactive traces from missile launchers and underground missile silos, came to life. Its sensitive instruments recorded the escaping radiation in the Syrian Desert below.

Cameras activated instantly, focusing on the exact spot where the caravan was situated. Telephoto pictures were being taken and instantly transmitted to the National Security Agency at Ft. Meade, Md., near Washington, D.C. In a soundproof room, a lone military officer keeping a constant vigil at the computer screens, abruptly leaned into the console. He shut off the alarm blasting in his headset.

"Something's coming in from InSat I," he said analytically.

"What is it?" another analyst said joining him at the console.

"I don't know yet. It appears to be some kind of radiation from Sector 23," he said. "It only lasted a few seconds."

"Where's Sector 23?"

"Uhhh . . . somewhere in the Middle East. I think it's Saudi Arabia," clicking on the cross-reference chart.

"Yes, that's right."

"Saudi Arabia? Maybe we'd better have a look?

Turn on the photo receptor."

"There. Right there. It doesn't seem like much. Could be an aberration in background level radiation?"

"No . . . a bit too strong."

"Pinpoint it some more. Focus in on that spot. Right there. Move it to the center a little. What's it look like?"

"Hmmm . . . uhhh . . . still doesn't look like much."

"Try zooming down to five miles. Enhance it with the computer. O.K. Now, what's the reading?"

"464. Wow, that sure as hell isn't background radiation? What the hell could that be?"

"Zoom down farther. Try a mile. What're you showing now?"

"Good God. You're not going to believe it if I tell you."

"Come on."

"Uhhh . . . it looks like a caravan."

"A what?"

"A caravan. A hot caravan. You know as in camels," the officer said.

"What the hell is making them radioactive?"

"You've got me. Think we ought to have a closer look?"

The NSA man was in an awkward moment.

"You know, there ain't a God-damned thing the Arabs got that I'm interested in . . . not their women, their food . . . not anything, except maybe their oil. But, I am interested in radioactive camels. When InSat 3 comes around, fire it up for a closer look."

Three hundred miles out in space, looming fast over the horizon of Saudi Arabia, InSat 3 received an electronic order to photograph and transmit color

261

pictures of the area in question.

The cameras beamed at the precise spot where the radioactivity was emanating. The high-resolution cameras would record anything the size of a thumbnail and could take photographs of a newspaper well enough to read from that altitude. It could also tell whether or not a person was breathing using its infrared equipment.

InSat 3 was indeed remarkable. It could also monitor all types of electronic communications from telephone calls to radio transmissions. It was a superb piece of multi-million dollar military genius placed into orbit by NASA's space shuttle years earlier. The spy satellites could detect underground construction of nuclear test sites in Russia, China or elsewhere. They were the ultimate eye-in-the-sky spies.

The U.S. had 24 of them orbiting the earth one hour apart, each with the capability of being diverted to different orbits and altitudes. This enabled the U.S. to cover virtually any part of the earth for intelligence purposes. The president could order the surveillance of any country in any part of the world at a moment's notice. This is what the nation's defense dollars were being used for. At times like this, everyone in the intelligence loop appreciated their own capabilities.

The NSA day officer swept into the room with a contingent of experts at his side.

"What've ya got, Jim?" he asked positioning himself behind the computer snapping his infrared glasses into place.

"Looks like something hot."

"O.K. How soon do we get a fly-by?"

"We're ready to transmit in 30 seconds."

The screen lit up in front of him. He focused the

infrared glasses and angled the screen to correct for the slightest glare. He didn't want to miss anything the first time around.

As InSat 3 began transmitting the pictures, the NSA officer jerked his head back.

"Holy Jesus! What do you make of that?" he asked incredulously. "The readings match-up to nuclear warheads. 475. Boy, that's sure fucking hot! Christ, I don't believe it. What the fuck are they doing out there in the middle of the Syrian Desert?" he pressed the others.

"Hold on . . . they're moving! They're changing positions!"

"How are they being transported?" the NSA officer asked.

The technical man looked at him.

"You aren't going to believe this."

"C'mon, spit it the fuck out. I haven't got all damned day."

"They're moving them by . . . caravan . . . camels."

The NSA officer swung around in his chair, flipped-up the infrared glasses and looked at him in disbelief.

"What the fuck did you say?"

"I said they're moving them by camels," he shouted back to him with all the seriousness he could muster.

"No shit?"

"No shit . . . " Jim answered.

"Christ, what'll they think of next? He isn't fucking kidding! Get me a closer look. I want to see those fuckin' camels fart radioactivity."

The technician pressed the automated tracking unit.

The Palestine Conspiracy

Visually, the high-resolution cameras whirred down onto its target from the edge of space. As the technician focused, there was absolute silence in the room.

"Jesus H. Christ. Look at them, will ya? Radioactive camels . . . warheads and all. What a way to run a transport unit," the NSA chief said without realizing he was being funny.

"What do you suppose they're going to do with them? Who are they? And, where are they going with them?"

The technician turned, "They're Bedouin. Authentic Bedouin."

"You can tell that from here?" the NSA chief asked. "And, what the hell is a Bedouin?"

"Look closely, they're wearing Keffiyeh's, held in place by a cord. And, besides, they're the only ones I know that carry nuclear warheads by camel," he joked.

The NSA chief's mood turned very serious.

"Where do you suppose they're taking them? Shit, the Arabs aren't supposed to have nuclear weapons. Where in the hell do you suppose they got them?"

"Who in the hell knows? But, there they are. They were bound to get them sooner or later. The readings look like Russian K-3 warheads, but I can't be sure yet. The missile compatibility is designed for a capable range of 500 miles, each carrying one warhead."

"Terrorism is one thing. But, these Arab bastards might want to start a nuclear war somewhere. I'm going to notify the President what we've got immediately. No one in this room is to breathe a fucking word about this to anyone . . . is that clear?"

Nobody in the room had to be told, but they were glad to hear it from the chief, anyway.

The Palestine Conspiracy

The chief ordered prints of the photographs to be delivered within the hour.

"I want tapes of the intelligence data, too, so I can show the president. I really don't think he's going to believe me unless he sees it for himself."

With that, he strode out of the operations room shaking his head, his hand clenched tightly around his notes.

The brief episode had begun in light humor, but now the seriousness of the situation was sinking in on everyone who had just witnessed it.

Something big was brewing in the Middle East.

Something that could take the world to the brink of war.

NSA had to find out what that was?

And, very soon.

CHAPTER 28

Beirut: June 16, the next day. 1:00 p.m.

Adrienne and Ahmed had taken Waite to the same field hospital where they had taken the boy the day before.

The youth had survived, and it was a good place to get medical care for Waite. His fractures and bruises needed immediate attention.

The PLO guard had worked him over pretty good. Waite had paid the price for venturing into the sector alone without telling anyone where he was going.

"We must leave Beirut. It is too dangerous for us here. You must come with us. Ahmed and I have decided that you will join us, and when the time comes, we can write the story after the summit is announced," Adrienne told him.

Waite nodded feebly from his hospital bed.

Still weak and unable to speak, he would do what was necessary if their lives depended on it. Certainly, nothing could stop his tracking down a story as good as this one, especially with so much at stake. Not even his broken nose and fractured face would take him off the scent.

"You know, I'm not supposed to leave here for another week," he managed to utter.

"But you must. We must leave Beirut now. If you stay, your life is in great danger. The Mossad knows you are here. They will try and kill you."

Waite knew what that meant.

The Israeli's didn't fool around once they targeted someone for death. Even though he was still groggy from the painkillers, he knew he had to move right away.

"Then, let's get out of here. We're going to do this in a way that will make the world stand on end."

Adrienne smiled.

Waite stood up from his hospital bed, teetering for a moment, and then regained his balance allowing Adrienne to help him get dressed. Ahmed kept watch in the corridor. He could hear the hospital staff checking on the patients, and he whispered that they would have to move quickly or not at all.

"Quickly!" Ahmed urged from the hallway. "Put pillows under the blankets. Turn out the lights. Now, quickly down the hallway. Hurry!"

Adrienne drew the curtain around Rick's hospital bed to make it look like he was sleeping.

Meanwhile, Rick struggled to get through the doorway moving gingerly down the darkened corridor, dragging his badly injured foot behind him. They left through a side door guarded by three PLO militiamen. If the Israeli agents caught them in the open, there would be a problem.

Still in his officer's uniform, Ahmed ordered the militiamen to stand aside and let them pass. They obeyed immediately.

"Hurry!" Ahmed intoned. "We must hurry! When the doctors find that we have gone, the Israeli agents won't be far behind."

The three moved quickly to a waiting truck. It was nearly dark, now, and Ahmed helped Waite board the vehicle. Adrienne jumped in behind him and quieted his groans. She removed the bandages and administered to his cuts and bruises while the truck started its journey through the streets of Beirut. The doctors had done a decent job. Waite had been lucky. He suffered no other broken facial bones. His nose looked terrible though, all swollen and black-and-blue. Adrienne sponged his face with water from a canteen.

"I always knew I had a hard head," Waite tried to joke.

"Shhh . . . be quiet . . . we have a long way ahead of us," Adrienne scolded.

She knew it would be a long, dusty, hot ride as they crossed the scorching Syrian Desert.

"Where are we going?"

"We are driving to Fasi's base camp on the border near Syria," she answered.

"It will not be dangerous for us there," Ahmed said. "There are no Israelis there to hunt us down. We shall be safe."

Waite breathed deeply and closed his eyes. If that's where they had to go to meet Fasi, then so be it.

Adrienne sponged his face as the rocking motion of the truck put him into a deep sleep. Hours later, he awakened when the rocking motion of the truck stopped.

Placing her hand over his mouth, she intoned, "Not to worry."

Ahmed touched his arm reassuring him, "We're simply taking on more fuel and water. How do you feel?"

"Somewhat better. My head still hurts. Where are

we?"

"We still have many more miles to travel. Sleep as much as you can. It will be several more hours before we reach the camp."

Ahmed lit a cigarette and offered it to Waite. Rick saw Adrienne sleeping, propped-up against the wall of the truck. He knew she was in much torment, but she hadn't shown it yet. He knew it would come out later.

As if reading his mind, Adrienne opened her eyes and looked at him.

"Shall I call you Aminah or Adrienne?"

She reached for the canteen and took a long drink, then offered him some.

"I am Adrienne," she replied without a smile. "For now."

"Whatever you say," he answered. "I'm in your hands, now."

"More importantly, how is your pain?" she asked.

"I'm all right. The sleep felt good. But, it's not my pain I'm worried about."

"How is your pain?"

"I will do what I must. It is already written for me."

"I love you," he whispered to her.

"And I, you."

"Adrienne, there's something I want to ask you."

"What is it?"

"You've lived in England for the past fourteen years. You speak with an English accent, but you're not who you say you are. You're, in effect, an agent for the PLO and working for a large London newspaper, leading a double life. A few days ago, you told me you were living with a British intelligence agent, and now you say you love me? What can I believe?"

"I suppose you don't really have any reason to?"

"That's just it. I don't know anything about you. Only what you have told me, and what I overheard. Why would you fall in love with me? I'm just another encounter along the way in your obsession with the Palestinian issue. Why did you choose me?" he challenged her.

"Rick, you don't have any reason to believe me except the way we both felt when we were alone. We did not plan our encounter. We just happened to be there. Love is that way."

She moved closer to him and put a wet cloth on his forehead.

"I do not pretend that you are one of my people.
But, I noticed something, which attracted me to you from the very beginning. You, like myself, want to see justice and truth. That's why we're both journalists. I like that in myself, and I admire that in you. We are both the same.

"Beyond that, I have heard about your reputation among our people in Beirut. You have the capacity to understand our suffering and keep an open mind about our cause. I know that you cannot sympathize completely with our cause because our people can be just as ruthless as the Israelis when it comes to defending their homeland, one we have yet to re-establish.

"I think it is this open-mindedness and courage which draws me to you. In the end, it does not matter whether we agree or not. I respect you for showing a side of this war which has gone unnoticed for too long by the American press."

Waite leaned over on one elbow and with considerable effort, kissed her on the cheek.

Her eyes welled-up in tears.

"I do love you, Rick."

"And, I love you more than any woman I have ever known. We will see this through together, and in the end, we will survive no matter what happens," he promised.

"Tell me more about your life in the desert?"

Adrienne had anticipated the question knowing that he would want to know.

"I still don't remember too much about that part of my life. I grew up among the Bedouins, and I was fourteen at the time of the plane crash. You already know how I became Necomis' wife. Such a practice is not uncommon among the tribes in the desert in return for an act of kindness. Perhaps, by your own cultural standards, you think of it as uncivilized. But as Bedouins, we think of it as a blending of families. It is Bedouin law. It is as binding to us as western law is binding to you.

"I went into the desert to live the life of a nomad's wife with Necomis' tribe. Several years went by and Necomis accumulated much power and influence in the region. By then, my father had become king and chose Necomis for his military chief because of his shrewdness, loyalty and cunning ability to outthink his enemies. He became an aviator and trained in the United States and Great Britain. He has served my father well. . . and Saudi Arabia equally as well."

Waite tried to absorb it despite the throbbing in his

head. Here was a woman, he thought, whom while merely a child, was taken as a wife by a Bedouin chieftain, taken away to live in the desert, and in only a few years became a member of one of the most powerful families in the history of the Middle East.

"Eventually, Necomis tired of me and sold me in the slave markets in Riyadh after consolidating his power with my father. When I escaped to Cyprus, I became an undercover agent for the Palestinian cause.
I moved to England after an English couple adopted me, and became a journalist winning a Pulitzer Prize on foreign affairs," she reiterated.

The Bedouins had courage all right. It was one of their trademarks. But, how could he be absolutely sure she wasn't using him like the others in Beirut had.

Ahmed climbed back into the truck.

"We are ready to proceed again. I bring sandwiches of roast lamb. You must eat."

Neither of them needed any coaxing. But, before taking a bite, they bowed their heads in prayer giving thanks for the food.

The Bedouins prayed all the time. In actuality, they prayed five times a day. There were morning prayers, noon, afternoon, sunset and final prayers, before retiring. Prayer was an essential part of the Bedouin life, and considered their highest value. Everything in life revolved around prayer.

The Bedouin was expected, during his lifetime no matter where he lived, to journey at least once to the holy cities of Mecca and Medina. The Bedouin would travel thousands of miles for this, pitching his tent in the desert sands with the sides of the tent tethered down for safety. During the day, when the sun was hot, the sides of the tent were rolled up to let the desert winds blow in. The tent itself was waterproofed and provided a sanctuary with several "quata's" dividing it into separate living areas. The quata's were hand-woven fabrics and hung into place dividing the inside

of the tent. Quilts, rugs and blankets were generally stored in the back of the tent, along with leather water bags, and grain for making specialty foods. Coffee, yogurt and dates were staples of everyday life.

The family usually owned a large tin trunk, beautifully painted in an assortment of bright colors that had been handed-down from generation-to-generation. Or, it might have been purchased from a nearby family. If the family had a newborn, the mother would hang a hand-fashioned cradle from the middle of the tent. To Waite, this struck down the misconception by Westerners that the Arabs had little regard for human life.

The Bedouin's entire existence seemed to center around their religion and family. In any case, no matter how strong a believer an Arab was, there was

little of anything else in the desert but prayer, family, and life.

"Amen," Waite said, as he finished the prayer.

The truck lurched forward as they ate the sandwiches and drank the warm tea. After several more grueling hours, they stopped once again at a grove of trees. The driver opened the back of the truck letting in cool, fresh air. Nearby, there was a small stream where they could bathe.

Adrienne helped Waite climb down from rear of the truck. He stood up for the first time since leaving Beirut, carefully leaning against her as they looked out across a beautiful, mostly green valley.

"What is it?" he asked of the beautiful sight.

"It is Jordan. And, over there, Syria. Isn't it wonderful? Beyond, that large expanse of hills is Saudi Arabia and the desert, where I am from."

It was one of the most beautiful natural setting's that he'd ever seen. They had made it this far alive. But, was this enough to die for? As long as he was going to die someday, it might as well be for a good reason. But, the question persisted, was it a valid reason? In the end, it was better to let God make that decision.

"How far?" he asked.

"Perhaps another twenty-five miles," Ahmed was evasive, taught by the terrorists never to give away information to anyone who might be memorizing the location of their secret campsites.

"I've not been to my uncle's camp, either," claimed Adrienne. "I've not seen him since I left Saudi Arabia."

"Then it will be a reunion of sorts?" Waite offered.

"Yes . . . a good word . . . a reunion . . . . a Bedouin reunion of family."

"Do you wish for a nuclear war in the Middle East? Do you want to see Israel destroyed?" Waite asked her.

"My uncle has fought for the Palestinian cause all his life. He cannot stop fighting now."

"That is not the question. What if it means the destruction of BOTH Israel and Palestine?"

"No. I don't think it will come to a nuclear war."

"But, how can you be so certain if Fasi is allowed to assemble those missiles? If we stand by and do nothing, we will be equally as guilty for letting it happen," Waite said, trying to get her to see his point-of-view.

Adrienne already knew that if men were pushed far enough, and long enough, that the unthinkable could happen.

Countries had yet to learn that they could not allow themselves to get to the point-of-no-return where the use of such terrible weapons seemed acceptable. Could the warlords be trusted to avoid that ultimate decision?

The United Nations and the League of Nations could not reconcile the differences in nearly 100 years. What made them think that they could now? World opinion didn't matter much, either. In fact, world opinion often worked to the detriment in many instances, fueling the hatred and animosities.

Certainly, instant access to news inflamed the process.

When events dictated a retaliatory response by another country, the news media was unremitting in its capacity to transmit the wrong idea or thought to the opposite end of the globe either by intention or by accident.

Such international events were extremely volatile when saving face was considered a valuable asset.

Sometimes, leaders just needed time.

And, the pressure of instant communication did not allow that.

That's why journalists were so dangerous.

CHAPTER 29

Haifa: June 16. 8:00 p.m.

The computer siren wailed an alert that a message of special importance was being transmitted from the United States.

The Israeli technician leaned over the laser printer as it began printing-out the message in code for deciphering. He switched on the decoding software and read the text.

"Washington: June 16, 1989 - 12:01 p.m. EST. NSA - Nuclear detonators confirmed inside Saudi Arabia. STOP. Destination believed PLO near Damascus. STOP. Purpose unknown. STOP. Satellites confirm missile-sites being readied near Syrian-Jordanian border. STOP. President Burrell has been informed and requests urgent phone conference via secure line with your prime minister. STOP. Iraqi military detected mobilizing air force and naval units for attack against Saudi Arabia oil refineries and oil tankers. STOP. American 8th fleet placed on full alert. STOP. If Saudi Arabia or U.S. navy is attacked, response will be heavy air strikes against military targets in Iraq including Baghdad. STOP. President Burrell will contact prime minister via hotline at 9:30 p.m. Israel time. STOP. End of message. STOP."

The computer operator tore away the printout and sealed it inside a brown unmarked opaque envelope. He transmitted a confirmation code back to NSA that the message had been received, then picked up a telephone and summoned a special courier to take the message to Prime Minister Glaenis. After that, he switched the computer to standby and resumed his watch.

Twenty minutes later, in Tel Aviv, the prime minister opened the intelligence pouch carrying the secret communication from the president. Prime Minister Glaenis switched on a special lamp that emitted a high-pitch audio tone, which could scramble sound waves so they could not be picked up by a hidden listening device.

Then, he read it aloud into a tape recorder set up inside his private study for historical purposes. Glaenis studied the message again as if to make sure it said what it did, and looked at his watch. It was nearly 9 o'clock.

When Defense Minister Prahoe arrived five minutes later out-of-breath, Glaenis read the message again.

"President Burrell is calling at 9:30 p.m. on the hotline," he told Prahoe.

"What did the message say?" Prahoe asked.

The prime minister was grim.

"The United States has evidence that nuclear warheads are now at this moment being delivered to the PLO inside Saudi Arabia, and that they have lost the radioactive track. Also, there is additional evidence that Iraq is going to attack Kuwait, and Saudi Arabian oilfields and loading facilities in Dhahran."

The words of the prime minister rendered Prahoe nearly speechless! He slumped back into a chair near the Prime Minister's desk.

"My God! Are they mad!" Prahoe said unable to contain himself at that point. The threat to Israel was paramount.

The prime minister's arms hung limp after he handed the message to Prahoe to read for himself. Prahoe took several minutes to absorb the full impact of the text.

"So, they have succeeded in obtaining nuclear weapons. We knew this day would come sooner or later. I would have preferred not in my lifetime. Will they stop at that or do you think they will use them Mr. Prime Minister?"

"Israel must assume they will."

"Do you think the Americans know about the meeting with Fasi and Thayer?"

"No. We haven't shared that with them yet," Glaenis said.

Prahoe interjected, "How far do you think the U.S. will go to defend Saudi Arabia? Can we count on them to defend Israel, too?"

"The implied message is that they will destroy Baghdad if it comes to that. As for the American hostages in Lebanon, they will be sacrificed, but it will be at a horrendous price to Iraq. That is my interpretation. We will know more after we talk with President Burrell."

"What do we do for now?" Prahoe asked.

Glaenis stared down at his desk.

"After we speak with the president, I want a secret session immediately with the members of the Knesset to discuss the immediate threat to Israel. Inform all military commanders that I want to meet with them immediately afterward to discuss the full implications of what our response will be to any nuclear attack."

"What will you say to the American president?"

"When he calls, I will listen to any new facts in the situation. I want to know how serious the United States is regarding the threat to Israel."

Prahoe cut himself off. He didn't want to influence the prime minister anymore until after he heard what the president had to say. But, he still managed one question.

"Do you think it could mean a nuclear response by the U.S. against Iraq?"

The prime minister answered cautiously.

"It would take an extreme set of circumstances against the U.S. naval presence for it to escalate to that. But, then, there's also the Russian presence. What would their response be? How would they react? Would they come to the aid of Iraq? They had been allies in the past and still remain friends."

Prahoe got the point.

It was a critically dangerous situation.

He unconsciously tried again to read the prime minister's position.

"What would our response be to the PLO if they attacked us with nuclear weapons?"

Glaenis leaned forward on both elbows and clasped his hands. He knew what Prahoe was after.
But, he didn't answer. Instead, he let the silence fill the room.

"Listen carefully at the Knesset meeting, then we'll both know."

They had to wait another twenty minutes for the president's call.

Then, Glaenis picked up his secure link to the Israeli Intelligence Chief at his home.

"Can you get here, immediately?" he said. "An urgent phone call from the U.S. president is coming over in twenty minutes. We want you to hear it."

Glaenis hung up the telephone.

"We'll, of course, use the voice scrambler, when the president calls," Prahoe said without realizing he'd said it.

"Would you like a cigarette, Mr. Prime Minister?"

Glaenis had quit smoking five years earlier. With a sigh of capitulation, he knew the situation called for one.

"All right, my friend, I'll join you this one last time."

They both smoked and waited. And, waited some more.

There was nothing else to do.

CHAPTER 30

Fasi's PLO base camp near the Syrian-Lebanese border: June 17. 7:00 a.m.

The trio of Waite, Adrienne and Ahmed sweltered inside the truck as the desert sun angled higher in the sky.

The truck bumped along the narrow, dusty, rocky road. They braced themselves by clutching the sides. The driver worked the truck perilously close to the edge of an overhang, its tires grabbing the ledge as it left the Lebanese border and trundled into Syria.

"It will be a little more dangerous now, but Fasi's men know we are coming," the driver shouted through a rear portal in the cab over the noise of the motor.

"How much farther?" Waite yelled back. His forehead throbbed as he spoke.

"Another eleven kilometers," the reply came in a thick Bedouin accent.

Adrienne felt relieved. It had been a long, hot, tiring journey. The heat inside was stifling. There were no windows for security reasons, and little ventilation, even with the back flap of the truck pulled up. To be exposed to the direct sun would have been worse.

Outside, the blazing sun bore down on them and heated the inside of the truck to more than 115 degrees. They couldn't stay inside much longer as the perspiration and body stench was making them sick. They hadn't traveled much during the afternoon

281

because of it. It had taken them more than two days and two nights to reach this point. Tired as they were, they found renewed energy now that the end of the journey was in sight. Soon, this hell would come to an end, and a new one would begin. Soon, they would meet Fasi.

Exhausted as he was, Waite was anxious for the meeting. He had to see firsthand just what Fasi's state of mind was. With only a few miles to go, Waite could feel his adrenaline pumping as he mentally prepared himself for the meeting.

It had been several years since his interview with Fasi. He hadn't known then that Fasi was Ahmed's uncle. But, he had appreciated the favor just the same. He appreciated being alive even more.

Here was a chance to do something constructive. It was hard to imagine, a more difficult challenge facing a journalist with the kind of knowledge he had in his possession. He had an opportunity to change history. If he had learned anything worthwhile at the School of Journalism at Kent State University, he was damned sure going to put it to the test.

It sure wasn't Journalism 101. It was the real thing.

The truck plied along the narrow roadway and came to an abrupt stop at a PLO checkpoint. There had been several such delays along the way, but this one was different. Waite knew in his gut they had arrived.

There was much excitement outside the truck. Militiamen shouted orders to the driver.

Waite bolted upright.

"We're here," Adrienne broke the silence inside the truck. Her voice trembled with the anticipation of seeing her uncle for the first time in fifteen years.

The Palestine Conspiracy

"What will I say to him, Ahmed?"

"Speak as you wish, but speak the truth," he counseled. "He will want to know more about your activities in England. You must tell him everything you know."

"Yes," Adrienne said. "I shall. Allah be praised."

"Everything?" Waite interjected.

"Yes, all."

"But, he already knows everything. It's his plan," Waite said.

Adrienne looked away.

Was there more to know?

The soldiers opened the bottom gate of the truck and ordered everyone off. The sunlight was so bright it nearly blinded them as they crawled out from beneath the greenish-brown tarp.

Waite surveyed the situation squinting across to a hillside. He could not believe what he saw. Encamped on a hillside were more than 27,000 Bedouin soldiers dressed in military fatigues blending into the terrain. They wore the PLO insignia on their sleeves.

Alongside the dunes were several large Bedouin tents, their canvases flapping in the desert breeze. A flag flew over the largest tent, Adrienne and Ahmed spotting it at once.

They turned and hugged each other, then fell to their knees and gave thanks for a safe journey.

"What flag is that?" Waite asked.

"My dear friend, it is the flag of Palestine . . . the flag of freedom."

Ahmed and Adrienne were in tears.

They knew what it meant - the re-establishment of a

homeland, a free and independent Palestine, and a place for them to finally live and raise their families in peace.

It would be a homeland for the thousands of Palestinian refugees forced from their homes by the Israelis.

"But, why are they here?" Waite asked.

"The Fasi-Thayer summit is a month away."

Neither Adrienne nor Ahmed would answer him right away.

Ahmed finally did.

"No," replied Ahmed. "The meeting is tomorrow. At this very moment in the United Nations, King Fasaid is announcing a peace initiative with the British U.N. representative detailing what will take place here tomorrow. The entire world will be informed at that time."

"But you said I would be able to break the news story through my bureau in Damascus. You can't do this. I trusted both of you."

"It was not up to me. But, you will still have your chance to break the story worldwide. In a matter of a few hours, UPI newsmen from Damascus will be here to film arrangements for tomorrow's historic meeting. Fasi hasn't disclosed to them exactly what is happening, but they will learn soon enough upon their arrival. The U.N. announcement will take place this afternoon. Your story will air tomorrow at noon," Ahmed explained. "So you see, I have kept my promise."

"What about the nuclear strike?" Waite asked. "What happens if the world rejects the entire plan? What will Fasi do then?"

"You may ask Fasi for yourself," Ahmed said. "Come. It is time to meet him."

The Palestine Conspiracy

Things were beginning to happen now. Ahmed guided Adrienne and Waite over to the large tent and stepped past the PLO guards.

He bowed toward the Koran placed just inside the entranceway. Adrienne did the same. Waite looked past a quata to see several PLO soldiers and aides. Fasi was nowhere in sight. The trio walked to the center of the tent and waited. It was refreshingly cool. It was amazing how simple airflow could alleviate the desert heat. A Bedouin tent was designed in such a way to keep the cool air circulating along the outer tent walls and downward while letting most of the hot air escape through open roof flaps.

Suddenly, the guards snapped to attention.

The atmosphere changed instantly the moment Fasi entered the room with his bodyguards.

Ahmed stepped forward, with Adrienne, the obedient Bedouin princess, a step behind.

Waite did not know what to expect.

Perhaps, Fasi would recognize him. The scene unfolding before him was almost surreal.

"Uncle!" cried out Adrienne.

She embraced him, as did Ahmed. The three huddled alone for a moment reciting a Bedouin prayer. Waite instantly recognized it as the prayer Ahmed had recited when he was wounded.

With tension mounting, Fasi turned to Adrienne.

"Why did you wait so many years to return to Palestine?" he gestured toward the Palestinian flag draped inside the tent.

"Uncle," Adrienne offered. "I have been working for the Palestinian people in England all these years. I could not make myself known to anyone, until I was ready."

Ahmed interjected.

"Uncle Fasi, you know from my reports in Beirut that the cause is going well. Our intelligence units have kept the Israelis at bay, the same techniques I learned while working with the American CIA."

"Well, then. What news do you have for me on the eve of the most important meeting of mankind?"

"I wish for the three of us to talk with you alone, without any advisors present. I have something to tell you that even the most trusted of our aides cannot hear."

Fasi turned away from Ahmed and approached Waite.

He looked at Waite.

"I know this man. He is the American reporter from Beirut, is he not?"

Waite was impressed.

Here was a man who met thousands of people every year, and he remembered a lowly UPI reporter who had interviewed him once. Fasi had a good memory. He had not forgotten.

"I interviewed you on the issue of Palestinian rights in the West Bank. Did you like the article?"

"Yes and no," Fasi answered. "It was the first time anyone . . . any western reporter had given a true account of the facts from our viewpoint. You represented us fairly. For that I thank you. But, it is not that story which impressed me about you."

"What is it, then," Waite stammered.

"It is what you have done for my people in Beirut. I thought Americans hated all Arabs. You have shown me a different kind of American. I have heard of this reporter who saved the life of a little boy risking his own life under Israeli mortar fire. Why did you do this? Now, I am the curious reporter, eh?" Fasi quizzed.

"Yes, I am that man. I don't believe in your cause like the others. But, I believe it in part . . . that the children of Palestine have a birthright to a homeland, a right to live in peace, and a right to co-exist with Israel inside and alongside its borders. I believe children of all races should be given a chance to grow and prosper in peaceful surroundings. I acted out of an instinctive mercy for that boy. He was wounded and dying. I could not stand by and let that happen if I knew I could possibly change it. I would have done the same for an Israeli child."

Fasi understood the emotion in that.

He had been a child of the desert. He had felt the same desperation for a homeland.

"Uncle," Ahmed interrupted. "We must be alone. Time is at a premium. We must speak now."

"Leave us," he instructed his bodyguards. "I do not wish to be disturbed until the noon hour passes."

They sat down upon a large Bedouin rug at the center of the tent. Fasi instructed his aides to serve his guests the traditional Bedouin meal of yogurt made from the camel's milk, ghee, roast lamb, dates and unleavened bread served from a communal platter.

"Now tell me, what news have you to report?"

"Uncle, I have learned that you are prepared to use nuclear weapons against Israel if the peace initiative does not go as planned. I implore you to reconsider on this tactic," Adrienne pleaded true to her word. "Such an attack can only doom the people of Palestine."

The Palestine Conspiracy

"I understand your concern, my dear Adrienne," Fasi said. "But do you understand that for the first time in 60 years, all Arabs are finally united on this issue. We have agreed to establish a country of Palestine from our own lands, taking none from Israel. Never before have all Arabs agreed to anything like that among themselves. It will be the first Palestine since the Balfour Declaration of 1920, which ended in disaster in 1947. Egypt, Jordan, Syria, Saudi Arabia, Lebanon, Iraq, Libya, Morocco, Tunisia, Sudan, Ethiopia, Kuwait and Oman have all agreed to it. And, even some in Israel probably would agree to the notion.

"It is historical in precedent. Our Arab brothers have united on all fronts to defeat the Zionists. Tomorrow, we will achieve our objectives in the United Nations. But, if we fail to convince the world, then we will defeat Israel on the battlefield with nuclear weapons. I am committed to it. Our missiles are armed at this very moment.

"We have tricked Israel. We have tricked the Americans. And, we have kept it a secret from the English prime minister. The only American who knows of this is you, Mr. Waite, as of this very moment. If you could do something, what would you do?"

Fasi was direct.

"I understand the frustration the Arab people have experienced. You say these lands belong to Palestine. Perhaps so, but they equally belong to the Jew. The Palestinians and the Jews were once of the same family. In blood, they still are. The tree trunk remains strong with many branches reaching outward," Waite argued.

"The water feeds these roots from many

288

surrounding nations. The roots stretch deep underground and into the Nile, into the Jordan River, into the Tigris River, into Syria and into Saudi Arabia. If you attack with nuclear weapons, you give Israel no choice but to retaliate in kind. The Middle East would be doomed to destruction."

Waite paused, and asked Fasi.

"How did you acquire the nuclear missiles?"

"That is no concern of yours," Fasi replied. "The point is that we have them, and we will use them unless Israel acquiesces to our demands for a free and independent Palestine."

"You have moved up your timetable, Fasi," Waite pressed him.

"What do you mean?" Fasi countered.

"What I mean is that it has taken the Palestinians some 2000 years to get to this point, what difference can a few more weeks or months make?"

Fasi stirred uneasily, angered at what Waite was implying. Waite could see that Fasi was not the same man he'd interviewed three years earlier.

"Mr. Waite, I respect you for what you are and what you have done for my people. You have shown at times a genuine fairness. But, what is done has already been done for a reason. I do not seek anyone's approval in order to do this."

"Not even Allah's?"

"That is correct.""

"But, that is blasphemous, Mr. Fasi."

"What is blasphemous to one man is not to another. It is all in the interpretation."

My God. He was insane. Men like him were rare. Such men could be great leaders, but they could be driven to self-destruction and in the process destroy much of the world. Such men had to be stopped. He knew it was paramount that Adrienne and Ahmed work with him to stop Fasi. But, would their loyalties allow that?

"Our father, King Fasaid, brought us out of the desert so our people could exist in a modern world free from oppressors," Ahmed said. "The oppressor in the Middle East is Israel. Israel will continue to be an oppressor as long as they continue to annex new territories by military means. The very existence of Arab culture is threatened to extinction if it continues. Uncle Fasi is correct in his assessment. The people of Palestine may have no choice if the treaty fails."

The logic stung at Adrienne.

"Uncle Fasi," she said, "You and my father have always provided guidance . . . you have given me life . . . and life to my brothers and cousins . . . but you cannot continue to live in the old ways. That is not enough today. We live in a modern world, yet much of the Middle East is not modern. Lebanon has been destroyed as a result of old worn-out policies, which have kept us at war with Israel for 60 years.

"It was my father who gave me away to Necomis in the desert when I was merely a child. It was my father who banished me to a man I never loved, a man I had never seen before, because of an old worn out tradition. It wasn't kindness in return for kindness. I was a sacrifice to perpetuate a way of life. I never saw my mother again, nor my brother, Akram, because of this foolish thing. Tell me, how great are the Arab people when they condemn women like me?"

The Palestine Conspiracy

"Silence, woman!" Fasi shouted preparing to strike her with his hand.

Waite quickly leaped up to protect her.

The move caught Fasi by surprise and he dismissed Waite's actions with a simple shrug.

Waite knew he could count on Adrienne's help if he needed it to stop her uncle. It was only a question of when and where.

Ahmed, who had sided with his uncle, would prove more formidable.

The die had been cast.

It would be Adrienne and he against Ahmed and Fasi.

The reunion broke apart angrily with Fasi leaving them alone to finish supper. The move was unprecedented even for a Bedouin, who could generally disagree with a guest while sharing a meal with him; yet keep him at ease with a courtesy not to disagree.

His sudden departure signaled distrust.

Several hours later, Ahmed left to join Fasi.

Waite crouched inside his tent and wondered what to do next. The meeting would take place tomorrow at noon. He had learned that Mrs. Thayer would arrive via Damascus then journey to the camp by helicopter to join the Arab leaders in signing the pact. Where were the missiles hidden?

He had to speak with Adrienne about them. If they could locate them, perhaps there was a chance they could destroy them before Fasi's technicians could launch them.

Waite walked outside and over toward the separate tent where he knew Adrienne was staying. Several guards stopped him at the entrance. He told them that

Fasi had given him permission to visit with her. They let him pass. He was feeling stronger now, nearly recovered from his wounds. He pushed aside the tent flap and entered.

Adrienne, lying on the floor, arose immediately and embraced him. They both sensed what had to be done.

"Adrienne, we've got to locate those missiles. If we can't destroy them, then we must reveal their existence to the world."

She knew he was right.

"What do you propose we do?"

"The UPI bureau crew from Damascus has just arrived. The men are staying over in the tent at the far side of the camp. They don't know I'm here yet. I've got to locate the missiles and tell them what is going to happen. If we can film and transmit the pictures of the missiles with their warheads ready for attack against Israel, it will shock the world. It may not stop Fasi, but it will galvanize world opinion against him. At the very least, it will warn Israel of the impending attack."

"It is a good plan. We must make it work, even though I feel like a traitor to my own cause."

"Look, if your uncle attacks Israel, there won't be any cause. Nor a Palestine. Without your help, all the well-intentioned spying for your people will have gone for naught."

As they left the tent, Fasi's guards followed them. They must get rid of them, Waite figured. But, how?

Suddenly, he was holding Adrienne in his arms and kissing her. That unusual display of public affection in an Islamic country clearly embarrassed the guards. They shuffled uneasily as the two continued to kiss and nuzzle each other in the moonlight. Adrienne followed Waite's lead.

Waite reached into his pocket and offered the guards each an American cigarette. Then, gave them the entire pack. They were pleased by the gesture, even if it was by an American. Waite tried to speak to them but they could not understand him.

Adrienne covered Waite's mouth and spoke to the soldiers in Arabic. The two men said something and laughed. To Waite's surprise, they departed leaving them quite alone. Adrienne smiled at Waite and nodded with a wink - an idiosyncrasy she had learned from him.

"What did you say to them?"

"I simply told them that we wanted to be intimate. That even Fasi would see no harm in that."

She was good.

Now they could look around the camp for the missiles. They searched one end of the camp to the other encountering little resistance as they walked along with their arms around each other. They approached an area of the camp more heavily guarded than Fasi's personal tent.

"This must be it," he whispered, nuzzling her ear as they approached the guards.

The guards immediately challenged the two.

"Why can't we stroll here?" Adrienne asked in Arabic.

"No one is allowed here. It is forbidden," the first sentry said.

"But why . . . it's a beautiful part of the camp?" she demanded.

"That doesn't concern you," the soldier answered.

Waite tugged and pulled her away.

"That's it all right."

Waite could feel the tension mount inside him as they walked away from the guards. Now, they must contact the UPI reporter pool from Damascus. That should be easy enough. Just find out where the most noise was coming from in the camp. Radios. Yelling. Cursing.

As they neared the reporter's tent, they heard a voice call to them from the darkness.

"Pssstt. Over here, Waite. What the hell are you doing wandering around at this time of the night? Do you want to get shot? And, just what the hell are you doing in Syria?"

It was Joe Glazer from the Damascus bureau.

"Boy, are you a sight for sore eyes," Waite said greeting him with a solid handshake.

"Yeah, so are you old buddy. How are things in that rat's nest, Beirut?" Glazer asked as if he already didn't know. "Fasi told us you were inside the camp. What the fuck is going on?"

"You heard about my bureau boys in Beirut?"

"Yeah, Christ. It was pretty gruesome I understand. What the hell happened?"

"We really don't know except we suspect it was the work of the Mossad."

"Israeli intelligence? Why in the hell would they do something like that?"

"It's a long story, and I don't have time to explain. But, we need to talk fast before we're discovered together. There are some important things about to happen here which you aren't aware of. I'll fill you in as

The Palestine Conspiracy

much as I can because we're going to need your help,"
Waite whispered to him.

"Any listening devices in your tent?" Waite asked
him.

"None that we could find," Glazer said indicating
such routine searches by his crew were commonplace.

The crew gathered around after Waite made the
introductions. At first, they were skeptical, but Glazer
knew from Waite's solid reputation as a journalist that
he would not bullshit them.

"How fast can you set up your equipment tomorrow
morning? Can you be ready to transmit once we get
inside the missile base?"

"Are you kidding? For a story like this, we'll be
ready. The signing ceremony is set for noon. We can
do a simultaneous broadcast within two minutes after
you begin rolling the tape showing the missiles. I can
page New York via satellite phone that we're
interrupting for a special bulletin."

"How about the satellite dish? Is it ready?" Waite
asked.

"It's already hooked into the New York feed. All
you have to do is aim the microwave gun toward the
dish antenna and transmit a few hundred feet to it. It
automatically beams the signal up to the satellite, and
hotter than piss on a cold night, you're in New York."

"Sounds good," Waite said. "But, we'll need an
excuse to get into the missile site. Adrienne, do you
think you can handle Fasi?"

She was impressed that Waite would trust her to
be alone with Fasi. She would not disappoint him.

"I think I can convince him that I've had a change

of heart."

"O.K. I want to time it when there are a minimum number of guards near the missile site. The best time should be right before Thayer and the Arab nations are signing the treaty. We can get into the base, interrupt the regular broadcast as the signing is taking place, and do a live remote via satellite warning about the nuclear threat."

"Sounds risky, but O.K.," Glazer said. "You know, you could both be killed when Fasi's men get to you . . . once they realize what has happened."

"Yeah, we'll be living on borrowed time," Waite said matter-of-factly. "Well, life is risky anyway isn't it? Adrienne, do you still want to do it?"

"I have no doubts. We're in this together from the beginning," she answered.

"Can you operate the camera?" he asked her.

"Yes, I've used that type before. They're standard bureau equipment, right?"

He knew he could count on her once this thing got started.

The plan was for Adrienne to talk Fasi into letting them see the missiles. Waite would kill the guards if he had to using the silencer on his 9mm he had smuggled into camp. Most of the camp's attention would be focused on Mrs. Thayer's arrival and Fasi. A special hospitality tent had been set up for the signing ceremony. Mrs. Thayer and the Arab leaders would watch the U.N. special telecast announcing their historic meeting.

Everything was planned precisely in advance with King Fasaid at the United Nations.

If Waite had calculated right, Fasi's and everyone's

attention would be diverted by the special coverage and he could do his work.

But, they would have to work quickly and efficiently, and they would have only one crack at it.

They broke up the meeting and agreed to meet the next day at 11 a.m.

* * *   * * *

The next day: 11:00 a.m.

They waited in Glazer's tent for Adrienne to do her part with Fasi.   Waite was becoming impatient. Where was she? What was taking so long?

The crew was readying the equipment for the broadcast.   They beamed the satellite dish to the northwest quadrant of the sky and locked it into place for the feed to New York.

This aroused no suspicion.

They had to set up for Mrs. Thayer's arrival anyway.

"Where is Adrienne?" Waite asked worriedly. "She's taking far too long."

"Shhh!   She's coming now," Glazer answered, peeking through the tent flap.

Adrienne entered the tent with a thumbs up.

"I told him Palestine comes first above all, but that I had to see the missiles for myself before I would help. He's instructed the guards to let me pass."

"How do we get the equipment through the gates?"

"Let me worry about that," Adrienne said. "I will tell the guards that Fasi has ordered historical film footage to be taken of the missiles.   They will not

297

question the niece of Fasi."

Waite nodded.

It was a long shot, but this whole thing had been one big long shot from the very beginning. Anyway they had no choice. Time was running out.

"Is Thayer on time?" Glazer asked one of his news team.

"Yes, she'll be arriving in just under ten minutes," he answered.

"Good. So far so good. Everyone check their watches. One minute after they sign the agreement, we'll cut into the broadcast with a special bulletin," Waite explained.

"Joe, inform the network in New York that something especially urgent will be coming over the feed, and that we might have to interrupt the U.N. broadcast with a bulletin from the live coverage from here. O.K.?"

"Gotcha," Glazer said, picking up the cellular telephone connecting him with the satellite.

"We're all set-up here. You'd better get started on your end. Good luck, Rick," Glazer wished as he shook hands with Waite.

Adrienne and Waite grabbed the portable mini-cam and set-off for the other side of the camp where the missiles were located.

Glazer whispered a last minute reminder to Waite.

"For God's sake, don't forget to aim the micro-gun directly at the center of the dish first thing to lock-in the signal. Use the tripod. It's steadier than the hand-held, and will transmit a better signal."

Waite waved him off lugging the special equipment on his shoulders.

The Palestine Conspiracy

Adrienne followed right-on-his-heels, like a Bedouin princess, with the camera.

CHAPTER 31

Aboard Royal Air Force 1: The same day. June 17. 11:35 a.m.

Mrs. Thayer propped her feet up on the special footrest next to her seat. She had finished correcting her speech earlier in the flight and needed the time to rest before she reached Damascus before taking the helicopter flight to Fasi's base camp in the Syrian Desert.

This was a special moment in British-Arab history. She had summoned an aide to arrange official photographers so they could film the historic signing. It was a gutsy, politically strategic move. But, she had made such moves before.

Britain would go it alone, something it hadn't done in nearly fifty years, in an attempt to alter a stagnating foreign policy that was going nowhere in the Middle East.

With the agreement in hand, Britain would establish a naval base in Beirut, at Basra, Iraq, and once again in Suez. It would establish the British philosophy of dealing with problems in the Middle East on a non-confrontational basis. In return, the Arabs would guarantee a continued flow of oil to Britain, Scandinavia and Western Europe.

These were her political objectives; her personal objectives were far different. If she succeeded, then history would judge her as one of the most effective prime ministers of all time. If she failed, history might record that she had made the effort.

"Mrs. Prime Minister, we will land in Damascus in five minutes. The trip by helicopter to Fasi's secret base will take another ten minutes," the aide informed her.

"Thank you. Have my escorts stand by, please."

She readied herself for the landing and checked her notes one final time.

It would be a great moment in world history.

And, as usual, she was fully prepared for it.

CHAPTER 32

New York: The United Nations. 4:00 p.m.

The gavel sounded at the special meeting of the Security Council.

Television work crews had been standing by since five o'clock that morning. A crowd had been on hand since early afternoon waiting to be seated in the gallery.

Everyone sensed that something extraordinary was about to happen. Delegates were already filing into their seats for a 7 p.m. announcement of utmost urgency.

The gavel sounded again as delegates milled around the tables speculating on the reason for another special session so soon after the first one. As they located their seats, their attention was drawn to the general-secretary from Switzerland getting ready to speak. TV crews moved perfunctorily down the aisles, efficiently positioning themselves to record the reactions of the U.N. delegates.

"Ladies and gentlemen of the United Nations General Assembly," began Vensberg. "I have called a special session of all United Nation members this evening to hear a most urgent announcement from the governments of Saudi Arabia and Great Britain."

The U.S. representative leaned forward on his elbows, clasping his hands, transfixed by the unfolding drama. What could they be announcing that they hadn't communicated to the U.S. government?

The Palestine Conspiracy

"I introduce to you King Fasaid of Saudi Arabia and the Ambassador of Great Britain, Sir George Handley."

The secretary-general left the speaker's podium and network cameramen swung into action, their cameras riveted on the two representatives.

Mrs. Thayer, aboard Royal Air Force One, linked by special satellite communication, watched the beginning of the speech from her specially equipped helicopter now approaching the Lebanese-Syrian border.

In Tel Aviv, the prime minister and defense minister watched with the entire Knesset assembled. At the PLO camp, Fasi, Ahmed and his cousins watched in fascination.

King Fasaid stepped toward the microphone, the first to speak.

"My dear delegates and friends of the United Nations General Assembly. I wish to speak to you today jointly with the representative from Great Britain, Sir Handley, about an urgent matter, which has come before this great world body but never solved.

"It is the question of a homeland for the Palestinian people - the soldiers, the refugees and the children of that war.

"Heads of state from seven Middle East nations, which include Egypt, Syria, Iraq, Lebanon, Saudi Arabia, Jordan and Kuwait, all bordering or near Israel, are at this very moment meeting with Palestinian Liberation Organization leader Fasi Etebbe near the Syrian-Lebanese border at a secret encampment where they have gathered to sign a historic pact which will create a new nation of Palestine within specific territorial borders.

"The country of Palestine is to be created from land volunteered for this purpose from five of these countries in the area of the West Bank.

"In exchange for this homeland, the PLO has agreed to take the following steps when the pact is ratified by the United Nations and Israel: (1) to stop world terrorism in the Middle East and throughout Europe and the rest of the free world. (2) to disengage all subversive activities designed to impede the right of Israel to exist in peace, as so long as Israel agrees to the defined legal borders of the newly created Palestine, and (3) Palestine will limit its army to the confines of the territory within its own borders."

A murmur swept through the assembly room. The PLO representative listened intently as the requirements of his people were read.

"At this very instant, broadcast by global satellite, an agreement is being signed by these Arab leaders and the head of a major government from the free world, the Prime Minister of Great Britain, Mrs. Margaret Thayer.

"Mrs. Thayer conceived the peace initiative and proposed it to Chairman Fasi Etebbe.

"I now introduce to you the ambassador of Great Britain with his government's announcement."

The delegates were frozen. Never before had such an agreement been announced simultaneously in front of this world body. The delegates knew the impact would be tremendous. It would put great pressure on them to ratify the pact with the world as witness.

The delegates greeted the British ambassador's

introduction with applause.

"Your majesty, Mr. Secretary-General, delegates and friends of the United Nations . . . my government has instructed me to read the following prepared statement from Prime Minister Thayer:

"I have brought forth this agreement among seven Arab nations in the war zone in the Middle East for the purpose of creating the nation of Palestine.

"The plan is two-fold: First, it will create a homeland for the Palestinian people who deserve to live in peace like the rest of the world's peoples; and secondly, to reverse the tide of world terrorism that has increased on both sides.

"I am asking the government of Israel to support such a move in the interests of world peace and security for everyone in the region.   I am signing this pact with seven other Arab U.N. member nations in the

Middle East today thereby taking what I see as an unprecedented historical step in establishing a peaceful solution to the continuing tragedy on both sides of this terrible war.

"I urge all present in the general assembly room to please view the television screen at the left, and please watch the signing ceremony taking place at this precise moment at Mr. Fasi Etebbe's base camp on the Syrian-Lebanese border. My government will seek your

support for this action on the floor of the assembly hall tomorrow in the form of a binding resolution accepting Palestine into this world body as a nation. Furthermore, the main sticking point from the Israeli side and Palestinian point-of-view, has been Jerusalem.   That problem can be addressed by allowing both countries – Israel and Palestine – to claim Jerusalem as their joint capital. This can be accomplished by using congruous or concentric zones, drawing the boundaries of Jerusalem so that they simultaneously represent the capital of both countries at the same time. That is, when the Israeli's draw their map, it will include the entire boundaries of Jerusalem. And, when the Palestinian's draw their map, it also will be drawn to include the entire boundaries of Jerusalem. A committee from both governments, equally shared in representation, to form a neutral, international open city, where the Knesset and Palestine government bodies can legislate, and can then govern Jerusalem itself. This new Jerusalem would take the form of a

district, much like the District of Columbia, where representatives from the various states govern the United States.

"Think of it. The concept is revolutionary, and has never been attempted in the annals of history. Dual capitals? It would be a first in the history of mankind, unprecedented, and historic. It is brilliant. And, it is the only way to achieve peace. Thank you."

The applause was deafening as the delegates responded with an enthusiasm unseen in the U. N. general assembly.

The British ambassador stepped away from the microphone. The lights dimmed and the network feed from Palestine came onto the giant screen set-up in the assembly room.

The noise level fell to a hush as the delegates watched Mrs. Thayer's personal military helicopter touch down at Fasi's camp. They were captivated by the moment, watching in complete silence at what they were witnessing.

At the encampment, Fasi greeted Mrs. Thayer with a handshake and a polite Bedouin greeting, his head moving side-to-side of her.

The seven Arab leaders emerged from a large adjoining tent for the signing. UPI cameras whirred into action. Photographers clicked away recording every gesture and movement.

Meanwhile, Adrienne and Waite worked their way unnoticed toward the opposite end of the camp and confronted the guards at the missile site.

"We have orders from Fasi, my uncle, to film historical footage of the missiles at the ready. You shall let us pass," Adrienne commanded.

The two soldiers were caught off-guard, but they recognized Adrienne.

"Shall I be forced to call Fasi here himself to verify it?"

Before they could reply, Adrienne, with a sweep of her hand to Waite, pushed past them lugging the television equipment.

She turned once more to the guards and admonished them with instructions.

"Let no one else pass through these gates until we return from our assignment. Is that clear?"

They obeyed the order as though it had been given by Fasi himself.

Adrienne and Waite hurried to the missile site enclosed behind barbed wire jacketed posts and dug into an area, which would protect technicians from the blast of firing the missiles.

Waite could hardly believe his eyes.

The Palestine Conspiracy

Already in place were Pakistani-made Shriek nuclear missiles with a range of 1,500 miles.

The 20-megaton warheads were already in position and armed.

Indeed, the caravan had arrived on time to complete their part of the mission.

Not only could these missiles hit Israel, but they could also reach across the Mediterranean to Turkish-U.S. bases and possibly into the Ukraine.

The thought paralyzed him for a moment.

"Hurry!" Adrienne said, "We must be quick. The broadcast is already underway!"

Recovering instantly, Waite began setting up the equipment as fast as he could. First, the micro-gun to shoot toward the satellite dish some 600 yards away had to be in place, remembering Glazer's words.

"O.K. The tripod is set. The gun is locked-in with 1/2-power. Do you get a reading on your camera?"

"Yes," Adrienne responded quickly, pointing the camera at the missiles on the mobile launchers.

"I'm focused and ready to go."

"O.K. When I get the signal from Glazer, we'll interrupt the broadcast with our own signal. I'm scaling up to full power on the antenna gun."

The red light on Adrienne's camera changed to green, signaling transmission readiness.

"Why are we waiting?" she asked nervously. "I told Glazer to let the world see the signing. We've come this far; we might as well let the world see it for themselves. After Thayer and Fasi give their statements, we'll cut in."

Adrienne rolled her eyes skyward. That wasn't part of the deal, but it was obviously part of Waite's.

The Palestine Conspiracy

"O.K.," she relented. "But they'd better hurry or we're dead."

They waited in the noonday heat for the ceremony to conclude. Minutes were precious. They could not afford to be caught now.

They had come so far to reach this delicate attempt at world peace. Waite pulled out his 9mm just in case he needed it and slammed home the 11-shot magazine.

At the hospitality tent, each Arab leader signed the pact with Fasi signing last. Mrs. Thayer grasped the pen handed to her by Fasi and signed the agreement.

Cameras recorded it as part of Middle East history.

The ceremony was complete except for the speeches.

At the U.N., members spontaneously broke into applause and stood in the aisles. It was a moment of first rank in history.

Fasi was the first to speak.

"My people have fought many, many years to reach this moment. Israel must accept us now. Israel must accept our right to exist with them in the region of Palestine. We ask Israel to join us in this signing tomorrow at the United Nations. Thank you."

Next, Mrs. Thayer spoke.

"Representatives of the United Nations. England has taken a bold new step in an attempt to find a peaceful solution to the 78-year-old problem of the Palestinian issue. It is quite simple. It is a basic need for all people in the world to desire a homeland. Israel understands this.

"It was Israel who helped establish this principle. The great Exodus, which occurred in 1947-48 brought forth a small but great nation. To abandon its responsibilities at a time when we now have a genuine agreement for peace in the Middle East would be to forsake the entire heritage of the region.

"I urge all members of the United Nations, especially the United States and Russia, to endorse and support this measure to its culmination.

"As you now understand, secrecy was of the utmost importance in this process so that progress could be made without public posturing.

"England is now a historical part of this agreement, and will put forth its efforts behind passage of U.N. Resolution #439 to be introduced jointly by Britain and Saudi Arabia at tomorrow's general session.

"To the Prime Minister of Israel, I ask for your support and open-mindedness to move this issue forward to completion. Thank you."

The applause was deafening. The delegates were on their feet with a resounding ovation. The Saudi Arabian king and the British ambassador clasped hands and held them above their heads. News anchors were astonished but standing by for a flash announcement having been notified by the news directors in production vans outside the U.N. building that something important was coming over the feed from the Middle East.

The president, watching the events with top aides in the Oval Office wondered what the hell was up.

At the base camp, Waite's beeper went off.

Glazer had signaled New York, and Waite to begin his broadcast.

Waite brought his microphone to voice level.

"Joe . . . can you hear me?"

"Affirmative. Start rolling whenever you're ready. We're cutting you in on the New York feed. The networks are primed for this and standing by. You're on your own now. Good luck."

Adrienne aimed the camera at Waite who was standing in front of the nuclear missiles. When the green light began flashing indicating she was transmitting a signal back to the United States, she gave Waite the thumbs-up.

Glazer counted down into the headset for Waite . . . "Four . . . three . . . two . . . one . . . go."

In New York, the delegates had returned to their seats after the long ovation, the chairman's gavel echoing throughout the assembly room.

"Quiet please! Quiet please! Please . . . please clear the aisles. Newsmen . . . please clear the aisles so that delegates can return to their seats," Secretary-General Vensberg pleaded.

At that precise moment, the network anchors stating that a special bulletin would be announced within a few seconds interrupted the broadcast feed from the Middle East.

"We have just been handed a message that a special bulletin will be coming over our network from the Middle East involving events you have just witnessed near the Syrian-Lebanese border. Again, we interrupt this program to bring you this special bulletin to be broadcast in a few seconds. Please standby."

The president of the United States swung his chair around in the Oval Office to get a better look at the TV. His intelligence chief edged closer.

"Anything going on in the Middle East that we don't know about?" the president asked the NSA chief.

"Nothing you haven't already been briefed on, sir," he answered crisply.

The Palestine Conspiracy

Suddenly, the color scan was interrupted. The signal was again coming directly from Fasi's camp. Waite stood in front of the missile launchers, as he began his broadcast.

"We interrupt this formal signing of the Fasi-Thayer Arabian-Palestine Peace Pact to bring you this special announcement regarding information we have just uncovered posing the most serious threat in the history of the Middle East.

"I am Richard Waite, a United Press International foreign correspondent stationed out of Beirut. I am standing here inside the base camp of PLO leader Fasi Etebbe where the signing of the treaty has just taken place. Unknown to Mrs. Thayer and the United Nations British delegation, my fellow reporter from the London Times, Adrienne Waters, and I have just discovered a secret plot to launch a nuclear attack against the State of Israel in the event this treaty fails.

"If this treaty is renounced by Israel at the United Nations, PLO leader Fasi Etebbe is prepared to launch these two missiles that you see poised behind me at the cities of Tel Aviv and Haifa. Each warhead carries the destructive power of 20-megatons, roughly 200 times the destructive power of the Hiroshima and Nagasaki atomic bombs.

"Millions of lives are at stake if these weapons are launched. Certainly, Israel would launch a counter-strike against the Palestine region; most probably the cities of Damascus, Beirut, Amman or Riyadh.

"These correspondents uncovered the plot several weeks ago, but we have not attempted to bring this out into the open until we had substantial proof of the missiles existence. Although both reporters covering this incident agree with the integrity of the peace pact, establishing a free and independent Palestine, we by no means agree with the last resort effort of PLO Chief Fasi Etebbe to use nuclear weapons as a final bargaining chip to establish a homeland.

"I must warn the members of the United Nations that at any moment, this broadcast could be interrupted by PLO leader Fasi Etebbe who is watching this broadcast with Mrs. Thayer and the Arab leaders. In the event that we are killed in the process of bringing this urgent message to you . . . we ask . . . "

The television screen in the U.N. assembly room flashed several times when PLO soldiers struggling with Adrienne and Waite interrupted the signal.

Delegates and newsmen at the U.N. could see part of the fight on TV as Waite was wrestled to the ground while Adrienne kept shooting with her camera.   A hush swept over the assembly hall. Such a thing was unthinkable. Nuclear weapons had been delivered into the hands of the PLO.

The U.N. secretary-general struck his gavel once more in an attempt to silence the delegation body. Everyone was scattered into small groups talking to different delegations on what they had just witnessed.

Vensberg announced that another special meeting of the U.N. security council would be held immediately.

Pounding his gavel once more, he ended the special session.   Reporters scrambled to interview individual delegations from the Arab countries involved in the peace proposal.

The Israeli delegation was outraged. In Tel Aviv, Defense Minister Prahoe and Prime Minister Glaenis were grim as they watched with Knesset members.

The Palestine Conspiracy

In the Oval Office there was silence.

"My God, if they fire those missiles, it's World War III," the president said to his NSA chief. "Get Glaenis on the hotline immediately."

* * * * * *

In Palestine, Fasi and Thayer looked at each other in dismay. Thayer had been double-crossed by Fasi on international television. Fasi tried to reassure her that the missiles were purely for defensive purposes. But, she would have no part of it.

Fasi moved quickly as Thayer announced her departure. He ordered thousands of PLO soldiers to seal-off the missile base. Tanks were brought up to protect the perimeter. He asked Syrian President Amal Messih to alert his air force to counter any Israeli air strike. Messih ordered his aide to transmit the alert.

"Bring the American reporter and my niece to me immediately," Fasi ordered. "I want them alive."

Adrienne and Waite had done it. Whether or not they would live to tell about it, they had changed Fasi's plan.

The plot was now out into the open. The whole world now knew what had been going on in the Middle East.

Let the world deal with it now.

They had done the heavy lifting.

The PLO soldiers bound both of them by their hands and took them to Fasi's tent.

"Aminah . . . you have betrayed your own people!" Fasi screamed at her as the guards dragged her into the tent.

The Palestine Conspiracy

"It was a great moment in Palestinian history and you ruined it all!"

"Better to lose the dream this way, uncle, than to lose it forever," Adrienne countered.

"You little infidel. You are a traitor to Palestine!" he shouted.

"No uncle, you are the real traitor. Perhaps, we have saved Palestine from annihilation."

"You have not saved Palestine, fool woman. You have saved Israel!"

"Ridiculous! There need be no war!"

"Stupid, Aminah. You always were rebellious! But, I can still launch the missiles if I choose. There is more than enough time to destroy Israel."

"You are insane!" she shouted, struggling to free herself.

Fasi was in a sheer rage. He could order them killed at any time.

"You must reassure the world that your missiles will not be used against Israel," Waite said. "Britain won't dare trust you unless you issue an apology, and turn those weapons over to the United States. They won't just stand-by and let this happen. Your people will be destroyed, along with them the dreams of a Palestinian homeland."

"Never! Let Israel tremble. They must agree or be destroyed!" Fasi screamed like a fanatic. "You will be executed for this in the morning!"

"What do you suppose your father thinks of what you have done today?" Waite asked her.

"I don't believe King Fasaid had any part in this. He does not seek to destroy Israel. He only knew of the peace plan and that alone. I am sure he is stunned by our announcement."

"So David did meet Goliath," Waite said. "Only this time, everyone will lose."

"Not quite," a voice spoke from outside the tent.

In walked Ahmed, and another person - General Necomis.

Adrienne nearly fainted with fear. Rick held her close to him as Necomis approached.

"What is the meaning of this?" Adrienne shouted at Fasi.

"Be still. We are going forward with our plan to destroy Israel tomorrow morning. The attack goes forward as planned. Necomis himself will direct it."

CHAPTER 33

At the Lebanon-Syrian border: June 17. 2:00 p.m.

Israeli agents infiltrated into eastern Lebanon then crossed the Syrian border under the cover of darkness carrying Uzi's and several satchels loaded with Semtec.

The Czechoslovakian-made explosives were lethal and packed enough punch to blow up the entire camp.

Dressed in black-hooded masks with matching uniforms that made them almost impossible to be seen in darkness, the three set-up up a reconnaissance position to observe the stronghold from a safe distance. They hid at the base of a cave along the roadside where they could get a good view of Fasi's campsite, and began making preparations for the assault.

Israeli military intelligence had learned of the camp's presence only a few weeks ago from American NSA. Now, their objective was to blow up the missiles and neutralize the nuclear warheads.

Moshe peered through his binoculars along the ridgeline toward the encampment, some two miles away. He pulled the cord tightly around his neck to steady the special night binocs, Stargazers used by American and Israeli army special forces.

It was a far cry from his eavesdropping assignment in London. That was a piece of cake compared to this. But, he had wanted some real live action, even lobbied to get it. There would be no boredom tonight. He

317

would see plenty of action when they went in for the attack.

"My friend, what do you make of all the activity around the missile site? According to our intelligence, the PLO had posted only a few guards around the camp," Moshe commented.

Nooka looked through the stargazers and was astounded at how brightly they illuminated the target and the amount of detail he could see through them.

"Several hundred, maybe close to a thousand troops around the perimeter. Impossible to penetrate with just the three of us," he said. "It will be suicide."

"Nothing is impossible if you're an Israeli," Moshe replied. "We will have to adjust our plans for the attack. But, we will succeed. Contact Gen. Sharn to direct an air strike against the north end of the camp as a diversion."

"Why not just knock out the missiles with our fighter-bombers?"

"My friend, we cannot be sure the missiles aren't already armed. If the warheads explode, everything in a 5-mile radius will be destroyed by the blast and deadly radiation will surely follow. Our own people would be affected by the fallout," Moshe explained.

"Once we get inside the compound, we can disarm the detonators rendering the warheads harmless, then we can destroy the missiles with the plastic explosives."

"Do you think we will survive?" the third Israeli sapper asked.

"My friend, there may be only one time in your entire life, however short that may be, that Israel will ask you to do something to save our people, perhaps even save the State of Israel itself. This is that moment

318

in time. There is a good possibility you may even die tonight, but you still cannot refuse. This is a special moment in your own personal history of what it means to be a Jew. It must be done. And, we must be the ones to do it. Do you understand?"

Both understood.

Moshe knew better. He knew they had already become heroes of Israel. He was proud of what they would do tonight.

Nooka got on the radiophone to Israeli intelligence in Haifa and gave the go-ahead for the attack, articulating the coordinates from the computerized readings on his range-finding binoculars. The coordinates had to be exact for the Israeli Air Force to make the precision night raid. Fasi would have to mobilize his men to fight off the attacking jet fighters and there would be certain panic at the campsite.

The rest of the PLO soldiers would have to take cover as the attack mounted in intensity. Moshe knew from experience that the attack would be brutal and deadly and there would be a lot of casualties, but it would make penetration of the perimeter much easier. It would be one helluva diversion. The night was clear, dry and moonlit. That would make it more dangerous, but with their black clothing, it would conceal them until they started the attack. That fact alone could make the difference between failure and success. The air strike was set for exactly 2300 hours, when the moon was at its lowest apogee.

"Try to get some sleep now," Moshe ordered. "We will move closer soon."

They slept fitfully, like men waiting on death row to die the next morning. During the next few hours,

The Palestine Conspiracy

Moshe and his men slept, ate rations for energy and prepared to make their move.

"It's 2200," Moshe said. "Time to move closer to the objective. From now on, no voice communication unless absolutely necessary, only hand signals. Sound has a way of traveling far in the night air."

Nooka and the third man nodded, and moved out among the rocks descending 100 feet to the road below. Moshe signaled to arm the Uzi's. The cocking sound of the machine guns broke the silence. Moshe grabbed his satchel of plastic explosives and pointed the trigger mechanism to ready. The timer needed only to be activated for the correct number of seconds before detonation. He could do that instantly and without looking if necessary. Moshe signaled to leave the roadside and begin angling toward the barbed-wire fence surrounding the encampment. He checked his watch. It was nearly 2245 and pitch black out. They laid down under cover about 20 yards from the barbed-wire perimeter. They would wait there for the bombardment to begin in fifteen minutes.

They went over the attack plan again.

The plan was to cut through the fence killing any guards on the way in using their Uzi's with silencers and muzzle-flash mounts. It was a deadly weapon in the hands of an experienced soldier, and especially accurate at close-range fighting. The Israelis were all trained in the use of them. But, some were better than others. These Israelis were the best.

They would be impossible targets because of the element of surprise and the blackness of their sleek commando uniforms enabling them to melt into the blackness of the night. They would attack crouching

320

low to the target.

Moshe's job was to disarm the warheads as a technical specialist, while Nooka planted the satchel charges and set the timing device. The third Israeli commando would provide covering fire. It was a desperate mission by desperate men from a desperate Israel.

They waited. The minutes ticked by agonizingly slow. Moshe checked his military watch. It read 2254 hours. Almost eleven. At six minutes to the air attack, the men became more fidgety. They knew the Israeli fighters would be on time. Exactly on time. This would be their moment in hell.

The Israeli fighter pilots would be extremely precise and deadly accurate on their bomb runs

And, if he guessed right, the first bombs would take out Fasi's tent.

He had learned an hour ago from Haifa intelligence that Mrs. Thayer had left the camp by helicopter only hours after the conference broke apart and flew to Damascus. That was good. They hadn't wanted to harm her unless she got in the way of the

mission. But, even if she were there, Israel would still bomb the camp. Israel always would do what it had to do for Israel.

Thirty seconds to go. Moshe listened for the sound of the jets he knew were out there in the night skies. With five seconds to go, Moshe counted down to himself and listened for the roar of the jet engines in their attack dive.

Suddenly, he heard the shrill whine of the three Gabriel dive-bombers and saw the flash of the Maverick laser-guided missiles fire from underneath the wings.

The Palestine Conspiracy

Six in all. On a trajectory toward the north end of the encampment. When the missiles hit with thunderous explosions, the PLO soldiers knew they were under attack and opened up with anti-aircraft batteries and machine guns. The planes swooshed-in low and fast making it difficult to track them by sight. Tracer shells lighted the night sky. The entire scene resembled attacking fire-spitting dragons spewing out

their vengeance upon an unseen enemy. All six missiles hit their mark. Fasi's tent was blown to smithereens. Two hundred PLO soldiers went to certain death on the first pass by the Israeli jets.

Moshe knew the Gabriel's would circle and come in for another bomb-run using the 1,000-pound incendiary bombs. He knew it would be horrible for the militiamen caught in the open trying to seek cover.

"Now!" Moshe yelled through the noise of the explosions to his men. "We move now!"

The roar of the jets was deafening as they passed low over the camp just missing the satellite dish. The ground shook from the shock of the exploding bombs. Now was the time to cut through the perimeter.

The soldiers had taken cover just as Moshe had anticipated and their attention was drawn to the sky overhead filled with jet fighters. The jet fighters dropped their incendiary bombs creating a huge fireball in the middle of the camp.

Moshe cut a three-foot section of the fence and marked it with white flags so they could find there way back. When he was finished performing the 20-second job, he tossed the wire-cutters to the ground and motioned Nooka and the other Israeli through the opening.

The Palestine Conspiracy

Nooka and the other commando made it through the barbed-wire fence with ease. Moshe followed them through.

Running toward the missile batteries, they encountered no resistance at 200 yards out. Moshe signaled for them to stop. They crouched low to the ground, still unseen, and waited for the third and final bombing pass.

The Gabriel's would come in low and slow this time to gravity drop the 2,000-pounders. He motioned for his men to lie still until the bomb-run was made. He looked for the missiles. When he spotted them, his heart pounded. The warheads looked as though they were already in place.

The arming mechanisms were right below the warheads. They simply had to climb atop and remove the arming pins. That was simple enough. The missiles could then be destroyed by the plastic explosives. And, then they could get the hell out of there.

"When they drop their bombs again, cover me," Moshe ordered.

He watched as the fighter-bombers circled overhead for their final run. In they came, like beautiful avenging angels to drop their death and destruction. Six more bombs fell alongside Fasi's tent as if the Israelis wanted to punctuate the importance of killing him.

Napalm.

Moshe was now certain that Fasi was burning in hell.

He smiled.

And, in the next milli-second, he sprang into action when the bombs exploded. Nooka prepared the satchels and activated the timer mechanism for ninety seconds while the third Israeli covered them with his Uzi. The PLO didn't even know they were present.

Moshe climbed atop the twin missiles after running the last fifty yards and frantically looked for the arming pins.

"They're already armed," he shouted down to Nooka. "You must hold off the enemy if they come. I will need more time."

Nooka reached down and reset the timer to three minutes.

Moshe reached for the arming pins, then felt a sharp stab of pain rip through his neck, throwing him headfirst from the missile. He was dead.

"Shoot! Shoot!" Nooka ordered the Israeli gunner. "They're coming on your left!"

The Israeli commando spotted movement and opened fire with his Uzi killing the first three PLO militiamen running toward him. Nooka knew he would have to disarm the missiles. Moshe was dead, but he could still accomplish the mission. There was still time.

He reached up and hoisted himself onto the rocket launcher and climbed to the top of the warhead. The third Israeli kept firing.

Ahmed himself was leading the PLO attack brandishing Waite's 9mm he took from him. Ahmed dropped to one knee to get a better aim at the man climbing atop the missiles. He steadied himself and squeezed the trigger twice with incredible calm despite the bullets whizzing around him.

Two shots struck Nooka in the chest and throat before he could disengage the pins. He fell to the ground mortally wounded.

Ahmed rose again, and continued to fire at the attacking militiamen. The Israeli gunner saw Nooka hit the ground out of the corner of his eye and pointed his Uzi at Ahmed now only yards away from him and fired. He hit Ahmed at point blank range. It was a deadly burst.

The Israeli gunner turned and activated the timer.

He reset it for thirty seconds, enough time to protect the mechanism and be killed in the process. He made no attempt to run. There was no escaping his rendezvous with death, and if a nuclear blast followed, what would be the use. He continued to fire at the attacking militiamen. Ten seconds elapsed. Bullets hit all around him as the PLO closed in for the kill. They struck him in a hail of gunfire throwing his body violently backward, killing him instantly.

Ahmed had been fatally wounded, but struggled to his feet again, stumbling forward toward the satchel charge in a desperate attempt to reach it. The seconds ticked off.

Bleeding badly from the head and chest, he fell and reached out in a desperate lunge to shut it off. He squeezed the trigger mechanism, and the timer froze at 2 seconds.

He had done it. He had saved the missiles from destruction.

The soldiers lifted a dying Ahmed onto a makeshift stretcher. And, as he let out a last gasp, the ancient Bedouin prayer left his lips a final time.

It was 1113 hours. The attack was over.

Fasi had miraculously survived the bombing attack by retreating to an underground bunker. When word was brought to him that over four hundred of his men had been killed in the raid, including Ahmed, he was enraged.

"I will destroy Israel!" he shouted to the officers assembled. "Prepare the missiles for launch immediately."

Technicians surrounded the launchers and readied the missiles for firing. Fasi trembled with anticipation as his technicians locked the inertial guidance systems into place targeting the cities of Haifa and Tel Aviv.

When everything was ready, he looked at his watch and prepared to give the order to fire. It was five minutes to midnight.

It was not supposed to happen this way. Israel was to have accepted the peace plan on his terms. Instead, they had attacked. Now, destruction would follow. He would strike back now.

"Where is General Necomis?" Fasi shouted.

"He was killed in the attack. The American reporter and your niece are being brought to you, now."

"Good! I want them here to witness the destruction of Israel!" Fasi barked out the orders.

Adrienne and Waite were brought to the missile site in handcuffs, the guards taunting them as they struggled to escape. Fasi scowled.

"You will die together after I launch the missiles!" he screamed. "Prepare to fire!"

Adrienne and Waite continued to struggle.

"Fire!" Fasi shouted through the smoke-filled launch site set ablaze by the Israeli Gabriel fighter-bombers. If he didn't launch them now, he risked losing the missiles.

In horror, Adrienne and Waite watched helplessly

as the missiles rose off the launch pads lighting up the night sky as they climbed in a reddish-orange trajectory toward Israel.

"You son-of-a-bitch!" Waite shouted, observing the launched missiles arc upward in the night sky. "You've just destroyed Israel."

Adrienne finally broke free from her handcuffs and seized a machine-gun from one of the guards. She pointed it at her uncle.

"You shall never see the gates of heaven! Only the underbelly of hell!" she cursed.

"Aminah. No! Allah will curse you! You fool!

She squeezed the trigger until she emptied the entire clip into her uncle. Fasi's madness froze on his face as the bullets tore through him, lifting him off his feet and jerking him awkwardly backward. He let out a primal blood-curdling cry, as bright red liquid oozed from his chest.

PLO and Israeli blood had been spilled, and, it seemed that nothing had changed in 2,000 years except the weaponry in which to do it. Did it really matter where the blood of such brave men was spilled? The hard, cold reality was that the degree of bloodletting would intensify as the missiles streaked toward Israel.

Within minutes, a nuclear retaliation by Israel would be delivered with deadly efficiency.

The sight of their leader's twisted body stunned Fasi's elite guards. In confusion, they ran from the launch bunker shouting that the world was coming to an end.

Adrienne seized the opportunity! There wasn't a moment to lose!

"Put down your weapons! Fasi is no more. There are no more Israeli attackers!"

She ordered the technicians to destroy the missiles in flight.

"It's impossible!" one of them said. "There are no self-destruction devices aboard, only the nuclear warheads."

"Then we must radio Israel that nuclear missiles have been launched against them. How much time before they reach their targets?"

"Twelve minutes!" came the reply.

"Can nothing be done to stop them?" Adrienne pleaded.

"Nothing," a technician answered.

Adrienne and Waite reached for each other.

They had done as much as they could to stop the attack but had failed to prevent it.

How valuable were they as journalists, terrorists or diplomats if the Middle East was going to be destroyed in spite of them?

They could do nothing now but to watch in horror, waiting for the inevitable nuclear strike, which would surely come from Israel.

Israel would strike back swiftly at the heart of Palestine.

CHAPTER 34

Tel Aviv: 12:02 a.m.

The hotline rang and the top aide rushed into the bedroom.

Prime Minister!

They have launched nuclear missiles against us!"

The utter shock of the statement startled the prime minister from his deep sleep.

Glaenis reached for the red chrome-barreled telephone on his nightstand and punched a secret code into the lighted dial.

But, the Haifa missile control command was already on the line.

"What is it? What the hell is going on?" he asked the missile commander, his heart pounding away.

"Nuclear missiles targeted for Haifa and Tel Aviv at this very instant. Estimated time of impact . . . six minutes!"

"Dear Jehovah, so Fasi has done it!" he recoiled to a nearby chair.

My God, Fasi had actually fired nuclear missiles at Israel in spite of today's events at the U.N. He hadn't even given Israel time to respond to the peace initiative. Glaenis tried to compose himself, but the silence in the room dissolved in a moment of personal terror. . . Israel was already doomed.

Tears flowed down his cheeks as he thought of the innocent women, children and soldiers who would die by the blasts. How could anyone, even anyone inherently evil, execute such a deed?

Both countries were armed for total destruction. At times, little else mattered more than having the last say in a centuries old religious war.

This time Glaenis knew neither side would win.

"Prime minister! What shall our response be?" came the voice over the other end of the hotline.

Glaenis searched for his last thought as a human being, then uttered the secret code that would launch a retaliatory strike.

"Destroy Beirut and Damascus with nuclear missiles. Immediately!"

He said it as an afterthought, without emotion. The very words froze in the air as they left his lips.

The general in the command post could not believe what he had just heard, but the codes spoken to him by the Prime Minister were exactly correct and corresponded to his own set. He must obey them by Israeli law.

Defense Minister Prahoe heard the order to launch the counter-attack as he entered the Prime Minister's bedroom.

The prime minister's eyes focused on Prahoe.

"If we don't counter-attack, we cannot extract revenge. But, will it really matter?"

Glaenis hung up the receiver and pressed a six-digit code authenticating the attack order to his military commanders in the field. The buttons on the telephone lit up in bright red. The final authorization was being transmitted.

"Is it too late to stop the missiles from hitting us?"

"There is nothing more we can do. We cannot

intercept the PLO missiles. We don't have that capability."

In Haifa, the missile commander obeyed the order he had been given by the prime minister. Radar trackers perfunctorily noted that the nuclear missiles were now only four minutes away from Haifa, and five from Tel Aviv.

They must launch their counter-attack now or lose that ability when the nuclear blasts came.

"Prepare to launch the missiles. Target sequence Beirut and Damascus," he ordered.

The giant stainless steel doors of the silos opened and the missiles moved into firing position.

"Have you verified the telephone code from the prime minister?" a launch control officer asked praying that some mistake had been made.

"Affirmative. I heard his very voice myself, confirmed it by computerized voice print, and received the correct verification code on my control panel," the intelligence chief said, pointing to the still flashing code numbers on the computer screen.

"Proceed with the attack," General Sharn agreed reluctantly.

The missiles were raised to their firing positions.

Two shiny, white David-and-Goliath missiles stood poised on their launch pads . . . . five . . . four . . . three . . . two . . . one . . . the launch officer stood by . . . his hand hanging above the red firing mechanism . . . zero . . .

"This is for Israel!" he shouted as his hand slammed down on the push button.

The missiles ignited in a ball white-hot flame and burst skyward toward their targets each loaded with

The Palestine Conspiracy

20-megatons of hydrogen bombs.

"My God!" Sharn shouted to his chief intelligence officer.

"It has come down to madness on both sides!"

CHAPTER 35

Washington, D.C. The White House: 2:07 p.m.

The President was in the Oval Office when NSA notified him that two Shriek PLO missiles had been launched toward Israel and they had counter-attacked with two David-and-Goliath missiles.

"Get me NORAD on the scrambler!" he ordered his secretary.

President Burrell had only minutes to decide a course of action.

The officer in charge of operations picked up the Washington hotline and received the proper computerized identification from the President.

He knew what the order would be as he was already tracking the missiles trajectories in the Middle East.

"Activate the Star Wars Defense System," the President commanded. "Destroy all missiles launched in Sector 23, immediately! Sector 2...3...understood?"

The President already knew the appropriate sector having been briefed earlier by NSA. He knew that region of the world especially.

"Sir," the colonel obeyed, pressing a button which sent a computer signal to the satellites overhead in deep space.

The President waited on the hotline.

"Mr. President, all systems activated!" came the instant reply.

"Destroy all missiles launched against their

333

targets," the President ordered. "All missiles. Is that clear?"

"Yes, sir!" the command officer of the SDI system responded, and flipped another switch activating the laser guns orbiting the earth over Syria and Israel.

The satellite reflector-mirrors swung around instantly and focused the laser energy on their targets identified by the computer-guided laser guns.

Immense amounts of energy were required to destroy a missile in-flight.

There was less than three minutes until the PLO's first missile would hit Haifa. The satellite-tracking device aimed the laser guns at the first Shriek missile, some 40 miles from its target, and fired a sharp, powerful burst of ruby-red laser light through the atmosphere.

It found its target and the warhead of the rocket was vaporized in a bright fireball. The second Shriek missile angling down on Tel Aviv was only two-and-a-half minutes away from its target.

Personnel at the Haifa defense complex scrambled to take cover from the expected blast. The computer operator shouted from his chair over the screams of panic in the room that one of the missiles had been destroyed.

"One incoming missile destroyed!"

General Sharn stopped in his tracks. What was happening?

Laser guns set deep in outer space had fired the three lightning-like bursts to hit the incoming missile at 19,000 feet to destroy it.

"What is happening?" General Sharn asked the

technician observing the computer radar system.

"I don't know, sir. Thank God something went wrong and the missile was destroyed!" the aide shouted.

"Maybe it was God himself who destroyed it!" the general rejoiced.

The laser guns kept firing at the second on-rushing missile angling straight for Tel Aviv.

"Intercepting David-and-Goliath missiles," the NORAD officer in the U.S. repeated to the President.

Instantly, another laser system far out in space began firing at the Israeli launched David-and-Goliath missiles targeted for Beirut and Damascus destroying them halfway to their targets.

One Shriek missile remained to be destroyed.

"Mr. President," the NORAD commander shouted into the telephone, "We're having difficulty tracking the last missile aimed at Tel Aviv. It's on a lower trajectory. I don't think we can get it, sir?"

"Dammit, you must. Do you understand? The world will never understand what happened."

The colonel ordered the low-orbiting close-in "Slammer" satellite laser weapons to lock onto the Tel Aviv missile. It began firing a multitude of fiery red-hot laser bursts expending nearly all of its energy in an attempt to blind the guidance system of the approaching PLO missile. The warhead veered off course several degrees to the south but was not destroyed.

"One minute to impact!" the star wars computer operator shouted.

"Keep firing!" the President ordered.

The laser guns, mounted on the computer-controlled space platform, energized again to maximum power. NORAD had one last chance to destroy the missile. The technician precisely aimed the laser guns to adjust to super-penetration. It was his last hope.

He would set up a laser curtain two miles in front of the incoming missile and attempt to destroy it as it flew through a wall of super-hot energized light. It would amount to what World War II fighter pilots referred to as a full-deflection shot.

The four laser guns beamed their energies in front of the onrushing missile. They could do this for 30 seconds at maximum power until the nuclear energy generator spent itself. The timing had to be perfect. If NORAD or the computers misread the target information, the power would be exhausted and there would not be enough time to try again.

A brilliant orange glow lit up the skies over Tel Aviv, awakening its sleeping citizens.

An orange shield descended over the city from the northeast like some biblical angel of mercy. It was a beautiful sight, outwardly miraculous in effect and divine-like to those who watched it from Jerusalem. Those observing it wondered what it could be?

An old Jewish man knelt near the entranceway of his home and said a prayer knowing it was some kind of miracle. It was the Messiah he knowingly told others gathering nearby.

"He has finally come."

The multitudes assembled in the streets, bowing their heads at the divine intervention.

Several shielded their eyes from the bright light, and some were afraid to look at the face of God.

Jews exiting from a late prayer service at a synagogue poured out into the streets to witness the phenomenon. They, too, fell upon their knees, awestruck by the power of Jehovah.

"It's the Messiah! He has come at last!" they shouted to each other. "God has come to save us all!"

The missile began its penetration of the laser curtain at 12,000 feet over Tel Aviv approaching the city from the east. As it penetrated halfway through the magenta curtain, suddenly the multitudes witnessed a tremendous flash of brilliant white light, followed by a great explosion.

"Jehovah!" they cried.

But, it was not a nuclear explosion.

Instead, the last warhead had been destroyed by NORAD.

Tel Aviv and Israel had been saved.

Damascus and Beirut had been saved. Palestine had been saved.

The millions of Jews and Arabs witnessing the event did not understand what had happened. To them, it had been some kind of divine display of lights.

Few would ever know just how right they were.

General Sharn understood what had happened. He picked up the hotline to the United States, dialed the President, and patched-in the Prime Minister.

At NORAD the commanding officer let out a sigh of relief.

"Mr. President . . . all missiles have been destroyed. Thank God, sir."

"Yes," the President said calmly. "Thank God, indeed, for such a wonderful defense system."

He took the call from Israel.

"This is President Burrell. We have destroyed all

nuclear missiles in the region of Palestine."

"But how is that possible?" the Prime Minister asked.

"Through our Star Wars Defense System," the President responded.

"Star Wars? But, that is a violation of the treaty negotiated between you and the Soviet Union?"

"Yes, but, I ordered our country to build it anyway, in secret. I think the world will be relieved that we went ahead with the plan. There was no other way to stop those missiles. Tel Aviv, Haifa, Damascus and Beirut would have been absolutely destroyed, and along with them most of the Middle East from radioactive fallout."

The words pierced the heart and soul of Glaenis.

"Yes, I understand. I don't think either we, the Russians, or the Arabs will complain," he said absorbing the reality of the situation.

"Tomorrow, I will address the United Nations to explain what has just happened. I will give my full support to the Middle East peace plan. I want Israel to be a signatory to that pact. Will you agree to it?"

After the near-catastrophic events, such a decision was now relatively easy for the prime minister.

"I shall assemble the Knesset tonight and brief them on the full implications of what has just occurred. You can expect our full support on the Palestinian issue. Good-bye, thank you, and God bless you, Mr. President."

CHAPTER 36

Fasi's campsite: 12:20 a.m.

The missiles should have exploded by now, but he and Adrienne could see nothing but beams of bright lights penetrating the night sky to the east and west. The lights were breathtakingly beautiful.

"I wonder what they are," he said holding Adrienne close to him.

They let themselves kiss for the last time as they heard soldiers approaching from the other side of the camp firing their rifles in the air. They both knew what would come and remained motionless.   The PLO soldiers rushed them but didn't shoot. Instead, they explained that Israel, too, had fired nuclear missiles in response to Fasi's attack. But, all the missiles had been destroyed by an "act of Allah."

"An act of Allah!" her own words shocked her. "But, how can that be?"

"It has to be," the soldiers repeated excitedly. "Who else could have destroyed them?"

Neither Adrienne nor Rick could answer.

"Come on, let's find Glazer, if he's still alive he'll know what the hell is going on."

They set off for the other side of the camp near the satellite-tracking dish that was left amazingly unscathed by the Israeli sapper and air attack. Good God, there he was - and busy working.   Glazer was already communicating with New York via the digital satellite circuit.

"What? Impossible! The United States has no Star Wars System. It's banned by a U.S.-Russia Arms Treaty."

Waite had heard enough. The network man insisted the report from the White House was true. The President himself announced the series of events just a few minutes ago on national television at the special session of the Security Council when the news broke.

It was unbelievable. Israel and the Middle East had been saved from nuclear annihilation because the U.S. had broken an arms agreement with the Russians.

"Well, son-of-a-bitch," Waite exclaimed watching a replay of the President on the bureau's television monitor. "What a story?"

President Burrell was calling for an immediate end to hostilities in the Middle East, and prodding Israel to support the Arab-English initiative."

The Thayer-Fasi pact had worked after all. "We shall have a homeland!" Adrienne cried-out. She hugged Waite in open triumph.

"Salaam, Alakam," she said.

"Salaam," he replied.

CHAPTER 37

New York: June 24.   Noon at the United Nations.

Adrienne and Waite were hailed as heroes as were the Arab and Israeli co-signers of the peace pact establishing a State of Palestine on Israel's borders.

Israel had signed the document as requested by King Fasaid, Mrs. Thayer and President Burrell.

Palestine had been created from the desert lands of the West Bank.

In Beirut, bells tolled from the few Christian churches left standing from the 40-year-war.

In Jerusalem, Jews wept at the Wailing Wall.

In Tel Aviv, thousands of people danced in the streets.

In Damascus, people read about the events chronicled by news accounts in the newspapers.

In Mecca and Medina, Muslims prayed at the holy mosques.

And, in the region of Palestine, two days later, Adrienne and Waite sat on the same hillside in the Jordanian Plain where she and her brothers had grown up.

They watched as two Bedouin brothers and a sister tended their flock of sheep, herding them toward the sparse desert grass. Tears came to Adrienne's eyes as she watched them graze peacefully in the gentle desert breeze.

The older boys looked much like Ahmed and Akram in their youth.

Both were gone now.

But, perhaps their legacy and others like them who believed in a free and independent Palestine would continue with the promise of a lasting peace in the Middle East.

The children waved to them and they returned the gesture shouting greetings to them. They reminisced about what had brought them to the Middle East.

Their lips met.

It would be the beginning of a new life for both of them.

Waite would keep his promise to her.

She longed to return to her Bedouin roots one more time.

"I told you when this assignment was over that I'd help you find your past. Now, we can begin," he whispered.

She kissed him again.

"Perhaps, we did something good for the world," she said. "And in the process, perhaps we did something greater for ourselves."

CHAPTER 38

June 25. In their hotel room in Beirut.

Adrienne and Rick worked their way back to the hotel room after leaving Damascus. A cease-fire had been arranged between the PLO factions and the Israelis occupying the city. All was quiet.

"God, do you realize how lucky we were?" Waite said.

"Without a doubt, we would have been killed by Fasi's security forces had it not been for the intervention of the United States and your American President."

"Without a doubt," Waite agreed. "And, without a doubt, we would have never seen the day when the Palestinian children would have a future established by their leaders.

"Can you imagine? The creation of an actual Palestinian State that has been dreamed about for decades?"

"Uh, yes. . . and a dream which began all because of you and Ahmed. May Allah smile upon him mercifully."

Good God, Adrienne noticed, Waite was beginning to sound Bedouin in his speaking pattern.

"I see," she said mocking him. "You are indeed a wise man beyond your years."

Waite grabbed her by the waist and pulled her close to him.

The Palestine Conspiracy

"Yes, I am wise to see that we must take some time to relax while we have the chance, because when we get back they'll be throwing assignments at us left and right. We're going to be writing a lot of stories about this."

She nuzzled his hair at his collar, kissing him softly across his ear. He began caressing her back and slowly worked his hand against her side, raising it methodically as her breathing quickened.

"Do you?" he said feigning permission.

"Perhaps . . . " she protested. "Maybe we could do this at some other time."

"Perhaps, that other time is now?" he said softly in her ear.

As they embraced, the door burst open and they found themselves staring at the barrel of a glistening chrome-plated automatic – Waite's own ivory-handled 9 mm.

"My God, it's Ahmed," Adrienne screamed.

Waite jumped from the couched and raised his arms.

Adrienne lunged forward and hugged him, as he lowered the gun barrel to the floor.

The hammer clicked shut. The gun had no clip.

Ahmed grinned at Waite and hugged his sister.

"Ahmed, you fool, we thought you were dead."

"You always think I am dead," he laughed. "And, I nearly was this time. I was in the camp when the Israeli jets bombed us and when the commandos attacked. I was shot at point blank range, not once but twice."

"How did you survive?" Waite asked incredulously.

"Oh, by the blessings of Allah, and with the luck of some Irish-American reporter named Glazer. I was hit

The Palestine Conspiracy

in the chest, right on my front, left shirt pocket. But, do you know what was inside that shirt pocket? The message from Akram. It was tucked inside a copy of the Koran my sister gave me as a child. The two bullets struck the holy book and saved my life. And, the rest, as you Americans say, is history."

It was a miraculous escape.

They had all three-made history, and perhaps had done something good for the world.

"There's just one thing that I can't reconcile," Waite said. "How did you manage to arrange Adrienne's coming to Beirut from London."

"Oh, my friend, that part was the easiest. You see I had done some work for British Intelligence in Beirut, and I orchestrated a well-placed series of telephone calls to Adrienne's editor at the London Times – anonymously. I knew they couldn't trace those mysterious calls. And, Brian, the ICE agent who was assigned to oversee Prime Minister Thayer's visit? He was one of my many contacts to set the plan in motion. Adrienne worked him over very cleverly . . .he never knew that she was in on what was going on over here. Unfortunately, he was killed in the air-raid."

Waite was amazed at how cleverly sophisticated the PLO operatives had become. Was their anything they wouldn't resort to?

One thing for sure, he figured, was that world terrorism had to stop by everyone involved if there was going to be a genuine peace.

"Do you think that it can work in the end?" Waite asked Ahmed.

"Yes, my friend, because the Palestinian people as a whole support it. The Israeli people now support it, too. They are tired of all the killing. We are all tired of it. The whole world is tired of it."

Ahmed was right.

The entire world was ready for peace. It was an opportunity for future generations to fulfill their promise after the old warriors died-off. It was an opportunity to end the fighting once-and-for-all.

CHAPTER 39

London: July 5. In Adrienne's Apartment.

Alone, Adrienne reached into her purse and swept the room with an electronic device smaller than her hand.

She listened carefully for the tones, which would tell her that the room was still bugged or her phone wiretapped.

The device was silent.

She dialed a number.

It rang four times before someone answered.

"I have returned. What further do you wish of me?"

(pause)

"Yes, I understand. No, he is not suspicious. I have allayed his fears about me."

(pause)

"When can I see you again?"

(pause)

"Must it be that long?"

(pause)

347

The Palestine Conspiracy

"Yes, I know. Security rules your life, and mine, too."

(pause)

"I realize he must never suspect that I work for the Mossad. Yes . . . as far as he's concerned, you were killed in the Israeli raid on Fasi's base camp. That is what Ahmed told him."

(pause)

"Goodbye, I love you. I'll see you soon, God willing."

(pause)

"Shalom and Allahu Akbar, Abdulla Necomis."

THE END

The Palestine Conspiracy

REVIEWS

"Mr. Spirko has written a riveting book with revelations about the Middle East that have all come true during the past decade. His astonishing predictions and ability to penetrate the mindset of the Arab and Jew alike makes his book one of the most intuitive, compelling, descriptive analysis of Middle East affairs of our time. He should have worked for the CIA." – A FORMER INTEL INSIDER

"One of the most provocative reads ever. I wish the manuscript had been available prior to the Persian Gulf and Iraqi wars. Remarkable in its scope and of his understanding of the Middle East." – A COVERT OPERATIVE OF THE U. S.

"A terrific read! One of the best spy-thrillers ever. Mr. Spirko has a genuine ability to grip the reader and bring, action, suspense and drama to all sides in the Middle East. His peace proposals nearly won-out at the Camp David Peace Talks in 2000. Those ideals should be resumed for the benefit of both sides – the PLO and Israelis, equally. The BBC termed his ideas as "brilliant." – A NEW YORK CITY BOOK REVIEWER

"An extraordinary, accurate analysis of the Middle East issues as they faced the world 15 years ago. Guess what? Those same issues haven't changed and Mr. Spirko has done a remarkable job of bringing them into proper focus via a compelling book that not only tells a story, but offers ideas for peace, fair to all sides, so millions may see the wisdom of working for peace instead of war. God, Jehovah and Allah, the same deity, can bless us all regardless of political or religious convictions." – A BOOK STORE BUYER

The Palestine Conspiracy

About The Author

Robert Spirko is a graduate of the Kent State University School of Journalism and studied for his MBA at the same school. He is currently an investment advisor and owns his own firm, "Herd On Wall $treet" near Cleveland, Ohio, and analyzes stock markets, economic and geo-political trends, predicting many before they occur.

His remarkable ability to forecast events before they occur has been described as truly uncanny by his friends and acquaintances. His predictions about the Middle East were even more important and remarkable than his predictions about the stock market. He did a stint in the United States Air Force. Mr. Spirko later became a stockbroker for Merrill Lynch and Prescott, Ball and Turben. In 1992, he became an investment advisor of his own firm, Herd On Wall $treet, and currently writes a stock market newsletter discussing geo-political events and investments. His average total return on his portfolio is 20.32% each year over an 11 year period.

At the 2000 Camp David Peace Conference, Mr. Spirko was instrumental in establishing new ideas between Ehud Barak and Yasser Arafat, and his contributions nearly culminated in a peace agreement – but the effort ultimately failed because neither side would take that final step to agree to Palestinian reparations and the abolishment of settlements on Palestinian land. The BBC termed his ideas on the

The Palestine Conspiracy

Jerusalem problem as "brilliant," recommending the use of the Holy City as dual capitals of both nations, something that has never been done in history.

Mr. Spirko has been an advocate for peace in the Middle East for decades.

He states, "Why can't there be peace in the Middle East? Everyone shares the same God whether He is called Allah, God or Jehovah. All will die equal in the end. Why not agree before that?"